HEATHER BOYD

USAT BESTSELLING AUTHOR

AN AFFAIR SO RIGHT

REBEL HEARTS 4

Rebel Hearts Series

Book 1: The Wedding Affair
Book 2: An Affair of Honor
Book 3: The Christmas Affair
Book 4: An Affair so Right

AN AFFAIR SO RIGHT

Edited by Kelli Collins

DEDICATION

This book might never have seen the light of day without the patience, humor, and enthusiasm of my editor, Kelli Collins. She rescued Quinn and his true love from a future gathering dust under my bed. You are priceless and I'm in your debt!

CHAPTER ONE

IF THERE WAS anything in life surer to turn a man's stomach, it was a blatant attempt at matchmaking over a mahogany dining table. Quinn Ford, formerly a captain in His Majesty's navy but now more happily Viscount Maitland, would rather be run through in battle than be the focus of his father's machinations to see him miserably wed to the mouse of a woman perched at his side.

"Have you visited Tattersalls yet?" he asked her to be polite.

Miss Genevieve Cushing uttered a negative squeak to his question and then buried her face in her water glass again.

He sighed in resignation. Miss Cushing was without the courage to answer anyone with confidence, or even to look his mother in the eye it seemed. He fell silent and turned his attention back to his plate.

Quinn had not resumed a public life in society to put up with missish nonsense. He admired forthright women. Prim and proper Miss Cushing, daughter of a wealthy London merchant, a connection most likely indebted to his father in some way, was most certainly not his type of female. She had none of the presence required to be a future Duchess of Rutherford when the title fell to him eventually. Not that he had ever wished ill on his beloved grandsire.

Which was not the case when it came to his own father—Lord Templeton—seated farther down the table from him.

Quinn glanced along to where his father sat holding court. Father was probably destined to live forever.

"You should have your brother take you one day," he said to Miss Cushing.

"He's very busy," she whispered.

George Cushing was probably visiting brothels with his intemperate friends right now. He was young and reckless. But who was Quinn to judge another man's priorities?

He was only concerned about people who affected his own life, and Miss Cushing would never be one of them.

Quinn's future wife would need to be possessed of firm convictions to survive his future, because when Templeton became the Duke of Rutherford, there was no telling what evil would befall him and the gentler members of the family. The family had already suffered due to Templeton's grasping nature.

He considered what other arrangements his father had made with Mr. Cushing besides attending this dinner. Nothing good for the Cushings, most likely. Quinn knew firsthand it was never wise to make any deal with Lord Templeton. People who did tended to be vastly unhappy with the result.

"Gentlemen, if you will excuse us, we will leave you to your simple pleasures," Mama, the Countess Templeton, announced as she set her napkin aside and rose from her chair at the end of the meal.

Quinn was quick to reach his feet, as were the other gentlemen, who protested she was leaving them too soon. His mother was an exceptionally popular woman in London society, hardly meek and most certainly not missish, and still attractive at fifty years of age.

Quinn adored her, and so did everyone else. Quinn's mother was respected, whereas his father was feared.

Mother urged the women to go with her, giving way for the gentlemen to partake of port and cigars after dinner. She gave Quinn a brief but pointed look that spoke volumes from her husband's shadow. *Tread carefully* it said.

Quinn inclined his head to her as she moved toward him at a stately pace. He'd grown accustomed to such unspoken warnings from his mother, and where he could, he heeded them all. Thwarting the Earl of Templeton's manipulations had become their life's work.

Her attention strayed to the young woman lingering by his chair, and her eyes narrowed with a hint of displeasure.

Mama had shared her guest list with him yesterday, and at that time, the Cushings had not been included for this remembrance dinner in honor of his late sister. They had not known his sister Mary. The Cushings were new additions; included, most likely, at Lord Templeton's express demand.

Mama grasped Miss Cushing's elbow and led her by subtle force toward the drawing room and away from Quinn. He hid a smile, grateful that when it came to matrimony, he and his mother were of the same mind regarding his future. She wished him to marry for love, so she thwarted her husband at every opportunity.

The other women trailed after Mama, chattering happily, and laughing among themselves as they fled into the drawing room for tea and a good gossip.

With them gone, Quinn took a turn about the room to stretch his legs and then headed for the decanters of port set aside for the gentlemen to partake from. He poured himself a drink and downed the lot. Dinners with his father required liquid reinforcement be deployed at all times.

He poured another and slid the bottle back into the spot.

Quinn joined Lord Deacon, who was nursing a brandy glass already at the end of the room. "My apologies for missing your cousin's ball last week," Quinn murmured to him.

Deacon, an earl near his age, was widely regarded as an idiot. Deacon did not excel at manly pursuits except for drinking; he did not seek to distinguish himself in parliament, claiming there were wiser voices to be heard. What Deacon did exceedingly well was friendship. He knew—not assumed, while wringing his hands—that sometimes his friends needed to use him as a shield. That was why, when he was invited to dine by the Earl and Countess Templeton, he could always be counted on to attend if Quinn would be there too.

Deacon smiled, glancing around the room as he did to see who was nearby. "The usual business?"

"Is there anything else that prevents me seeing my friends but my father's orders?"

"None so far, but I am sure that your future wife might have the ability to sway you one day." Deacon's eyes sparkled with mirth, glancing toward the distant drawing room, where Miss Cushing had vanished. "Did Templeton's latest matrimonial prospect catch your fancy?"

"Hardly," Quinn grumbled. Deacon knew the challenges Quinn faced thanks to his overly ambitious father. "I swear she squeaked."

"Could be amusing in the right setting. At least you could find Miss Cushing in the dark, should you ever misplace her." Deacon laughed suddenly. "Mary would have set down a plate of cheese for her, had you expressed the slightest interest in marrying the girl."

"She would have, too." Quinn raised his glass with a deep sigh. He missed his little sister, but never more so than today—on the anniversary of when she'd ended her life.

"To Puddleduck," Deacon said, raising his glass, too. Deacon was one of the few friends who knew today's significance to them. Suicides were rarely spoken of in polite circles.

Quinn's sister had been seventeen when she'd drowned herself. Three and Twenty in a few weeks' time. It still shocked him that she was gone. Quinn's nose itched, and he forced a laugh out to fight his sadness. "She adored the name you gave her."

"She was a good sport. But at least Puddleduck is better than the nickname *you* gave her," Deacon scowled. "The Pestilence was hardly a respectful name to give any lady."

Mary had been something of a pest as a child, and calling her *the Pestilence* had stuck until her last year. "She never minded the names."

In hindsight, perhaps the nickname hadn't been the best choice to give to his younger sister. No one had sensed her unhappiness or known her emotions were so fragile. Mary had died so young, for reasons that to this day baffled him. His second younger sister had appeared happy one day, full of plans for the future, her season, marriage, and babies, and yet had waded out into the sea at the family estate fully clothed and drowned—as she must have known she would.

Quinn surveyed the room, his thoughts stuck on that tragic day. The sun had been shining, and he'd had good news to share about his new command and had run out to the cliffs to tell her about it. Discovering Mary face down in the churning sea was a shock Quinn would never forget. He hadn't been able to save her. She'd already been gone too long by the time he'd pulled her from the water.

"She gave as good as she got. What was her nickname for you again?"

"Bumblefoot, on account of my lack of prowess on the dance floor," Deacon said glumly. "At least that was accurate. I still can't dance well enough to please the ladies I like."

Mary had been Deacon's friend. Quinn had assumed they'd marry once Mary came of age, and she finally noticed Deacon had adored the ground she walked on. They had always been whispering to each other and laughing over the silliest things no one else had found remotely funny. Deacon had taken her death as hard as any member of the family.

All except for Father. Templeton hadn't shed a tear.

Quinn regarded his parent as he spoke loudly and with great enthusiasm without any respect for the anniversary they had planned to mark today. Templeton had covered up the suicide swiftly and had told everyone to forget her.

Quinn couldn't do that and had suffered for his disobedience.

Mother openly marked each anniversary just to spite her husband.

"Maitland?" Deacon regarded him solely, and the softly spoken word drew him back from the dark abyss of his grief and anger. It was always there, catching him off guard. He couldn't accept that he'd never know why she'd died.

He forced his fists to uncurl. "Father and Mr. Cushing are as thick as thieves tonight, but I'd rather die without an heir than marry his daughter."

"I'd like a smart wife who was happy to put up with a fool like me." Deacon's grin faded to apprehension. "Watch out. He's got that look about him. Oh, damn and blast it. He's coming our way," Deacon complained.

Quinn quickly turned his back on the room to peer out the window. Outside, Londoners were going about their business without a care in the world. And the world was finally at peace. Napoleon was locked up; the French army and navy thwarted by the might of the British forces. Life should be pleasant.

Except that it couldn't be while his father pursued his own agenda to direct Quinn's life.

"Ah, Lord Templeton," Deacon bellowed with great enthusiasm.

"Excellent dinner as usual. Your dear wife has outdone herself yet again. My sincere compliments to your cook and staff, too. I can't remember the last time I've ever felt so full, except for Lord Sanderson's dinner last week. But do you know I had to turn down a second helping of that fine pork chop that night because it left the faint aftertaste of lemon in my mouth? None of that at your table here, of course. Lady Templeton would never allow such culinary faux pas beneath your roof, would she?"

Quinn struggled not to grin. Deacon could natter on about dinners, and the food served to him, for hours on end. He bored everyone with his little speeches—always on purpose. It was a useful skill Quinn couldn't hope to emulate but appreciated. Deacon could play the fool at will without breaking a sweat.

"A man can indeed have too much of a good thing," Quinn agreed, bravely joining into the conversation because it would irritate the hell out of his father that he would side with Deacon.

"I require a word with my son, Lord Deacon," Father said abruptly.

"Oh. Oh, yes of course. Certainly. Go right ahead," Deacon offered.

Quinn turned slightly to acknowledge his father, but nearly laughed out loud as it became clear that Deacon wasn't leaving them, and remained planted at Quinn's side with his arms crossed over his wide chest.

Immovable.

Seeming unaware he wasn't wanted.

"In private," Lord Templeton growled, before jerking his head toward the hallway door. "Perhaps you could deliver your compliments to Lady Templeton in person."

"Oh, of course." Deacon smacked his forehead, eyes wide. "I'd best rejoin the ladies then."

With one last happy smile to Father, Deacon rushed away like a hapless schoolboy.

Lord Templeton scowled. "You should end your friendship with that dullard."

"He's a good man," Quinn replied, having suffered the demand many times before.

"Forever nattering on about pork chops and lemon as if I care about such things."

Father couldn't abide idle conversation. He was too impatient to care about anyone but himself.

"Mary liked him," Quinn said with a sincere smile. Mention of Mary was one spectacular way to stop any topic of conversation in its tracks. It worked every time. "She was the one who asked me to include him in my circle of friends, and I promised I would watch out for him."

Father tossed off his head, jaw clenching briefly. "What did you think of her?"

Ah, there it was—the real reason for Templeton's rude interruption. "Of whom?"

"The Cushing chit. Her father owns a thousand acres at Colchester and has no heir apparent. She'll inherit everything I hear." Templeton gestured to the gentleman in question, eyes narrowed and assessing. "She would be a good match for you."

For anyone but Quinn. "Doubtful."

Father looked at him with the dead-eyed stare of a furious man. "It is time you gave up these foolish notions and made an advantageous match."

"I'm not marrying a woman I don't care deeply for."

"That's your mother's new nonsense clouding your head."

Quinn snorted out loud. "You and Mother married as strangers and never became the closest of couples. No wonder she highly recommends love matches over cold alliances like yours."

Father's hand finally twitched at his side as Quinn scored a hit. The topic of his parents' union was a tricky one. His parents barely spent any time together these days and everyone knew it. Father had married Mother for her enormous dowry. He had kept a mistress since Quinn was at least ten years of age.

Templeton's glory days were over though. His hair was more gray than black, and he'd developed a definite paunch these past few years. When angry, his face mottled an unhealthy red, as it did now.

"Do not speak ill of your mother," Templeton warned.

"I would never disparage *Mother*." His mother put up with so much and never complained except for lack of grandchildren to hold in her arms. However, his sister Sally was well on the way to fulfilling that request, thanks to her recent marriage.

Father grabbed his arm. "Impertinent whelp. How dare you?"

"I won't allow you to choose my bride for me," Quinn said in a mild tone. "I will make up my own mind about when I marry, too. You may scheme until your face is blue, but when I marry, believe me, it will not be for the good of my purse alone."

The grip on his arm tightened to painful levels. "You will call on Miss Cushing tomorrow," Templeton insisted.

Quinn had borne worse punishments and kept his face impassive. "I will not. I came to dinner tonight to remember Mary, with people who knew and loved her. I've no idea why you would disrespect Mother *or* Mary by forcing strangers upon us at such a time. We loved her more than you ever did."

Father dug his fingers deeper, just as the other gentlemen stood and began to move noisily about the room. Quinn remained still, enduring the pain without flinching or pulling away. He'd been doing so for years. "Do not embarrass Mother, tonight of all nights," Quinn warned.

Templeton released Quinn immediately.

Deacon returned, his face beaming an idiot smile. "Ah, Maitland. Are you free now to complete our conversation?"

"Indeed." Deacon's timing was impeccable. Despite his father's plans, Quinn was determined to make his own way, to live his own life in peace now that the war was over. That was why he'd resigned his command so quickly after the war, before his father could hatch a new scheme designed to keep Quinn in his clutches.

He moved toward his friend without a backward glance for his father's permission. He slapped Deacon on the shoulder and turned him toward the drawing room. "Now, tell me more about this problem you have?"

Deacon winced. "I'm afraid I'm going to need rather a lot of your help."

"For what?"

"Finding a woman for me to marry, of course."

"Oh." Quinn stared at Deacon in astonishment. "I didn't think you were serious about that."

"Well, I am." Deacon protested. "I'm tired of women who just want to sit on my lap a few times and then pretend they didn't fancy me after all."

Quinn choked on an oath. Now there was a picture he'd rather not have in his mind. "Ah, Deacon, now is really not the time for specifics of your intimate relations. When we're done here, we could talk at my home if that suits?"

Deacon nodded quickly. "I knew I could depend on you."

CHAPTER TWO

THEODORA DALTON SHIELDED her face from the heat even while trying to see beyond the fierce blaze into her home. "Father!"

"It's no good, miss," an older neighbor insisted, arms held wide to prevent her from continuing her search for her missing parent. "It's too late."

Above Theodora's head, the country home she'd shared with her parents on the outskirts of London since their return from abroad two years ago crackled and groaned ominously as it was consumed by ever-expanding flames. Theodora was fortunate she'd awoken and found her mother before the smoke had choked the life from them. They had fled via the rear of the property, where they had expected to find her father.

"Father might be in the library," she told the man over the noise. "He is always there at this time of night. We must rescue him!"

"No one could survive that." The man grasped her shoulders and pushed her back none too gently.

"Unhand me, sir!" she screamed indignantly.

He did just as the house groaned again. They both staggered back, shielding their heads from another blast of heat.

"It's too dangerous to stay here," the man yelled before backing all the way to the street and leaving her as the only soul brave enough to remain near the blistering fire.

Theodora held her ground, blinking through the intense heat and smoke, determined to be on hand to assist her father. The street behind her was filled with people taking in the horror of the situation.

She heard a disturbance, and cast a quick glance for her mother, grateful to see her at a safer distance. The local firefighters had arrived and parted the crowd by yelling, finally bringing the water wagon to begin pumping water toward her home. A line of men and a few women carrying buckets also began to fling water toward the open doorway, sloshing most on the ground before it could do any good to prevent the blaze from spreading.

Theodora took a bucket herself and approached the doorway. Flames had reached the front door hallway, dancing up the walls and licking the stucco ceilings until they blackened and cracked. Small clumps of fire fell like raindrops in places, scorching the hall runner she'd chosen in India and brought home to England.

She tossed her inadequate bucket of water ahead of her, desperately hoping for some sign of movement within. She took a step closer and called out.

Her arm was caught suddenly. "Everyone is accounted for," a man shouted over the din of the crackling blaze.

Hope surged, and she scanned the crowd. "My father?"

"No," the unfamiliar voice replied. "There is no sign of Mr. Dalton anywhere."

Theodora damped her handkerchief in the bucket slops. If she covered her mouth and nose, she just might get closer. "He depends on me."

"The minute you step inside that house, you'll be lost too," the man warned in a harsh voice, and then he cursed—like a sailor who'd never been around a proper woman before in his life. His arm curled around her middle and, before she could protest, the fellow hefted her off her feet. Although she struggled, Theodora was moved back, without apology or permission.

The cooler air filled her lungs and made her cough hard enough to bring tears streaming from her eyes. She struggled but was carried to her mother, who was staring at the building in her blanket-covered nightclothes with huge, fearful eyes.

"Thank heavens she's safe," Mother whispered to the women flanking her, women who had dressed in such a rush that their hair was down, and their costly jewels had been left at home. "Thank you for bringing her back to me."

Theodora fought the restriction of the strong arm that remained around her waist, holding her off the ground like a child. "Let me go!"

"Not until you accept it is hopeless," the man growled. "Anyone who goes near that house again will surely lose their life. I won't risk yours, and anyone fool enough to follow you will die too," he insisted harshly.

She twisted around to view her captor, and her eyes widened in surprise. She barely recognized the hulking, soot-covered giant who pinned her to his body. No wonder her feet dangled in the empty air. Lord Maitland, formerly Captain Maitland of the *HMS Reckless Hope*, held her fast against his broad chest. She knew little of the man for all they'd been neighbors these last two years, but since his return to shore, he was forever entertaining friends in his home until all hours. His comings and goings entertained a whole host of gossips each morning. Theodora knew him enough to nod to, to admire his muscular form as he rode past.

He had seemed a merry sort of man under normal circumstances, but today she barely recognized him in his temper.

"Lord Maitland. Help us!"

"I am," he promised, holding her closer still. His attention returned to the burning house. "I'm doing exactly what your father would have wanted me to do. I'm keeping his daughter alive. Ladies, you must remain here."

Her home groaned again, and crashing could be heard within. Maitland dropped her to the ground as he ordered everyone to move back until they were pressed against the stone wall bordering his property.

Theodora stared at the blaze. Smoke billowed toward them, pushed by a strengthening breeze, obscuring her vision. "Dear God, Papa."

"That was probably the upper floor falling in over the east rooms," Maitland suggested in a soft voice full of soft sympathy.

A chill swept her skin, and she shivered. "My father's library was beneath."

Lord Maitland's arm slipped around her again, and he rocked her. "I know."

She stared in horror, unable to believe there was no hope. She clung to Maitland's arm, praying her father might yet be all right. But it seemed hopeless.

The fight left her legs suddenly, and she would have fallen if not for Maitland's continued support.

"Get those men back!" he suddenly shouted over the top of her head.

He held her to his chest tightly another moment, and then the pressure eased. "There's nothing we can do. Stay with your mother. Those people are too close. I must move them out of harm's way. Deacon, help me bring them to order, will you?"

Maitland released her, stripped off his coat, whipped it around her shoulders, and then left her to stand in silence with the scent of his cologne filling her lungs. He strode away with the other man, Deacon, she assumed.

Maitland and Deacon took command while Theodora huddled inside the warmth of Maitland's perfectly tailored evening wear.

She followed his movements as he argued and gestured to the house and the people standing about idly while her home was consumed. Eventually, he convinced them to move to safety, and she could tell, even from this distance, that he was a man who expected to be obeyed without question.

Another section of the roof collapsed, falling into her own bedchamber, spraying sparks of light out over the street where just moments before a group of bystanders had lingered. Theodora stroked the exceptional-quality material wrapped around her. If not for Maitland, they'd all have been showered in sparks.

If not for Maitland, she'd have been injured.

She shivered again and hugged his coat closer about her body. Everything they had was inside that burning house. Possessions and money.

Theodora glanced toward her mother as the horror finally sank in.

Did Mama realize it too? They had nothing but the clothes on their backs.

Theodora moved to her mother and inserted herself in the little group surrounding her. Her mother was quick to link arms, and together they stared at the destruction of the home they'd shared. "What can we do?"

Her mother tightened her grip on Theodora. "I don't know."

More of the house collapsed as Maitland hurried toward her. His arms folded around both her and her mother as everyone took cover. A blast of heat and smoke swept over them all in a thick choking cloud, along with a deafening roar. Theodora held her face against Maitland's chest as they began to cough together.

"It's over. I am so sorry," Maitland whispered for their ears alone when the smoke had thinned. "I'm so sorry nothing could be done to save him."

Her mother sobbed then, grasping both Theodora's and Maitland's clothes tightly as she grieved and wailed for the loss of her husband of thirty years. Theodora did her best to soothe her, but there was no stopping Mama once she began to cry.

She was surprised Lord Maitland allowed it since they were strangers to each other.

When Maitland stepped back a little while later, Theodora was free to see her home had reduced to a pile of ash, broken, and burning timbers, and a thick plume of smoke drifting upward toward what had been a perfectly clear, starlit sky. There was nothing left that she could recognize of the pretty house they'd lived in.

Theodora cried for her father then, never noticing Lord Maitland's fine coat had slipped from her shoulders until he placed it back around her again. "How could this have happened?"

Maitland squeezed her shoulder. "There'll be an investigation."

Anger filled Theodora. "Whoever was responsible for my father's death must be punished."

"Punished? Why would you say that?" The man appeared horrified. "Surely an accident caused the blaze."

She drew away from Maitland, wiped the tears from her eyes and straightening her spine. "That was no accident. My father was always very careful with open flames. You don't know how particular he was about such matters. Someone started that fire on purpose. It is the only explanation that makes any sense."

Maitland held her gaze a long moment, still patting her weeping mother's shoulder. "The coroner will discover how this *accident* occurred."

The other fellow returned. "I say, this is turning out to be a sad night all round," he muttered to Lord Maitland.

"Indeed, it is, Deacon," Lord Maitland agreed.

"Where is Mr. Small?" her mother asked suddenly, pulling away from Maitland and glancing around wildly.

"Who is that?"

"My father's secretary," Theodora explained as she looked around. In the chaos, Theodora had forgotten Mr. Small often worked after she'd retired for the night. Mr. Small did not reside with them, but he occasionally fell asleep over his desk. The man had still been hard at work at his desk when Theodora had retired that night.

"Mr. Small! Mr. Dennis Small!" her mother cried. "Are you here, sir?"

Theodora stared at the soot-covered crowd anxiously. "Mr. Small! Are you here?"

Her mother continued to call out, in a voice that soon became laced with pain and exhaustion.

"Mr. Dennis Small. Show yourself." Lord Deacon lent his louder voice to Mother's, and they moved away. Deacon continued to call out in a huge voice that slowly faded as they disappeared from sight.

"I'm here," a croaking voice suddenly replied to Theodora's left.

Theodora searched for the sound, and found the man prone on the ground, soot-covered and almost unrecognizable as Mr. Small. He raised one hand toward her and then let it drop.

Theodora rushed to his side, astonished he'd been so close all along, and that she'd been too wrapped up in her fear for her father to notice his suffering.

Part of Mr. Small's hair had been scorched. His right cheek, from eyebrow to jaw, was red and blistered down one side, and his coat sleeve was in tatters, too. "Mr. Small! Oh, how terrible that you are hurt. But do you know if my father went to his club tonight?"

"I tried to reach him, but the flames were too thick between us,"

Small croaked. "He wouldn't listen. He could have saved himself if he'd not been so stubborn."

"It's all right. You tried." Theodora slumped onto the ground at his side, all the fight leaving her as she accepted that her father had perished in the blaze. "I'm sure he would have listened to you if he could."

Theodora wiped away her tears and noted a man kneeling at Mr. Small's other side. Big and brawny, the fellow wasn't in their employ, or known to her, either. He too was covered in soot though, so he must have tried to fight the blaze. "Thank you for all you have done tonight, sir. Might I know your name?"

Mr. Small grasped the other man's coat. "Don't," he wheezed.

Theodora glanced between the men. "Do you know each other?"

"No," Small gasped. He coughed, and kept coughing so violently that the other man had to support him through the worst of the spasms.

Theodora blinked back tears and raised her face to the gathering crowd. Maitland had lingered, his face inscrutable beneath the black soot. "This man needs a physician."

Maitland shouted out to another man to come running.

Small grasped her arm suddenly, pulling her near until they were eye to eye. "He started the fire, Theodora."

"What?" Theodora stilled. "No."

"Your father. Started the blaze. He killed himself." Small sank back, hissing in pain as a well-dressed man arrived and made an attempt to examine Mr. Small's wounds, despite his protests. "He would have killed us all!"

The physician darted a glance in her direction, then focused on his patient without looking at her again.

Theodora was tugged to her feet, too stunned to do more than stare down in horror at Mr. Small. The accusation her father had started the fire was ridiculous. He would never endanger his family. He would never shame them by killing himself.

She glanced up and found Maitland looming over her again. She swallowed at his sour expression. "What did you hear?"

"Enough." He shook his head. "The smoke has confused the man," he said in a loud voice that carried well beyond their immediate surroundings. "I've seen it many times in battle."

A reasonable explanation, but when Maitland grabbed her elbow, she shook him off and crouched down next to Mr. Small instead. "My father would never have done that. Take it back!"

"I saw him," Small insisted, and then cried out in pain as his burned sleeve was cut away, exposing seared flesh. He bared his teeth as liquid from a flask was poured over the arm. "I saw him. I saw him! He started it all. I swear," Small said through clenched teeth, hissing and spitting in pain. "He had a pistol to keep me back," he said in a voice rising in volume. "I had to leave. He would have killed me, too."

Theodora sucked in a sharp breath. Death by suicide always brought shame and scandal to those left behind. And endless gossip. Small's ridiculous claim could ruin them. "You are mistaken. He wouldn't have done that. He was murdered. Speak the truth!"

The crowd began to mutter and draw closer to hear what was said next.

The physician pushed at Mr. Small's chest with just his fingertips and then sighed. "There doesn't seem to be much wrong with him beside the burn, and there are others who need me. I'll return shortly," the physician announced before he stood and pushed his way through the crowd.

"He was dead before the flames took him," Small insisted. But then his eyes rolled back in his head, and his heels drummed on the ground suddenly.

The man sitting beside Small grabbed him, but then Small

exhaled and slumped in his grip...and never moved again. The big man fumbled for Mr. Small's wrist, seeking a pulse, and then exhaled. "He's gone."

Theodora had no strength to do more than stare.

Mr. Small was dead—and the accusation her father had killed himself, had tried to kill them all, remained.

Maitland captured her about the waist and carried her away.

"No." Theodora could not accept anything she'd heard tonight. She clutched at Maitland's arm as darkness closed around them. "He couldn't have done it."

"My condolences, Miss Dalton," Lord Maitland said softly against her ear. "You'll need to be braver than ever now."

She looked up into his face, trying to see his expression in the fading light. "I can't let Mama hear of Mr. Small's accusation."

He shook his head as a sudden breeze blew his dark hair into his eyes, which by day she knew seemed lightened by wisps of gold, most likely made by years of exposure to the sun and sea. "Keeping the gossip from your mother will be impossible."

"It's not true! Father loved us. He would never willingly leave us without his protection." A tight band of tension closed around her ribs, leaving her almost breathless.

Maitland glanced back at the house, a concerned expression in his eyes as he set her down. "Had he had any problems in his life?"

"No, none," she insisted. "Father was a shrewd and respected businessman. Very much liked."

"It is possible to be shrewd, respected and liked, and deeply in debt just the same," Maitland suggested.

"We had no money problems." Theodora glanced at her fingers, attempted to scrub some of the soot from them as she considered the truth. "Not before the fire. My father distrusted banks so much that he kept his money close and at home. That was why he was so particular about flames. He knew the risks of carelessness as much as we did. We are destitute now because the fire destroyed everything we had saved."

Maitland gaped at her in shock. "No."

"Everything is gone," her mother announced in a small voice as she joined Theodora and Lord Maitland.

"I'm afraid so, Mama." Theodora quickly embraced her mother and held her tight.

They were both aware of her father's distrust of financiers, and solicitors particularly. They'd discussed it, argued about it with him, but he'd never made any better arrangements. They were always uncovering pound notes tucked away in books in his library.

Now, everything that made them wealthy had been inside that burning house.

She released her mother, beaten down by helplessness, raw and with no sense of what to do next. For the first time in her life, she had no one to turn to for advice. She was responsible for herself, and for her poor mother, too.

She glanced around, noted the women who'd stood by her mother earlier had withdrawn to whisper among themselves at a distance. Given the way Mother bowed her head, she must have already heard Small's claim that Father had taken his life.

They were already made outcasts because of a liar's dying words.

Theodora put her arm around her mother's shoulders again and squeezed. She addressed Lord Maitland, determined to put on a brave face. "Thank you for your assistance tonight, Lord Maitland. And please thank your friend, too. If you would be so good as to convey our respects to everyone who helped to put out the fire, we would both be very grateful."

He nodded and glanced around at the crowd that kept whispering. His brow furrowed in consternation, and then he scowled. "I'll have a carriage brought out. Where shall I tell them to take you?"

Theodora exchanged a worried glance with her mother. They were bound for anywhere that would take them in. Anywhere people did not expect to see proof they had funds to pay for accommodation, or anything else. At the moment, she had no idea where such a haven might be. They'd have to live on credit now, something she personally abhorred. Theodora smiled to hide her anxiety. "That is not necessary. We can make our own way."

"I'm not leaving him," her mother gasped, as she faced their smoldering home.

Lord Maitland gently turned her mother away from the ruins of their life. "Mrs. Dalton, perhaps you would accept an offer of temporary lodgings, at least for today. From my home, you can oversee the collection of any of your property they recover."

"That is very kind of you," Mother replied, nodding slowly.

"It is the least I can do as a gentleman," he murmured kindly.

Maitland turned to Theodora. "Convince her to go in. My housekeeper is a compassionate woman who will look after you both. Ask for anything. Tea and food if you can stomach it. Clothing, too."

Theodora glanced down, suddenly awkward. They stood about in only their nightgowns, and her mother wore a shawl, but Theodora was still wearing Lord Maitland's coat. They undoubtedly needed his charity, but accepting a stranger's help for life's little necessities stung.

She'd been gossiped about before, and had hated it then, too.

She would clear Father's name.

For now, she had no other option but to accept Lord Maitland's kind offer of sanctuary. "We are grateful for your assistance, my lord," she said with as much dignity as she could muster.

He moved to her side, looking down at her with pity. "I understand only too well how you feel at such a time, Miss Dalton. I, too, have been left behind by a loved one without understanding why. Go in and leave me to sort this out for you both."

"My father is in there," Theodora reminded him.

He looked over both women's attire pointedly. "Your mother needs you more."

CHAPTER THREE

QUINN'S HEART stayed with the Dalton women as they headed inside, and he turned to survey the destruction of their home. A death by suicide left one floundering, unable to fathom the sudden absence. He'd felt the same when his sister had died, but had been protected from gossip on the family estate. But death by suicide in London was another matter entirely. It would not be an easy matter to cover it up. Even the suspicion of suicide would bring shame upon the Dalton women, and the word was spreading quickly already, thanks to Mr. Small's dying words.

Proof of suicide, a crime in common law, could have the Daltons' remaining property seized and forfeited to the crown. Without the support of good friends, the Dalton women would become outcasts in society in a matter of days, if not hours.

Seeing fresh men arriving to attend the blaze, he pulled his wilting valet aside, impressed he'd been fighting the fire along with everyone else. "You've done enough, Rodmell."

"Are you sure?"

Rodmell wasn't a particularly robust man; he'd more skill for knotting cravats than working up a sweat. He pointed around them.

The building was unstable now, too. "The rest of the work will be bloody dangerous."

"As you say, my lord," Rodmell said. He sagged, clearly exhausted.

"Go inside and clean up, then make sure the Dalton ladies are comfortable while I see what's being done with salvage. Tell the housekeeper to house and feed their servants, too, as I send them in. And keep them away from the windows if you can."

"Yes, my lord." Rodmell hurried away.

Quinn didn't want them to see Dalton's body removed.

Deacon reappeared, seemingly out of breath. It was such a relief to see him return that Quinn collapsed against the nearest object of support to catch his breath. "I thought you'd gone."

"I thought I saw an old acquaintance in the crowd, but I must have imagined it. Never mind. Are you all right?" Deacon asked.

"Yes," Quinn confirmed, taking stock of himself. He'd suffered no harm but this tragedy, today of all days, had hit him hard. "You should head home."

"Are you sure I should leave you? I heard it was a..." Deacon didn't say suicide, but he implied it by his silence.

"I'm sure it wasn't. I'm sure the two deaths have nothing in common."

Deacon opened his mouth but then closed it again. He shook his head. "About what I asked you for help with earlier..."

Quinn patted the man's shoulder. They'd briefly spoken of Deacon's request in the carriage already, enough to know he was sorely needed for moral support as Deacon pursued a bride. "Deacon, it would be an honor to help you find a wife, but let's not spread that about. I'm sure you will find the perfect woman soon enough."

Deacon nodded. "Someone smart."

"Someone kind," Quinn countered, slightly pained by the request made to him earlier that night. What was wrong with

Deacon? He was titled and had money enough to make any woman he liked notice him. Women should be flocking to catch his eye. "You have a right to marry anyone so long as they deserve you."

"If you say so."

"I do indeed. Now get yourself home to bed and leave me to think over the matter for the next few days," Quinn promised. They shook hands, and Quinn sent him on his way.

Once alone, Quinn surveyed the smoking ruin, his mood sinking. He could see far better now than he had at the height of the blaze, and it did not look promising. The outbuildings had survived unscathed but not the house. Most of the flames had been reduced to smoking timbers within the three-story dwelling. What was left to burn, the local brigade was doing a thorough job of dousing with water. He headed toward the local magistrate, a man he'd not had reason to speak to before today, and introduced himself.

"My lord. It's an honor to make your acquaintance. Mitchell Banks." They shook hands. "Bad business, this," the man remarked.

"It is. There could be a body inside."

Banks deflated. "None has been found yet."

"The daughter thought her father, Mr. Millard Dalton, might have been in the library. East side at the front, that would be."

Banks pursed his lips a moment. "Fire was worst there."

"I noticed that too." He nodded. He'd known saving the house was hopeless as soon as he'd burst from his carriage after returning from the Newberry House dinner with Lord Deacon. "Whatever your men find, I want for Dalton's widow. She's resting in the house behind us, my home, at present. I'll provide you with her new direction as soon as they decide where they are to go next."

"Rest assured, you can always count on me to do the right thing, my lord. Could take my men a few days to search such a large dwelling, though. What we find of value will be sent over to them immediately, of course. The Dalton's were prosperous people, I hear, and there are always a lot of light fingers around a wealthy home, unfortunately. We'll post men to guard the place tonight, too." A cart rolled up. "Ah, looks like the vicar has heard the news. I'd best have him cool his heels while we dig a bit deeper into the rubble."

Quinn glanced around and noticed Mr. Small had already been taken away for burial. Since the Dalton women knew the man, he called the magistrate back to him. "Mrs. Dalton might wish to pay her respects. Where was Mr. Small taken?"

"Who?"

"The other man who died here."

Banks' eyebrows rose in surprise. "No one mentioned another body to me?"

"Dalton's man died right there." He pointed to the bare patch of pavement the poor fellow had previously occupied. He glanced at his pocket watch to check the time. "He died...oh, it must have been no more than an hour ago now."

He shrugged. "I didn't hear about that death. Devil take it! I hope the anatomists didn't get him while we weren't looking, but it happens more often than I'm happy about. I will look into it. What did Small look like?"

Quinn shivered. Anatomists. They dissected the dead with no respect. Stole loved ones from their final resting places in the dead of night, usually. Quinn described what he had seen of the man while Mr. Banks took notes. "Short, I think. Fine-boned. Dark hair. That's all I know, but for his full name—Mr. Dennis Small."

Banks shook his head and then excused himself to speak to the waiting vicar. He directed the horse and cart to wait and then returned to supervising his men as they worked on the house.

Quinn found a spot out of the way and watched them shift their attention to the front of the house. He accepted coffee from one of his footmen an hour later, and then a cry rang out.

A body had been found.

He reconsidered the coffee and handed it back. "Perhaps later."

Quinn walked forward until he could see clearly into what had once been a library, much like his own, and gritted his teeth at the sight he beheld. The corpse was blackened, almost unrecognizable, huddled against the hearth. He stared long enough to decide it must be Mr. Dalton, and then let his gaze drift away. He'd known the man only a little. The length and size seemed a match for what he remembered.

"Is that him? Is that Dalton?" Banks asked of him.

"I would say so," he confirmed, but he looked again. He could not get out of his mind that there was something about Mr. Dalton's remains that did not seem to fit his expectations.

Dalton had died with both arms curved over his head as if he had tried to protect himself.

That did not fit with what he'd been told to expect.

If Dalton had been dead *before* the fire reached him, if he had taken his own life as Mr. Small claimed, wouldn't his limbs have been relaxed at his sides?

He faced Banks. "That is not what I expected."

Banks scratched his head. "The victims of fires are often like that. They always try to protect their heads. What were you expecting?"

Quinn gritted his teeth. Mr. Small had most definitely been wrong to claim Dalton dead before the fire had reached him. He'd been very much alive—but could he have been saved? Quinn shuddered at the idea of burning to death. "It was suggested that Mr. Dalton had taken his own life."

Bank scratched his head again and glanced around them. "Not the easiest way to die. Let me consider it properly. Now why did the fire start here?"

He watched Banks, who clearly had experience with such grizzly scenes, pick his way carefully through the debris with confidence, questioning and cataloging everything he saw out loud. Banks would be the man to spread the word that Dalton's death was not a suicide, and Quinn desperately hoped that was the case.

He could give the Dalton women the peace they would need in their grief.

"It started in this room. No doubt of that. There's too much destruction here for it to have begun anywhere else. I'd say a lamp was knocked over, somewhere near the window. Drapes caught, and it spread up and across to the book collection." Banks poked a stick into a blackened lump of thick ash by the inner wall. "See how a little evidence of the collection remains, but only at the bottom of the pile? This was paper."

Quinn nodded and then tried to picture the room before the accident. Unfortunately, he'd only called on the man once, not long after they'd taken up residence across from his home, and hadn't had any cause to return. He couldn't remember very much, but he did recall heavy drapes around the front windows and a set of over-flowing bookshelves where Banks prodded.

He glanced around, sizing up the space between the late Mr. Dalton and the doorway. The drapes were all the way across the room from where Dalton had cowered from the blazing heat. And yet Dalton had been close enough to a doorway that he could have escaped or called for help. But he hadn't done either.

He'd stayed in this room for some reason. But why?

"Death by accidental burning. No doubt in my mind." Banks dusted off his gloves. "I trust you'll be happy to provide a statement, my lord."

Quinn quickly agreed. "I'll write my account of events and have it delivered to you today."

"That would be appreciated." The coroner put a cloth to his mouth then hunkered down near the corpse to study Dalton in closer detail. His attention roamed the body from head to foot, frowning a little. He stood suddenly. "I'd best inquire about that other fellow."

Quinn quickly followed him out, grateful for a reason to leave the scene. He was no stranger to death, thanks to his naval career, but he'd hoped such sights might have been spared him, now he was ashore. He'd seen too much death in battle already.

As Banks began to give orders for the removal of the corpse, Quinn turned toward his home.

There at an upper window stood the dark-haired Miss Dalton, watching events unfold. He was not surprised she kept watch over the proceedings, even from a distance. She was a fierce little thing. He called Banks back to him. "Where will Dalton's body be taken?"

"Directly to the church for burial, I expect, given the state of the corpse." Banks pursed his lips. "I should like to speak to the deceased's family, but it can wait until tomorrow, when they are over the initial shock."

Quinn doubted a single day would be all that was required to achieve such a feat, but agreed. "Very good. I will make arrangements for your appointment tomorrow and let you know where they will meet you, and at what time."

Quinn tipped his head and started toward home with a weary heart. He was pleased suicide had not been the cause of Mr. Dalton's death, but nothing could prevent sadness over the loss.

CHAPTER FOUR

QUINN LET himself into his home, noting a hushed atmosphere prevailed. He trudged upstairs to speak with the Dalton women immediately.

Mrs. Dalton, still dressed as he'd first seen her that night, appeared to be asleep beneath a thick comforter on an upper sitting room chaise. He took a step closer, but his housekeeper waved frantically at him then raised one finger to her lips to silence him. He nodded, agreeing not to disturb the sleeping woman just yet. Quinn glanced around, anxious to discover where Miss Dalton had gone.

The housekeeper gestured behind him, towards another chamber.

Quinn turned to his private office, noting the door was ajar.

Miss Dalton stood by the cold hearth, hands pressed to her face, ebony hair twisted into a tight braid around her skull, her shoulders shaking as she sobbed silently into her hands. The poor woman. He was glad to know that she'd bathed and was wearing a day dress now, but not so pleased by her distress. He felt utterly useless under the circumstances, but he crossed the room and cleared his throat softly.

She startled, trying to wipe her face before he saw her tears. "My lord."

"Miss Dalton." He studied her face as more tears began to fall. Fascinated, he watched them slide over her cheeks. He'd never before met a woman who could cry quietly. Theodora was a classical beauty by societies standards. Flawless pale skin beside glossy dark hair. Her brows were two straight fine lines above a pair of fine silver eyes. "They found him exactly where you thought he'd be."

She nodded, and her full bottom lip quivered.

"It is natural to cry. My sisters often damp my shoulders when they are upset. If it will help, come here, my dear." He held out one arm, as he would to his sisters when they were upset, and drew her unresisting body against his chest.

The little woman sobbed brokenly against his waistcoat while Quinn stroked her shoulder, attempting to comfort her during this difficult time. Her hands clenched at his clothes, and he wrapped her in both his arms. They stayed that way for a long moment.

"It was an accident. The coroner believes a lamp fell against the curtains."

She looked up quickly, eyes narrowing. "What about Small's accusations? He said—"

"Small was dying. Confused and in pain. I'm sure he was mistaken about what happened. So is the investigator." Quinn stepped back. "The man wishes to speak with you and your mother tomorrow. His name is Mr. Mitchell Banks. I know of him by reputation only. He's said to be honest and compassionate. He also seems experienced at understanding how fire spreads. I promised to send him your new directions, since your home was destroyed. Have you and your mother discussed where you will go?"

Theodora's shoulders rose in a shrug. "Not yet, but I fear there could be a problem with my mother. She has taken my father's death very hard. She refused to be moved farther than that room or to dress in the clothes your housekeeper offered. I dread to think how she will take a complete relocation."

"A few hours' sleep, and she will be reasonable, perhaps, and understand decisions must be made."

Miss Dalton nodded. "I hope so. What happens now?"

"Banks will direct any recovered possessions to this address until you have secured new lodgings, and I can have them sent on to you. Everything of value or personal in nature will be recovered. He's also promised to post men to watch over the site tonight to prevent looters. I'll send my grooms out shortly as well, just to ensure it happens."

"Thank you." She held out the side of her gown. "Thank you for the clothes."

He squinted at what she was wearing now. It wasn't black, as required for full mourning, but a dull shade of forest green that would do for now. "My sister's, if I recall correctly. Louisa must have forgotten one again. For as long as I can remember, my sister has left something of hers behind, mostly so she has an excuse to return, I think."

Miss Dalton nodded slowly, then took a few steps away before sinking into a chair at his desk.

"It will be all right," he promised. Miss Dalton's quiet dignity at such a time concerned him. Shouldn't she be grieving harder?

"No, it won't," she said as she rubbed the desk with the flat of her hand. "You don't understand how much Papa meant to us."

Quinn followed and sat on the edge of the table. He took up her hand. "I'd often thought I should know your family better. Your father seemed an accomplished businessman."

"He was." Her expression tightened. "I expect we will never see you again after today." Theodora stood. "I should stir my mother so we can make decisions. I must also find employment."

"Surely not." He jumped to his feet, staying her with one hand outstretched. "This is not the time," he protested.

"Better to start now than wait until we are starving." Her expression grew amused; the first sign of levity he'd noticed. "Do you object to a woman engaging in honest work?"

"Of course not. For someone else and at another time. You're a lady in mourning," he insisted, despite knowing he'd no right to tell her what to do.

"I am in mourning, and that is why I must work." She leaned close to him. "I prefer to be busy doing worthwhile things. I've never had the temperament for doing little, as many ladies are prone to do. I have worked for my father, secretly, since I was a girl, and those skills will help Mother and I recover our lives now."

"I see. But..."

Her expression hardened, and he quickly fell silent. "Your disapproval reminds me that English society might not yet be ready to appreciate an independent woman who works for a living. I would have had a much greater chance of employment had this happened in India. No doubt Mother and I will return there as soon as I've amassed funds enough to travel."

He studied the woman, astonished by her quick decision-making ability at such a time. "I am surprised you already have half a plan in mind."

"If you knew me, you wouldn't say that." She regarded him with one brow raised. "They say you are not the usual frivolous aristocrat strutting about Town. Should I believe such gossip?"

He drew back. "Frivolous?"

"Carefree?" She rubbed her temple firmly enough to leave a red stain on her pale skin. "Forgive me if my words offend you."

"I do forgive you, and easily." He'd not truly been offended, only surprised that she thought of him at all. Truth be told, he'd rather have a reputation for frivolity than ruthlessness any day. "I can well imagine the strain you are under."

She sighed. "Don't worry. I don't faint."

"I never imagined you would." Smart, prickly, and impertinent—an intriguing combination in a woman. Ladies like Theodora Dalton were rare and would never fall apart in public. They would keep their pain private, as his late sister had. The thought brought a chill racing down his spine at the realization. He looked her over carefully, suddenly worried for her state of mind. He did not know her, but he had learned she did not have a great many friends of her own age coming to call. Who would look out for her now? "Did your father approve of your work?"

Tears filled her eyes again. Quinn cursed himself for uttering that foolish question. Perhaps the less said about the late Mr. Dalton today, the better.

"He believed in hard work." She cast a frown around the room. "Does your secretary believe in hard work?"

He glanced behind him to the untidy stacks of correspondence littered about the place. He'd get to sort it all out eventually. "I don't have a secretary at present. The last man abandoned his duties—to marry, of all things."

"How shocking."

"Well, he loved the woman he married, so I couldn't easily find a way to change his mind. Bribery did not sway him, and he's not the least bit sorry he's left my employment, either. Finding a suitable replacement has been a trying business, I must say."

She studied the desk. "Would you employ *me*?"

"I beg your pardon?"

She dragged a pile toward her and shuffled the unopened correspondence. "Employ me. I'll have this room straightened in under a day and your social calendar brimming with engagement you will enjoy by the end of the week."

He took the letters from her gently. "Miss Dalton, you're not thinking straight. You've just lost your father and your home. This is hardly the time to discuss what *I* need."

"This is exactly the right time and place. How else could I learn of the situation you find yourself in? You are in danger of being smothered by so much paper as I've never seen. Employ me and save us both. You will gain the services of a dedicated employee. The work will distract me from my loss and from here, I can keep an eye on the recovery of my mother's property."

She began flipping through the papers on the desk in earnest, sorting fresh mail into neat new stacks as if she intended to start immediately.

Alarmed, he stilled her hands again, discovering them very cold. He rubbed them briskly to warm her. "Absolutely not. Think what your mother will say about this when she wakes? She will need you, and she surely will not approve of you working for me."

"My mother is in no fit state to think, let alone disapprove. We can help each other, my lord. I must have funds, and you," she glanced away, her breath shuddering past her pretty lips, "you need someone to throw out scented letters you clearly were not desperate to open."

He winced at that.

"If you require further incentives to employ a woman, I could be of help in other ways."

Miss Dalton glanced up at him under her lashes, and he was alarmed by the desperate gleam in her eyes enough to clutch her slightly warmer hand tightly in his. He wanted to help her, and he had the means to do so. He could set the ladies up in a residence until they found their feet.

Theodora laid her other hand firmly on his chest.

His pulse kicked up a notch as she toyed with the buttons of his waistcoat, and by the way her lips parted. Her tongue flicked out, wetting them.

He swallowed hard and released her hand. "What did you mean when you suggested you could help me in other ways?

"You watch me."

Quinn raised a brow in surprise. He had never hidden his appreciation of women. Beauty and grace deserved a man's full attention and respect. He admired many women, but Theodora Dalton had shown no interest in him before today. "I imagine many men do."

"I've been alone for two years," she murmured, teasing his chest with a gentle caress that he felt all over. "There are things missing from my life."

"You're a spinster," he reminded her, frowning. Spinsters were not meant for dalliance, not unless one wanted to end up leg shackled. Quinn wasn't so generous that he'd marry this woman out of pity.

"I was to be a bride once," she whispered.

It was hard to miss her meaning when her hand slipped downward purposefully to the waistband of his breeches. "I did not know that about you," he struggled to say.

"Daniel, my betrothed, did things with me. In private." She bit her lip. "I enjoyed those things very much."

Quinn blinked in shock at her confession. Many an engaged couple anticipated their wedding night. However, he was not such a fool as to believe her serious in her offer. Too much had changed in the past hours for him to believe she knew what she was doing or saying right now. "You miss him, and I do understand. However, I'm sure you will agree that tomorrow, you will regret this discussion. We will not speak of this again."

"I miss the warmth and companionship of a lover." She drew his hand to her breast and held it against her softness. "The touch of a man's body against mine at night is not something easily forgotten."

Stunned, Quinn could only nod as she moved his hand a little, so he caressed her breast. Miss Dalton wasn't thinking straight. "I hope you are not suggesting that your employment be a mutually beneficial arrangement?"

"It could be. I know how to keep your days and nights full," Miss Dalton promised. She smiled slowly, her eyes glazed, and lowered her hand to cup his cock through his breeches.

Gods! The woman most definitely had experience when it came to the male of the species. That had not been an exaggeration on her part. Quinn couldn't remember the last time a woman had come right out and offered pleasure so abruptly without any form of prior flirting.

He caught her wrist and held her still. "Do you keep this experience of yours a secret from your mother?"

"From everyone." She lifted to her toes to whisper in his ear. "No one will ever know what we do together."

CHAPTER FIVE

EVEN WITH HER heart in danger of breaking, Theodora knew exactly what she was doing in offering herself to Lord Maitland. Men were uncomplicated creatures and often required an added inducement to render the right sort of aid. Although in Lord Maitland's case, he did really need her. The moment she had stepped into this house, and discovered the disorder of Lord Maitland's private office, she'd decided where to seek employment.

She had fleetingly studied Quinn Ford since his return to shore and resignation from the Navy, after what was reported as a distinguished and lucrative career. She had noticed his interest on more than one occasion, but had been too busy with her father's concerns to do anything about encouraging him. He was a man with presence and sense, and that appealed to her more than his handsome face and easy smile for other ladies.

She was looking forward to finding out if the handsome viscount lived up to her expectations—but that would be after she'd straightened out his affairs.

She eased back before he could try to claim a kiss, heart hammering against her breast at her boldness. Sensations she'd set aside for so long stirred her blood a little too strongly for their current location. She had made her offer, and she'd not offer more until he agreed.

Daniel had taught her that timing was everything—in business and in pleasure, too. As much as she missed the man, she was to marry two years ago, she couldn't mourn Daniel forever. She had loved him with her whole heart and body, and not a day went by when she didn't think of him or regret the future they might have had together.

Quinn Ford was real, flesh and blood, and available by all reports. And he suited her immediate needs for employment if he could be persuaded. She wanted only brief employment, a casual liaison, and then she'd return to India to take up her former life and mourn her father properly.

This house was perfectly positioned for her needs, too. She wanted to keep an eye on the recovery of their remaining possessions. The coroner would also not ignore the importance of Lord Maitland's wishes for a speedy investigation if she nudged the viscount to lend his weight behind her request. The viscount would help her get to the bottom of her father's death, whether he intended to or not.

"I do need a secretary," he mused, but then smiled broadly. "However, as tempting as your offer is, I must decline."

Theodora was taken aback by his refusal, and obvious amusement in her surprise. She had propositioned him in no uncertain terms. And she had no doubt Lord Maitland was fully engaged in her suggestion that they share a bed.

Despite the rebuff, she was quite desperate to win him over by any method she could. She stroked him, a firm caress, because he'd not stepped back out of reach yet. She dug her nails in at the last moment to heighten his enjoyment and earned a grunt in return. Daniel could never resist that. "I've no interest in capturing your heart, my lord, if you fear I have designs on marrying you to support myself," she promised.

"That's actually comforting." His smile grew, and then he laughed softly. "But I still decline. I have a mistress. She's the jealous sort. Hates to share."

Theodora released him with an oath, turning away to quickly form a new plan. There had been no gossip about him keeping a mistress. Mistresses were often as immoveable as wives. She grew aware Lord Maitland had followed her, though, and she hid a smile of pleasure.

Perhaps he had no personal need for her now, but she would not be so easily thwarted in other areas. She wanted his employment, and to forget that her father had just died horribly. "I accept the restriction."

"You accept what?"

She turned. "The position of secretary only. I can start immediately. I prefer to be paid by the month, in advance. Lodgings, for myself and my mother, until we can arrange our own close by. In return, I am available to you at any time of the day or night for any correspondence you need written."

His brows had risen high at her statement. "You are determined, aren't you?"

Theodora prided herself on her commitment to everything she did. He could wake her in the middle of the night if the mood struck to write a letter, and she'd never complain. "I am my father's daughter." Her grief surfaced for a moment, but she quickly suppressed the urge to cry. Weeping would get her nowhere in a world controlled by men. "That will be to your advantage."

"How so?"

"As you saw earlier, people gossip. Particularly women. Husbands tell their wives many things they don't know what to do with, so they discuss the matter with other women. Mother and I may be on the outer at the moment, but that will not always be the case. I will share my discoveries with you, and you can use that knowledge to make yourself richer."

"I am rich enough to last two lifetimes." His jaw worked, and then he leaned forward suddenly to stare into her eyes. "Let me make one thing clear. I am *not* my father's son. I do not now, nor do I ever want to, employ peddlers of information. I do not deal in intrigue."

Theodora stepped back from his anger, recognizing she'd made a disastrous assumption about Lord Maitland. She had assumed, deep down, he was the same as every other man. Theodora had assumed the former captain to be well connected with the East India Company, too—a company that delighted in political machinations that had ruined many. Perhaps she had underestimated the viscount. "Understood, my lord."

His lips pressed tightly together as if he were fighting the urge to berate her further. For a long, horrible moment, Theodora feared she'd lost whatever advantage she had gained in her search for employment. She had blundered, and very badly, given the way he stared at her now. His scrutiny was actually quite terrifying.

"You may begin after the funeral, if that is still what you want," he said suddenly. "I'll arrange for rooms to be prepared for you and your mother for an extended stay."

She nodded, and Lord Maitland walked away, hands clenched at his sides.

Theodora rushed to follow him but when she reached the top of the staircase, he was already gone from sight.

Apparently disturbed by Lord Maitland's abrupt departure down the stairs, her mother stirred. "Millard?" she called.

"Oh, Mama." Theodora hurried to her mother.

Her mother sucked in a sharp breath as Theodora sat at her side and took her hand. She stared at their joined hands, bare of rings and still grubby from the ash and soot of the blaze under their nails, and fought not to cry again.

"Oh, no," Mama whispered. Her mother raised her face, showing that tears filled her eyes and her lower lip trembled. "For a moment, I had forgotten he was gone."

Theodora hugged her mother tightly and kissed her hair as she wept anew for many long minutes. When her crying abated, Theodora released her. "Papa would want us to be strong. To that end, I must tell you, I have made arrangements to save us from utter desperation."

Her mother stared at her in confusion. "What arrangements?"

"Lord Maitland is desperately in need of a secretary, and has hired me. You will not believe the mess I stumbled upon in his private office while you were sleeping. It could take weeks to sort through, but I will straighten him out in the end, and we will find out who killed Father with his help."

"I cannot believe Lord Maitland agreed to that," her mother whispered. "He has been kind enough already. He barely knows us for all that we have been neighbors for two years."

"It did take some bold negotiation on my part, but it is done, I assure you. We have a roof over our heads and Lord Maitland's protection for the foreseeable future." Theodora glanced around to check that they were alone. "But he does not yet realize he will help us clear Father's name. Those lies Mr. Small told must be repudiated. The slander will surely spread until Father's memory is besmirched beyond all repair. We must have his help to prevent that from happening."

Mother bowed her head. "We both know it couldn't be true."

"That is not good enough for me," Theodora fumed. "I want everyone to understand that Mr. Small lied through his teeth about Papa."

Mother's breath caught. "Do you plan to deceive the viscount and investigate under his name?"

Theodora nodded, a little pained that her mother had correctly guessed her intentions so soon. In business, one sometimes had to get one's hands dirty to achieve the results one wanted. "If Maitland asks directly, I will tell him anything he wishes to know about my inquiries. I will not keep secrets." She wiped the tears from her mother's cheeks. "Do not worry, Mama."

"How can I not worry when you will not be honest with him, just as you weren't with Daniel?" Her mother captured her face. "Your father only asked you to be nice to Daniel, and you ended up engaged to marry him. What else have you bargained away to the viscount?"

"Nothing at all." She winced though, feeling a fool again. Her greatest bargaining chip was useless when a man had a mistress. He would be immune to flirtation, and his desires would be satisfied by another beyond her control. "My services in exchange for a roof over our heads, payment made month to month, and in advance. Generous terms. Maitland is rich enough that he can afford the expense of two extra women in his household with barely a ripple."

Yet, it still smarted that her seduction had been so thoroughly rebuffed.

The mistress had been an unknown factor in her assessment of Lord Maitland, but what was done was done. She would make do with a position and go from there. She just had to survive burying her father and do her job well enough to be kept on.

Timing was everything. Theodora had long since learned that in business, emotions only slowed one down and prevented clarity of thought. But not everyone thought as she did. After years of practice, Theodora could easily suppress her emotions behind the busy activity of work.

She longed for such a distraction now. The well of sadness

inside her was vast, and she shrank from the pain of losing another loved one.

She had cried copious tears for Daniel, and now would cry in the privacy of her bedchamber each night for years to come over losing Papa, too. In between, she had to be strong for her mother and wipe clean her father's tarnished reputation.

She would win over the viscount to her cause soon enough. Her first step would be to prove herself invaluable in managing his business affairs and earn his trust—and along the way, she would satisfy her curiosity about this jealous mistress of Lord Maitland's.

With those goals ahead, she convinced her mother to retire and rest in the hastily prepared bedchambers upstairs.

CHAPTER SIX

QUINN MOVED out of the shadows and clapped. "Marvelous."

On the stage, the performers turned to stare into the pit of the dimly lit Theater Royal as the echoes of his applause died down slowly.

"Maitland! You beast," Adele Blakely cried out once she recognized him in the shadows, hand clenched to her chest with all the dramatic flair of a superior performer in front of a captive audience. She rushed from the stage to meet him, golden blonde hair loose and billowing behind her as she threw herself into his arms.

"Why didn't you speak up sooner?" she chided, after they'd greeted each other with a passionate kiss.

He and Adele had been friends, and lovers, for years. They had an easy relationship, one that had survived his long absences at sea, when he'd not been able to see her as often as they both wished he could. For all the days and months apart, however, he'd never felt closer to another living soul.

"Forgive me, my dear." He kissed her again, and then caught her earlobe lightly with his teeth before whispering, "You know I like to watch you perform unobserved. It gives me a thrill to see you in your natural milieu."

"And I prefer to know where you are at all times when you are watching me." She'd complained of his sneaky habits before, but her smile grew as she leaned into him. "I'd rather have you seeing me work my magic on the crowd from the distinction of being in Rutherford's box."

He caressed her soft cheek, causing her delicate skin to flush with heat and her eyes to grow round with desire. Adele was a stunning woman. A virtuoso on the boards, as well as on her back in the home he provided for her on Wellington Street. "I'd prefer the melee of the pit over the indignity of public scrutiny watching me watching you. Imagine if my father arrived." He affected a shudder. "I'd never enjoy another moment with him hovering and scowling."

She pouted. "But the view from Rutherford's box is so much better than the rest of the seats of the theater. It can seem as if we are the only two people in the room."

He sighed. They'd argued this point far too often for him to yield now. "I wish I could oblige you in this, but my mind is set on the matter. I will never sit in Rutherford's box when there is a chance my father might join me," he promised. "You know what his presence does to my temper."

Thankfully, Adele pressed her lips together and said no more to try to persuade him. She had never really understood how much he detested his father's company. Unfortunately, Father had become an irregular patron of the theater this past year, invading Quinn's favorite haunt so often, he'd largely given up regular attendance. If not for Adele, he'd have stopped coming altogether.

Adele looked up at him under a flutter of eyelashes with the steady regard of a wife in training. He'd won this round, for now, but the next discussion was coming. He could see her mind had turned to other matters. "I waited for you after my performance last night. How was the dinner?"

"Dull." He took her hand in his. "I had intended to come as promised but there was a complication."

"What happened?" Her face grew tense. "Were you that overcome with passion for the society debutant you met at dinner? They say Miss Cushing is lovely and her dowry rivals that of your sister's."

"I've told you a thousand times, I'm not interested in debutants." He laughed heartily, but then sobered to pull her close. "Where do you get these silly ideas that money is all that interests me about a woman? I went home, intending a brief conversation with Deacon, but there was a fire. A neighboring property burned to the ground. I had to stay and help. Everything was in chaos, and two men died last night."

Adele's eyes rounded. "Oh, how dreadful. Were you close to these neighbors? Are you hurt?"

He brushed her long hair over her shoulder, heart swelling with love at her concern for him. "It was dreadful, but no, I wasn't so foolhardy as to put myself at risk," he assured her. "I barely knew them, in truth."

But he'd had a hard time all day, forgetting that a man had burned to death not far from his home, and that his daughter and wife were utterly overset by the experience. He could scarce imagine the desperation behind Miss Dalton attempting to seduce him just to prove they were worthy of his charity.

He was not like his father to believe such an offer sincere, but if Miss Dalton needed a distraction, she could make the futile attempt to straighten out his study for a few days. It would ensure she made no further inappropriate advances to anyone else in her fragile state of mind, and he would settle them in a good situation elsewhere soon. That was the only reason he'd agreed to employ her. The next time Miss Dalton propositioned a man, she might not be so lucky, and some lecherous scoundrel might take her up on her offer she'd eventually come to regret.

Adele, however, would not find his decision to take in the widow and daughter at all pleasing. He'd have to mention the Daltons were in his home, and hope Adele didn't become unreasonable. If she heard Theodora was pretty, and unmarried, she'd fly into a rage. He'd not lied that Adele was the jealous sort. She'd declared nothing would ever come between them on many occasions. "One of the men who died in the fire left a widow and daughter behind. The other man, we fear, was taken by anatomists."

"Oh, dear," she said, eyes filling with tears. "I'm sure you did all you could."

"The daughter would have run into the blaze after her father, if I had not prevented her." He'd certainly tried to help, but his help had been paltry at best and almost too late. "I offered the pair shelter until they recover what few possessions might have survived the blaze."

Adele pursed her lips and stared at him sourly. "You are too tenderhearted, always looking after everyone but yourself."

He laughed and held her against him a little more firmly. Quinn loved that Adele worried about him. They had a future together that nothing could change. "I took *you* on and have no regrets. Was that not the right decision, my love?"

Adele blushed prettily and patted his chest. "I would have been lost without you. You gave me the world."

They had met when she'd nothing but her extraordinary talent to her name. He'd admired her dedication and had opened doors so she might have her dream of performing on the stage. After the doors had been opened, and society had acknowledged her talent, her rise to prominence had been assured. Helping Adele was the best thing he'd ever done for another living soul. He had no regrets at all about his small part in her success.

"I only gave you a chance to impress those who mattered, and you did the rest." He lowered his face to hers. "I'm looking forward to introducing you to my new friends as we planned, too."

He was introducing her to Amy, his secret half-sister, and her new husband, Harper Cabot, the surprisingly amusing shopkeeper. He'd been planning this introduction since Christmas, but a great many distractions kept getting in the way.

"I wish things could be different, but I'm afraid I cannot make your dinner." Her gaze rose to his, and she quickly kissed his cheek. "I'm so sorry, Quinn. I must stay late for rehearsals for all of this week unless I want Mr. Arnold to scream like a fishwife. I must also be fitted for the costumes he insisted upon having made afresh. I have no idea when I will sleep, or when I will have a moment for amusement again. Mr. Arnold is planning one of his exclusive parties for after the first performance, too. He's already anticipating the play will be a wild success."

"But we made these plans weeks ago," Quinn reminded her. It was not possible to send his regrets at this late stage, and he didn't want to disappoint Amy and Harper yet again.

"I know, and I have apologized." Adele looked up at him, her expression firm. "You know how important the theater is to me. I want to make you proud."

"I am already proud." He understood her dedication to her craft but damned if he liked that he came second to the theater in almost every situation.

"Please understand." She toyed with his waistcoat pocket watch, glancing at the time. "I must go. If I disappoint Mr. Arnold, he'll make me understudy in the next production instead of lead."

"We cannot have that." He glanced toward the stage, noting Samuel Arnold's fierce glare had already turned in their direction. The man was strict and always made good on his threats to demote those who displeased him. "I'll send him a brace of goose for his feast as an apology for today's interruption. Send a note round when you are free again."

She rushed away to return to the stage without kissing him good-bye, leaving sourness in the pit of his stomach.

Quinn lingered a little while, watching with keen interest but confusion, too. Adele knew her lines well, and spoke them with authority and passion as she strutted the boards. Samuel Arnold would be a fool to drop her when the woman brought the crowds to the theater in droves. Quinn could not understand why Adele couldn't believe she was irreplaceable to both the production and to him.

He nodded to the manager before he strolled out, at a loss for amusement for the afternoon. He'd hoped to spend the evening with Adele, but if she was too busy, he'd best find other interests to occupy himself. Perhaps a trip to his club would fill the empty hours.

He was about to hail a hack for Whites when his name was called out. "Lord Maitland?"

He glanced around, noted the livery worn by the Duke of Rutherford's grooms and a familiar face. He groaned aloud. "Yes, Harrow."

"Your presence is requested." The man gestured toward his grandfather's gleaming black town carriage that had stopped a little down from the theater's main entrance. "Immediately, my lord."

He rolled his eyes but hurried across the street. Would Rutherford ever slow down? The old man did more than most gentlemen half his age. Quinn could barely keep up with him. However, it did not go over well to leave his grandfather waiting, even when he was not expected to be in London at this time of year.

He murmured his thanks as a groom held the door open for him and entered the plush leather and blue-velvet interior. "I didn't know you were in London."

"Where else would I be," Quinn's father answered in a biting tone that had terrified him as a boy as the carriage moved off.

Quinn was utterly taken aback by his father's presence, and the absence of the friendly face of the Duke of Rutherford in the carriage. "My apologies, Templeton. I didn't know you had claimed Grandfather's carriages for your personal use now."

His grandfather had been very clear that he preferred they did not use his carriages and such without good reason.

"Did you call on Mr. Cushing's daughter as I asked?" Templeton sneered. "No, of course, you did not. You disobeyed me."

Quinn knew better than to rush in to defend himself. That was the surest way to escalate an argument. He took a moment to straighten his coat before answering. "There was no reason to raise her expectations."

His father whacked him with a riding crop across his upper arm, something he had done all of Quinn's life. Quinn barely flinched from the sting.

"Of course there was a need," Templeton said, eyes growing hard. "Mr. Cushing expected you to call and grace his drawing room. You deliberately made me look a fool with your rudeness."

Quinn sat back as if the punishment had not occurred. "I'm no longer in the service, nor must I carry out your orders. I have more important things to attend to than beating your drum."

"Like calling on your flighty little tart," his father bit out, glaring at him with all the gentleness of a caged lion.

Father took too much notice of his relationship with Adele for Quinn's comfort. He chose to ignore the dig rather than defend her character yet again. "I have been renewing acquaintances, catching up with old friends I've missed over the years I was away from London."

"Those men are bachelors, and are chasing after the same women you should be considering for your bride," Templeton said with a definite sneer.

"Some are indeed wavering bachelors with much to say about the latest crop of debutants. We compare notes on our first impressions over coffee each day, and toss a coin as to who should have whom when the time comes," he confessed. The talk over coffee was often vastly amusing—especially hearing the lengths some women went to snare a husband.

His father's expression changed to anger, and the riding crop struck him again across the thigh. Hard. "Watch your tone, boy."

Had there been much of a tone to his words? He must be slipping. However truthful he'd just been in his discussions on the debutants, Quinn had learned to adopt a neutral manner to avoid unpleasantness. Lately, he'd found it hard to even pretend at niceties when they were alone. Templeton rarely needed an excuse for his violence anyway.

"Dinner tomorrow night," his father informed him.

That hadn't been an invitation. It was a demand Quinn couldn't immediately accept, for good reason. "Who will be there?"

"People who matter, so you will be on your best behavior. It is high time you started speaking to the right people instead of gallivanting around Town with those useless scoundrels you call friends."

"They do have titles. Crawley is a duke and Deacon is an earl."

"Deacon is an empty-headed fool, too stupid to see he embarrasses Crawley by always being in his shadow, and now in yours. You offer poor candidates as part of your inner circle. You need friends who are better connected than them, and cleverer. Powerful men who can support you in the battles to come."

"You mean I should curry favor with men I have nothing in common with, like you do." He sighed, resigned to the same old argument with his father and the next slap of the riding crop. His skin still stung from the last stripe, but he gritted his teeth rather than reveal that.

His father glared. "You don't know the sacrifices I have made to make your way easy in life. You owe me."

"No, sir," Quinn bit out instantly.

The crop lashed out again, but Quinn caught it before it connected with his face. He held it, staring into his father's hard eyes. "I do not owe anyone more than I have already given in the service of my country. I have lost friends because of your ambitions. I've often wondered if we lost Mary because of something you had a hand in."

Quinn released the crop quickly. He'd not meant to accuse his parent of such an unconscionable crime. There were some things even his father would not do in his pursuit of power. He looked to his father, believing the next punishment would be at last one he deserved.

His father paled at the accusation, swallowed quickly, shocking Quinn to the core by the first glimpse of guilt he'd ever witnessed on his sire's face.

"I had no part in your sister's death," Templeton blustered, schooling his features to blankness.

But it didn't matter. Quinn saw culpability in his eyes.

He observed his father even as he struggled to hide his contempt for the man. "I don't believe you."

"It's the truth." Father's eyes grew stony. "You'll never prove otherwise."

Quinn grew icy cold all over. He'd seen that look before—on the day they'd buried Mary, in fact. Father had a temper, but Quinn had always believed his sisters had been spared the lash of punishment over the years. Had he been wrong? "What did you do to her?"

"I did nothing."

"But you know why she took her own life, don't you?"

"I refuse to speak of her with you."

"And I refuse to speak to you of anything else." Quinn's anger grew. "You pursue your own agenda that has nothing to do with what your own children want or need. You should have protected Mary."

"I did protect her," Templeton claimed. "The girl was always high strung. Flighty."

He swung at his father, but Templeton deflected the blow, sending his fist into the squabs of the carriage.

They stared at each other across the dim interior. It was the first time Quinn had ever attempted to strike back at his father, and it would be the last. He would never be like him. He shook off his father's touch. "Don't you dare malign Mary ever again."

But he knew his father well—his obstinacy was legend. Quinn would get nowhere in a more prolonged confrontation. Templeton would rather die than admit fault in Mary's death.

It would be wiser to withdraw and continue investigating behind his father's back, and to that end, Quinn slammed his fist hard on the roof to make the driver stop the carriage.

He trembled in anger as the carriage came to a shuddering halt. It gave him intense satisfaction to notice his father had grown even paler in the last minute. He looked worried, and he should be. Quinn knew now to look for his father's involvement in Mary's death.

If Templeton had hurt Mary, he'd pay dearly for what he'd done. Quinn would lash out with his own brand of revenge until he was satisfied Father had been punished enough. There were plenty of ways to hurt him. "Goodbye, Templeton."

"You are not dismissed," his father roared as Quinn stepped out in the middle of Bond Street.

"You may not wish to acknowledge it, but we are done, my lord. I have nothing left to say to you, but that will not always be the case. I will have the answers I seek—and soon."

He set his hat on his head. He would walk the rest of the way to his club while he reviewed what facts he had about his sister. Mary had been in London at the same time as Father the week before her death. She'd returned to Newberry without Templeton and drowned herself the very next morning.

Something had happened in London, and he would find out what it was.

"A woman like her, in her situation, wants only one thing," Father called. "You will see I am right in this. She uses you!"

It took a moment for Quinn to understand that his father was not speaking of Mary, but had returned to the subject of Quinn's mistress. The old man was a mule when it came to his own agenda. Quinn knew precisely where he stood with Adele, so he wasn't worried. She was his future. The only woman he could imagine spending the rest of his life with.

Marrying Adele would not please Father one bit.

Quinn glanced at the store ahead of him. Cabot & Hunter Haberdashery was bustling with activity, and it was a warning to him of the consequences of underestimating Templeton. His father cared for no one, but innocent lives were forever changed by the man's interference.

Quinn returned to the carriage. "And how will *you* use *me*, my lord? Will you destroy my life and the happiness I've scraped together to further your own ambitions? I am not your dog to bring to heel anymore. If you want something unpleasant done, do it yourself."

"I'll show you who is using who, here," Templeton threatened.

Quinn turned away in disgust, flicking up a coin to the groom hanging off the back of the conveyance as it began to pass him by. "Next time warn me when it's not Rutherford," he called to Harrow.

"I was forbidden, my lord," the groom said by way of apology.

Typical. Harrow would probably be threatened with dismissal if he tried to warn Quinn. That had happened before, too.

CHAPTER SEVEN

QUINN HEARD A STRANGLED sob and glanced toward Miss Dalton. She was so pale, he feared she might faint and topple into the open grave, where her late father waited to be laid to rest.

He eased back a little, discreetly positioning himself closer to the woman and her mother. Her spine straightened as those gathered around the graveside regarded her. He was uncertain if the people attending the burial were true mourners or merely gawkers after gossip.

Funerals were always hard, but this was the first time Miss Dalton had shown her upset since the morning after the fire. He'd never thought her unfeeling, but he did think her strange to fight the release of emotion so commonly felt at such a time.

The vicar droned on, and Quinn listened with one ear, but the rest of his attention remained on Miss Dalton and what she might need from him. To be honest, he was quite worried about what her next request might be, given that she'd already propositioned him—a complete stranger.

When the vicar finished his graveside sermon, mother and daughter held each other. Fingers entwined so tightly, their knuckles showed white. Mrs. Dalton sobbed brokenly as the vicar attempted to speak words of condolence to her.

Miss Dalton put an arm around her mother's back to hold her up. Her face was blank of emotion, conquered by sheer force of will, he suspected.

"Thank you, sir," she said. "My father would have been honored by your words today."

"He was an exceptional man. I am sorrier for his death than you can possibly know."

Miss Dalton gently turned her unresponsive mother toward the waiting carriages. Their steps slow, measured.

Neither lady needed to remain while the coffin was lowered into the ground and covered with earth. But Quinn would. He would ensure her father's final resting place could never be disturbed by grave robbers.

Although more familiar with burials at sea, he gestured to the men he'd hired and waited while the mortsafe was lowered over the simple coffin. Only then did he allow the grave to be filled, and tossed coins to the men who would remain in the cemetery for the next ten days or so. Further security against those who would defile Mr. Dalton's final rest.

Mr. Millard Dalton had suffered enough, in Quinn's opinion.

As he turned from the grave, he noticed Mr. Banks standing nearby.

He moved toward the man. "Banks, it was good of you to come."

"I came to see you, actually." He glanced back toward the carriage briefly. "I called at your home, and your servants were kind enough to give me your directions."

"Oh," he said. "Is there a problem?"

"No. I have good news in fact."

"What is it?"

He winced. "I did not want to speak of this before his widow, but when Dalton's body was inspected more closely before placed in the coffin, these were found. They were embedded in Mr. Dalton's very flesh."

Banks opened up a square of linen to reveal a handful of bright gems.

Quinn gasped. "What the devil?"

"There was what seemed to be some gold inside his charred flesh, too, which makes me suspect that Dalton had these gems on a gold chain around his neck when he died."

Although his stomach clenched, Quinn picked up one gem, studying the color and shape in the light. "These seem perfect."

"Yes, I was unsure of what they might be, and took the liberty of having them cleaned by a colleague. Once polished, it became clear that what I had in hand was very valuable." He glanced toward the carriage where Miss Dalton and Mrs. Dalton waited for Quinn. "They should be returned, but perhaps you might oblige me in this errand? I understand the Dalton women are still guests of yours."

"They are." Quinn accepted the gems, stuffing them in his inner pocket. "Mr. Dalton was very well loved by his wife and daughter, and Mrs. Dalton particularly seems incapable of making any decisions. There will never be a good time to return these, I fear, but I promise I will do so at the first opportunity."

"I do understand, but it is not right to allow them to believe themselves paupers. I have it on good authority that you have a king's ransom there."

He smiled quickly, exceedingly happy for them. With these gems in their possession, they could be settled in a new home soon. They could live a life of ease, as Dalton would have wanted. He was also relieved Theodora would have no need to begin work for him, or for anyone. "I don't believe the Dalton women had any idea of this."

"I wonder why?"

Quinn did too. Those gems would set the Dalton women up for

the rest of their lives, though. "I'll return them to Mrs. Dalton when we reach my home."

He said his farewells to the investigator and joined the women in his carriage. Mrs. Dalton had turned her face away, and Theodora was curled against her mother's side. Neither lady acknowledged him. Quinn tapped the carriage roof and got them underway, regarding the pair with concern.

They remained silent until they reached Maitland House. Mrs. Dalton was the first to speak, thanking him for his assistance as she alighted from the carriage. Theodora said nothing at all, merely stumbled up the front stairs and disappeared inside faster than he expected. He held out his arm to Mrs. Dalton, allowing her to lean on his strength as she returned indoors.

"Mr. Banks spoke to me after the burial."

"Did he?" More tears slipped down her cheeks.

"Indeed." Once inside, and in private, he revealed the gems to her on his palm. "It seems Mr. Dalton did not leave you without means after all."

Mrs. Dalton poked at the gems without any real interest. "My necklace? He was supposed to have the clasp fixed for me. How did you come to have them?"

Quinn winced. "I'm told your husband was wearing them when he died."

Mrs. Dalton sobbed at that and pushed his hand away. "I don't want them!"

"But they are yours to keep. Madam, nothing is beyond your reach now."

"All I want is Millard returned to me." She backed away. "Keep them. I couldn't bear to wear them again."

She turned and dashed for the staircase.

"Mrs. Dalton!" Quinn called after her.

She kept going without looking back at him once. He heard her sobs and winced. "Madam, please. I'm so sorry. I had no choice but to tell you."

Mrs. Dalton waved a hand just before she disappeared out of sight.

Damn. He should have waited to tell Mrs. Dalton about the stones, but how could he allow her to continue to think herself destitute? That would be heartless. He couldn't have *not* informed her. The stones were hers by rights, and valuable.

Perhaps he should have told Miss Dalton first, instead, and allowed her to break the news more gently.

He followed Mrs. Dalton upstairs, intending to speak with her daughter next. The doors to his guest bedchambers were closed, as expected, and as he poised outside the first door, Theodora's, he heard the woman's heartbreaking sobs inside.

Determined not to further upset the women, he retreated to his bedchamber and the cold hearth next to his bed. He knelt, stretched his hand up inside the chimney, and removed a steel box from within. He pried the lid open and, since it was empty, dropped the stones inside and hid it again. The stones would remain there until Mrs. Dalton asked for their return. He would allow her time to grieve before broaching the subject again.

CHAPTER EIGHT

"IF YOU DON'T MIND me saying, Miss Dalton, his lordship has maids who dust and clean for him," Mr. Rodmell, Lord Maitland's valet, remarked at Theodora's feet.

Theodora shrieked, dropped the cloth she was holding and struggled to keep her balance on the chair. The large landscape she'd been peeking behind crashed back against the wall. "Rodmell! Don't do that."

"My apologies, but you still should not have been moving the paintings. That is a maid's job."

"Clearly, they have missed this spot for some time. I found cobwebs here, and now that I know for certain that there are no spiders behind it, I can breathe easily again," she said, shuddering.

Rodmell appeared less than impressed with her suggestion that there could be unwanted beasties in the library and took the cloth from her hand. "Mr. Layton had no complaints about the room."

"Lord Maitland's last secretary may have had no complaints about his books, but probably never lifted his eyes to the corners of the room. He's been gone for months. The study requires a thorough dusting." She wiped her gloved fingers down the picture frame and showed Rodmell proof of the dust.

"I'll have a word with Mrs. Burrows for you and have it attended to," he said quickly, and then sneezed.

"I would appreciate that." Theodora wasn't usually so picky about her surroundings, but wearing mourning colors revealed so much about a home. She already had a dusty hemline and a never-ending urge to rub her nose. The more time she spent in this room alone, the more irritated she was by the inattention to cleaning it. Rodmell helped her down to stand beside him. "What I was really doing before being distracted was looking for some clue as to the location of this charming scene."

"It is of the Duke of Rutherford's family seat at Newberry Park in Essex."

Lord Maitland's family had a similarly named mansion in the heart of Mayfair—some twenty minutes ride distant from Maitland House. Newberry *House* was said to be very elegant and quite large. Quinn's parents, the Earl and Countess Templeton, lived there with the Duke of Rutherford's blessing along with other members of the family when they came to London.

"Ah, I see. A pretty spot indeed." Theodora had heard much of the country estate too from a maid who'd grown up there, and she'd discovered a great many landscapes for the area spread around Lord Maitland's home while she'd been waiting to speak to him. She had thought they may have been of the same location, but hadn't been sure until now. She pointed across the room. "And who is the merry young woman in that small portrait over there by the fire?"

Rodmell sighed softly. "That is, was, Lady Mary Ford. The master's younger sister."

Theodora moved closer. Yes, perhaps there was a similarity she could see around the eyes. She'd heard mention of Louisa, Sally, and two brothers already from the chattering new maid Lord Maitland had seen assigned to her. "What happened to her?"

"It is not my place to speak of the dead," Rodmell said after a long moment of silence.

Theodora whipped around quickly to stare. Rodmell had been more or less an open book until now, speaking expansively of every member of the Ford family with great pride and fondness—except for this one girl. That he would not say very much was telling. It must have been a tragedy that stole her life away.

"When did she pass?"

Rodmell took a step back. "At seventeen. Five years ago, it would be now."

"So very young," Theodora whispered. "Was she a favorite?"

"Oh yes. The master and Lady Mary were very close. If there is nothing else, I must return to my duties?" Rodmell asked, appearing ready to flee.

She smiled in understanding. "If you could have someone start on this room today, I would be grateful. I'll move my work down to the dining room until the chamber is ready for use again."

Rodmell frowned deeply. "You'll have to speak to Lord Maitland about that. He prefers to keep his correspondence to the upper levels of the house."

That struck her as an odd thing to do, but a great many things about Lord Maitland jarred with what she had expected of him. Yet she did need a table to work upon. The only other one large enough to hold all of Lord Maitland's papers was in the dining room downstairs.

"Well, I could always work on the staircase while I wait," Theodora mused, but then laughed. "Honestly, Lord Maitland is still out and has left behind no word when he will return from Mayfair, so might we settle on a compromise. He employed me to work, and I cannot in these conditions. I would rather not explain to him that anyone might have been lax in their duties since Layton's departure. Do you not agree it is unnecessary to bother so great a man with every small detail of how his home is maintained?"

Rodmell eyed her warily, clearly unsure of her reasons for asking. "I do agree," he said slowly.

"Good." Theodora dusted off her hands again. "We are in agreement. He need never know about this discussion, or any others we might have in the future on similar topics."

She began to collect her papers so she might move to another room to work.

However, Rodmell lingered, and when she looked his way again, he was scrutinizing her with a small frown.

Theodora wanted him gone. "Is there something else?"

"I wanted to say how very sorry we all are for your loss," Rodmell said, his tone full of compassion once more. "Mr. Dalton was a fine man. A fair man. Everyone at Maitland House knew him by reputation to be a sensible and just employer. The staff will not pay any heed to unfair gossip we might hear."

"Thank you," her eyes misted with tears, and she brushed them aside quickly and firmed her jaw. The last thing she'd expected to affect her was the sympathy of a servant over the rumors of her father's demise. But it meant a lot to her to have her father's character acknowledged by Lord Maitland's servants. It struck her as both honest and painful. Her father had risen from very humble beginnings and worked hard to achieve much in his short life.

However, Theodora was only just hanging on to her composure right now. Conversations of this nature would only upset her. "If you don't mind, I prefer not to speak of the matter again."

"As you wish, Miss Dalton. Lord Maitland is the same way about his sister." The man stood to attention; his sympathy hidden again behind a professional bearing. "Perhaps you would like to tell me what you *do* expect. Lord Maitland has never employed a female secretary before."

Theodora drew in a deep breath, grateful for a practical question she could answer without too much thought. "I rise early, prefer hot chocolate and toast served to me in the morning room before I begin work. I like tea and a few biscuits or a single pastry at eleven. Luncheon is at three o'clock—something simple is preferred. Dinner is either on a tray here at my desk at seven or with my mother, if she is to eat in the dining room. I tend to work very late into the evening and will not ask for anything from the kitchens after eight o'clock. I prefer not to be disturbed when I work late at night."

"My God, that is a frightening schedule you plan to keep," Maitland remarked as he strode in and tossed his hat across the room. It landed exactly on top of a large bust carved out of marble, and then slid a little to the side until it stopped at a jaunty angle. Maitland came close, resting one hand on the back of her chair as he studied her. The pose showed off his tremendously elegant clothes to perfection. He frowned. "Do you ever allow yourself time to look out the window?"

"Of course." She took her seat and drew a blank sheet of paper from a drawer, pushing the feeling of excitement Lord Maitland's return stirred in her body. There was an open warmth about him, not just his body heat she discovered, that made her exceedingly aware of him. She wanted him to like her, and it had very little to do with her abilities as a secretary. "Four times a day at the very least. It is very good exercise for the eyes, and I recommend it to you. I was just about to remove myself to the dining room and enjoy the view from there, so I would not upset the household routine."

She glanced up when he remained silent. "My lord?"

"Dalton, what are you doing here?"

"Working, of course."

Lord Maitland stared at her for a long moment then shook his head. Had he changed his mind about her working for him?

"If there is nothing else?" Rodmell asked diplomatically.

"Nothing for me, thank you, Mr. Rodmell," she said quickly to the man, anxious to be alone with Maitland and prove herself capable of her new duties.

"You may go, Rodmell," Maitland agreed, still looming over her.

Once they were alone, she lifted her face to her new employer. "Who is that bust of?"

"My grandfather, the Duke of Rutherford. Don't worry, Rutherford is fond of hats. He gave the bust to me when I moved here so I would never be without him." He smiled slightly. "I thought you would be with your mother."

"Mama has asked me to leave her alone. I've checked on her several times, only to be sent away." She smiled quickly. "She just sits at the window, her hand at her throat, staring at nothing."

"Has she said very much since we returned from the funeral?"

"Not really." Theodora worried a little. "Was there something you needed to speak to her about?"

"It can wait." Maitland sighed as he picked up his mail from the corner of the desk and shuffled through it. "These are all open," he said sourly as he waved them toward her.

"Yes, I know. Do you always turn the mail upside down?" She sighed, committing his little quirk to memory. "The uppermost correspondence were only invitations. The truly important letters are now on the bottom and are mostly from your family, judging by the return addresses. Family correspondence remains sealed."

He reversed the pile and then grunted. "Layton never had such a system."

"Well, I am not Mr. Layton, and if he left *you* to open everything, that would explain why dust coated some of the letters that were buried on your desk, which you can now fully use."

While he'd been gone, Theodora had rearranged parts of the room to her liking with the help of a footman. She had placed her desk at a better angle, so she had a view of the door and so she could see who came and went up the stairs. She could also sit comfortably while Maitland dictated or discussed his wishes, and yet still give him the privacy of not looking directly at him.

Once the room was properly dusted, she could feel very comfortable here.

Theodora collected the pile of papers she wished to work her way through and stood. "Excuse me, my lord."

"Yes, I heard you were moving downstairs so the lax maids can dust, but you didn't intend to tell me about it," he said, a slight smile gracing his lips.

"You were listening?"

"Couldn't help it, and I always find it fascinating what people say in unguarded moments. *So great a man* you say? Old Layton never flattered me so well." He laughed softly as she blushed and took the pile of papers and folders she held before gesturing her to precede him from the room. "Ladies first."

Theodora hurried ahead, feeling her cheeks burning now.

CHAPTER NINE

THEODORA HADN'T REALLY NEEDED Lord Maitland's help, but she was grateful for it just the same. He'd saved her several trips up and down the stairs.

The dining room was a pleasant chamber, and she chose to sit in the middle of the table, spreading her papers around her in a circle. Maitland prowled the room, idly watching her arrange his papers without comment.

She wished Maitland would sit. He was elegantly dressed and disturbingly tall—and was making her concentration scatter away from his business affairs.

"Won't you sit down, my lord? I have a few questions that could take some time."

"Oh." He hooked a chair beside her with his foot and sat down untidily upon it. "I'm used to reading on my feet—an old habit from my days at sea. Old Layton was forever complaining about it too. I used to sway from side to side once."

Lord Maitland still swayed, though she would not dare bring it up on her first day. When her father had perished in the fire, and Maitland had held her, she'd been gently rocked from side to side as if she were a child. It had been oddly comforting to be held like that once more.

As he began to leaf through the thick pile, Maitland started to fidget. His legs seemed particularly mobile, jiggling up and down in the most distracting way. She watched him in silence for a few moments. However, Maitland didn't seem aware of what he was doing.

When she could take no more, Theodora placed her hand on his knee briefly to still him. Then she readied her pen to write. "What are your thoughts on the day's invitations?"

He exhaled sharply and sat at the table properly to study the invitations. "I'll attend Garrison's on the fifteenth, the Leavenworth on the eighteenth, but not the Fairborn route on the nineteenth. Lady Fairborn has grown particularly demanding, and I'd prefer to avoid her."

Theodora wrote notes quickly, but then glanced at him as his words sank in. "Do you not like forward women?"

His brows rose. "I do not like married women who flirt with me before their very large and possessive husbands for the fun of it."

"Ah, avoidance is a very diplomatic solution when it comes to unwanted advances." Theodora winced. That probably explained why she had not seen her employer for the last few hours. She'd made him uncomfortable, but not enough to see him turn her and her mother out. Perhaps he hoped she'd take herself away. Theodora straightened her spine, determined not to remind him of her faux pas by acting forward again.

"It can be." He set down the papers, his knee bouncing again. "I will need a brace of goose sent to Mr. Arnold of the Theatre Royal this afternoon."

"That is easy to arrange." She reached for a slip of Maitland's stationery. "And the note is to say?"

"My best for a memorable opening night."

"I had not thought you the type to enjoy the theater." Theodora bit her lip. A good employee would probably not remark on his habits or likes. A male employee certainly would not. She jotted down the note quickly, warmth rising up her cheeks once more. But, as she glanced at Lord Maitland's bouncing knee again, noted the theater would require Maitland to sit still for extended periods of time. He was sure to have a box, or access to one. That habit of bouncing his leg must be very distracting for his guests, as it was again for her now.

She stretched her hand toward his knee, but changed her mind at the last second before she touched him. Thankfully, he stopped moving on his own. "Have you been a patron of the theater for long?"

"Of a fashion." He stretched his legs out suddenly, crossing them at the ankles beneath the table. In that pose, he became very still at last. She bit her lip, unusually distracted without cause. Inappropriate remembrances of being in his arms brought heat to her cheeks and a pleasant hum to her body at the possibilities to be found in his bedchamber.

He had someone else in his life, she reminded herself. A mistress. A possessive type of woman. In her experience, jealousy only had reason to stir when a highly emotional being felt threatened by a romantic rival outside her sphere of influence.

She wrenched her attention back to his face. "Is your mistress an actress?" she blurted out.

Lord Maitland regarded her steadily, neither confirming nor denying. "Send the goose and note after four o'clock, Dalton."

His use of her last name alone was confirmation enough she had made a correct assumption—and had overstepped, too. Formality placed barriers between people as surely as a wall had been built. As much as his secrecy disappointed her, she couldn't force him to speak to her about personal matters or relationships. She wasn't any woman's rival. She'd already lost that particular battle. "Yes, my lord."

She quickly wrote and then passed the paper to her employer to sign. He took the pen from her, scrawled a wild signature, and then slid it back across the table.

"I had accepted an invitation for tomorrow night," he told her with a wry smile. "I will need to send my apologies."

She checked his sparkly filled appointment book. "You were to dine with Lord Deacon tomorrow in Town."

He nodded. "Deacon is a good friend. Please say the 'usual delay' prevents my attendance."

She frowned. "What is the usual delay?"

"My father. Lord Deacon will understand the reference without needing additional explanation." He took a slow breath, grimacing as he rubbed his thigh. "I will be dining at Newberry House instead with my parents. Eight o'clock until whenever the hell I can escape," he growled.

Startled by his angry tone, Theodora made a mental note never to mention Lord Maitland's parents if she could possibly avoid it. "And the other invitations?"

"Give them my apologies and best wishes for a pleasant evening as you decline them."

"Very good. I'll prepare replies directly." She quickly scratched out the necessary letters for his signature and passed them over, surprised to find he would wait for her to write every single one. "Is something wrong, my lord?"

He began signing. "Layton would have waited till I was gone before he even started."

She smiled quickly, bearing through yet another reference to her much-mentioned predecessor with as much forbearance as she possessed. "I don't like to waste time, and the hostesses will appreciate a speedy response so they can make their arrangements final."

"I see your point." He finished signing with a flourish and slid them all back. "What is your experience at arranging dinners?"

"I have always enjoyed it. We hosted some fabulously invigorating debates at my father's table when we lived in India. His circle of acquaintances in London was smaller, but always well attended and enjoyed."

"Good. Make arrangements for a dinner for twelve for Tuesday evening in two weeks' time. The housekeeper will help you. I will write you a list of my closest acquaintances to invite and leave it on your desk upstairs."

"How many courses?"

"Eight."

"Is the dinner for any particular purpose?"

Lord Maitland's brow furrowed. "Just get it done."

Although curious about his silence, she brought his appointment book closer and flipped it open. Lord Maitland tapped a finger to the specific date, where a single star had already been drawn. He said no more about it, but his tension was palpable. If the date was important to him, why would he not say what the entertainment was in honor of?

She made a note about the dinner, relaxing at the realization she would keep her employment until at least that date. "I can have the housekeeper draw up three menus for you to choose from."

"Thank you." He stared at her. "Desserts must be served for the first course."

"But the dessert course should come later."

"Not for this dinner."

Now she really *was* intrigued, but his expression suggested he wouldn't explain any of it. "Was there anything else, my lord?"

"No. But you puzzle me, Miss Dalton." He sighed heavily and rubbed a hand across his jaw. "I don't believe I've ever met anyone so entirely calm after a tragedy as you appear to be. When we suddenly lost a member of my family, my mother, and sisters, even my younger brothers, were distraught for weeks and months. Work really does the trick for you?"

Theodora set her quill aside carefully. "Perhaps I am abnormal not to vent my emotions and wallow in grief, as other people will. I've never enjoyed crying in public. Besides, I have learned the grief never goes away entirely, no matter how much I have cried and railed at the injustice of my loss. I worked very long hours after my fiancé, Daniel, died. If I am able to exhaust myself during the day, I sleep better at night and regrets are held at bay for a little while."

Lord Maitland stared at his boots. "What did you regret about losing Daniel?"

That perhaps she hadn't loved Daniel enough by the end of his life. In the beginning, she'd thought herself the luckiest of women, in love with a gentleman of great passion, but had been deceived by her own awakening desires. "Far too much."

Maitland waited for her to say more, but Theodora was too wise to divulge much else. A male secretary would not be so forthcoming about his private affairs. She must learn to keep to her place, no matter how easily she was drawn toward the man who'd taken her in. "You have a dinner tonight to prepare for," she reminded him.

"I do indeed, but there is plenty of time to change and return to Town by the expected hour." He remained seated, lost in thought. "If I go up early, my valet will have an excuse to fuss over my attire for longer than necessary. I am quite sure you've noted Rodmell's nature already."

"I like him. He's very loyal to you." She smiled quickly then glanced at his open appointment book, noting his hosts for the night lived not far away, and recognizing the surname from her previous shopping expeditions on Bond Street. "I would not have thought a viscount would have much to say to the proprietor of a prosperous London haberdashery, or his wife."

Maitland laughed suddenly and took up the day's newspaper to read. "Then I'm happy to have surprised you. Cabot is a new acquaintance and exceptionally good company. I see the newlyweds often, and I am always available should either one come to call."

"I see," she said, making a mental note that her employer's eccentric circle of friends included a couple many of his class would think far beneath them. On the surface, Lord Maitland had seemed like every other young buck about Town—concerned for appearances and ready for dalliances and fast thrills. Finding out he was also introspective and loyal to friends of all social standings was a happy discovery.

She made entries in his diary for the appointments he would keep and sealed his letters in readiness for dispatch. As she completed her work, she made notes of things to ask the housekeeper tomorrow when they planned Lord Maitland's dinner, and then thumbed through a great stack of old, untidy papers.

He glanced at his paper. "My investments. London properties and such. Rent day is not too far away if memory serves."

"Monday," she concluded after checking through a few of the files. "Do you employ a rent collector, or must I do that?"

"I employ a rent collector. A Mr. Albert Bellington. Mr. Layton used to tour the homes with him from time to time, but I cannot ask you to do that."

"Why ever not?"

He glanced her way, eyes skimming her from top to bottom and back again. "You're in mourning. Sometimes tenants do not want to pay, and it becomes an ugly business to extract the rents. I refuse to put you in harm's way."

"I have dealt with recalcitrant tenants before. My father owned property in India, too. I know the struggles of running a profitable enterprise while still being fair. I'll take along an extra groom or footman if it makes you more comfortable with the idea of me going.

Someone who knows how to use his fists, if necessary, and can apply his looks to charm the most reluctant tenant's wife out of their hidden stash of coins."

He lowered the paper completely, staring at her. "You are such a contradiction."

He was not the first to notice she possessed her own peculiarities. Usually, it was brought up at the end of a negotiation that she'd won. Most men did not like to be bested by a mere slip of a woman. "Compared to what, my lord?"

"To my imagination. When I first saw you across the street, you were cutting flowers in the garden. I thought then that conversing with you might be like speaking to any other society lady—a conversation full of empty-headed nonsense about the weather, or the cultivation of plants and such. Something I have little interest in or desire to learn more of, I confess." He grinned widely and leaned toward her a little. "You are never dull, are you?"

"I try not to be," she said modestly, but she was delighted by his approval and interest in her character, even if it was for naught but ensuring a pleasant working environment. "So far, I find you rather unique among men, too."

A warmer smile curved his lips, quickly hidden as he returned to his paper. His paper crackled as he suddenly dropped it again. "Theodora, when you had a problem in your life, who did you confide in? Your mother or your father?"

What an odd question, and even more so that it was delivered with him speaking her given name. With anyone else, she would have protested the informality, but she decided to let the use of her given name pass unchallenged, to see where the conversation would lead. "That would depend on the problem. If I had misplaced an item or could not decide what to wear, I would speak to my mother about it. For anything else more serious, I would have sought my father's advice."

He leaned toward her again, eyes alight with eagerness. "Would you have confided in him if it were about a suitor?"

Overwhelmed by his proximity, Theodora fought a blush. "No."

His eyes narrowed. "Who would you have spoken to about a gentleman you favored?"

She regarded him warily. Was he trying to find out if she was gossiping about him with the servants? "What is this about?"

"Please, bear with me and answer my question. Who did you trust with the knowledge that you were interested in Daniel before the engagement was announced?"

"Well, Daniel knew, of course. We were drawn to each other from the very moment we met."

"Anyone else?"

Theodora gave his question serious thought, curiosity about his need to know rising. "Well, my maid likely knew I was smitten with someone, but I don't believe I ever mentioned Daniel to her by name in the beginning, until our understanding was common knowledge. I had no particularly close friends in India to share such a personal confidence with. I did once ask a gentleman acquaintance about Daniel's reputation, though."

"A friend?" He closed his eyes a moment.

"Yes, I suppose you could call him a friend, but only because I knew he would hold his tongue about my interest."

"You truly trusted a man with so personal a topic?"

"Yes, my lord." She sat back in her chair, studying Lord Maitland openly. "Why would that be considered odd? I have just confided in you, haven't I? Besides, gentlemen often know things hidden from women. I wanted to know if he had any dark secrets that might harm my family or me if our acquaintance became permanent. Do you think I should not have?"

"I... No. I'm sure you knew what you were doing, but I never anticipated this direction." He raked a hand through his hair and bit his lower lip. He glanced her way and then stood. "Thank you. Go about whatever you were doing before, my dear. I have to think about this further."

Theodora could not quiet the pleasure that Lord Maitland had used her first name and called her 'my dear' in the space of five minutes. She looked down to hide her smile. Perhaps he was not immune to her charms after all.

CHAPTER TEN

"YOU KNOW, no one has ever suggested such a thing before," Quinn grumbled to his hosts, swiping the last of the cheese from the platter in the dining room of a property he'd once owned in London. Although calm on the outside and happy to be here once more, Quinn still couldn't shake the feeling he'd missed an important facet of Mary's life. He'd always thought that Mary would confide in her family before anyone. Thanks to his tête-à-tête with Miss Dalton today, he had a new direction. Never once had he considered his sister might seek advice outside of the family, but she certainly could have. The question was, who she might have turned to that wasn't a relation.

"I'm sure Lady Templeton has extolled the virtues of matrimony before," Mrs. Amy Cabot said, giggling around her half-empty wineglass. "I cannot be the first to suggest it was high time you made some woman very happy and married her. You are much too nice to remain a bachelor forever."

It was suggested far too often of late, but at least tonight's discussion of his bachelor status was harmless fun, rather than serious discussion. He scowled at Amy's husband seated across the table. "Mr. Cabot, your wife is under the weather. Control her impertinent tongue, man," Quinn complained with mock ferocity.

The older man merely grinned, leaned over to kiss his wife soundly on the lips, and then sat again. "Leave her be. She's happy."

"She's three sheets to the wind, sir!"

"I am not foxed," Amy protested, but then giggled enough to make it obvious she was indeed very foxed. "I'll have you know I am in full control of my sensibilities." Wine slopped from her glass onto the table, and she gasped in horror at the red stain. She glanced guiltily at her husband. "Maybe a little bit disguised, perhaps."

Cabot stretched to pat her hand, eyes brimming with laughter rather than irritation. "A first, my dear. Don't fret over the tablecloth. I'll get you another if the stain sets."

Quinn glanced between the pair; heart full of affection for the obvious bond of love between the newly married couple. He was proud of Amy, despite her current condition. She was deliriously happily married to a man utterly devoted to spoiling her at every turn, if tonight's excesses were any indication. Quinn had no grounds to complain that his secret half-sister was foxed. Amy was finally stretching her wings under the gentle guidance of a man who adored her and would keep her safe.

At least she had someone to look after her now. That had not always been the case, unfortunately, from what Quinn had learned. Amy had nearly been lost to him, too. He wouldn't allow anything to happen to her.

Quinn leaned back and patted his stomach, replete but clear-headed despite the wine consumed. "Another excellent dinner, Mrs. Cabot."

"Thank you for coming, my lord. You are the kindest man to make the time to visit us."

"I did warn you we'd not be strangers the night we met," he reminded her.

She smiled happily. "So you did. I'm sorry your friend couldn't join us."

"Another performance to perfect," he winced, realizing he'd made that same excuse before. "I swear, Adele becomes more obsessed with each new role she plays."

"Perhaps she does not like dinners." Amy exchanged a worried glance with her husband. "A pity neither of us has any talent for performance, Harper. We might have arranged an amateur theatrical. She might have consented to coach us all in our parts. That could have been far more exciting than merely overindulging."

Quinn cleared his throat, discomfited by the suggestion. Adele could be very demanding of those who acted opposite her. He had no talent for pretending, and Amy was the sensitive sort who took all criticism to heart. The pair would meet eventually, and he hoped Adele would accept his half-sister was as important to him as the real ones. "Once this play is over, things will be easier," Quinn promised, determined that Amy not believe for one moment his mistress thought her career more important than meeting a shop-keeper's wife.

There was a tap at the door, and Cabot stood to attend to the interruption and left them alone.

Quinn shifted Amy's glass to a safer location than the edge of the table just in case another wild swing of her hands might bump it. "So, you are happy here?" Quinn asked of Amy once her husband was well out of earshot.

Amy glanced about with pride shining in her eyes. "Yes, this is a lovely home. Thank you for making it available for Harper to purchase."

"He said you liked it best of all the properties he'd viewed. I could not let the man disappoint you," he said, then winked. When he had met the pair, Harper had been promising to debauch Amy in the adjacent drawing room. What he'd missed hearing was the earlier marriage proposal, but a wedding had soon followed, and given the way they still smiled at each other, lifelong bliss seemed assured.

"He never has failed to live up to his promises to date," Amy assured Quinn, and then glanced beyond his shoulder. Her smile faded. "What is it?"

"A messenger has come, Lord Maitland," Cabot said as he rejoined them. "The woman claims it to be an urgent matter that cannot wait."

Quinn turned and found Miss Dalton half hidden behind Harper Cabot's larger frame.

He blinked in surprise to see her; shocked Theodora would make the trip into Town just to deliver him a message. That was more than Layton would ever have done. Layton would have sent a footman.

"Ah, meet my new secretary, Mrs. Cabot. May I present Miss Theodora Dalton? I've employed a woman to manage me, and so far, have no complaints."

"It is not like you to ever complain," Amy promised, as she wobbled to her feet and stretched out her hand politely. "A pleasure to make your acquaintance, Miss Dalton. Forgive us for how you find us tonight. It has turned into something of a celebration."

"I'm happy to meet you, Mrs. Cabot, but..."

Theodora's gaze cut to his, and his stomach instantly knotted at her expression. "What is it, Dalton?" He took in her bearing, seeing the sadness in her eyes, and hesitation, and his breath caught.

"My lord, there has been a tragedy in your family."

He stood quickly; all amusement gone. "My grandfather?"

"No, not the duke." Theodora shook her head quickly. "I am so sorry to be the bearer of this news, but Lord Templeton has been struck down by a tragic affliction. He lives, but cannot move his arms and legs, or even speak."

Quinn's legs wobbled, and he grasped a chair back quickly to hold himself up.

No more punishments or demands.

Templeton might die.

And Quinn couldn't find it in his heart to be sorry.

Misunderstanding his feelings, Miss Dalton hurried forward and grasped his arms tightly, staring up into his face with huge eyes full of concern. "Are you all right, my lord? Quinn?"

"Yes, I'm fine." He licked his lips, and then patted Theodora's shoulder. The hope for an end to his father, though, remained and grew. Quinn steadied himself using Miss Dalton's shoulder, fighting the urge to rejoice out loud, to celebrate as he had at the end of the war against France.

He had been in battle against his father his entire life, striving to slip free of the yoke of family obligation and unreasonable demands without losing his freedom or his compassion.

That goal was so close, he could almost taste freedom.

He faced Amy to see how she had taken the news.

His half-sister held her hands to her lips, but her eyes were dry.

Cabot moved to support his wife. "You must go and take charge, Maitland. There will be much you need to do to aid Lord Templeton's recovery."

Quinn's mouth dried with bitterness. Recovery was not what he wanted for his father, but he couldn't say it out loud to anyone.

He walked to Amy and pressed a gentle kiss to her forehead. "I'm sorry to spoil your dinner, sister dear."

Theodora Dalton gasped out loud, but he didn't look at her or deny it. His concern was for Amy, who'd never met the man who'd kept her mother as his mistress for a time, and then deserted her once her belly was full.

Amy reached up to cup Quinn's cheek. "Don't think of me, Quinn. You have more important concerns now. Take care of yourself, and your mother and sisters. My heart goes out to them. They will need your strength very much."

He closed his eyes a moment, unable to fathom how he would cope with their grief in the face of his elation. He could have other responsibilities soon, too, a new title he had never coveted. "I will pass along your best for a speedy recovery as soon as I see them."

Cabot came forward, clasped him on the shoulder, and guided him toward the door. Miss Dalton followed close behind.

"If your family needs anything at all, day or night, just send word," Cabot offered.

Quinn nodded, grateful for the offer, and that a footman held his coat and hat at the ready. Miss Dalton grabbed his arm when he was suitably garbed for the outdoors and steered him out to the carriage. Once inside the dark confines, she tapped the roof, and they moved off toward Rutherford House.

Quinn covered his head and bent forward over his knees as his mind whirled in chaos.

His father could die.

The bloody tyrant might finally give him some peace.

There were things he needed to do. So many things he'd never considered.

He'd have to send word to the King, or would Rutherford want to do that?

All of a sudden, he became aware that Miss Dalton was witness to his collapse, and he sat up quickly. It was then he discovered her hand rested on his thigh, offering silent support while he'd been overwhelmed. Her touch anchored him, righted his keel in a choppy sea while he attempted to navigate a new future.

One where he might have a chance to be happy.

He glanced out the window as the carriage slowed, recognizing the street they traveled as he tried to slow his pounding heart to the point where he could think clearly. "Why are we here?"

"This is where he fell ill," she said in a soft voice full of compassion.

They stopped before the home he provided for Adele Blakely, and his confusion increased. "But..."

The door opened, the steps were dropped, and Miss Dalton scrambled from the conveyance before him. He stared at the doorway opening ahead. A severe gentleman in a dark coat lingered in the shadows of the house, and Quinn shrank from the truth glaring him in the face.

Surely Father had not been so incensed as to come here to berate his mistress in person?

He hurried out, still a bit dazed as he strode up the steps of his mistress' London abode to hear her crying piteously in the sitting room.

"Mr. Clifford Fletcher, physician," the stranger introduced himself.

"Is she hurt?"

The man appeared surprised by his question. "Oh, not at all. Not at all. Her gentleman friend is upstairs in her bedchamber. If you would be so good as to follow me, I will take you to him."

Realization dawned slowly as he glanced into the dining room, which had not been cleared of dinnerware. The table was set for two —an intimate dinner.

It seemed Adele hadn't been too busy for dinner after all.

"I know where the bedchamber is."

He took the stairs two at a time, turned left into Adele's bedchamber, a room furnished with soft silk bed linens and a delicate crystal chandelier to please her demands for superior furnishings.

He stopped and took in the candlelit scene.

Male attire was scattered haphazardly across the floor, mingled with Adele's delicate garments. There was a body in her bed. He forced himself to gaze upon his father—in Adele's bed, naked beneath the fine linen sheet he'd paid a fortune for.

Father was very, very still as he stared at the covered windows.

"Damn you."

Father blinked once.

Quinn gritted his teeth against the nausea that turned his stomach into painful knots. He had no words.

He was too full of anger.

"The ailment came upon him quickly," Mr. Fletcher told him, unaware of Quinn's inner turmoil. "Quite serious, as you might conclude, from his lack of response to anyone. He collapsed in the midst of...well. There is no saying if he can hear us or even understand. He cannot be roused and does not appear to be suffering any pain."

"Yet." He should suffer for this betrayal! Quinn jerked around. "A word, Mr. Fletcher. In private," he ground out.

"Yes, of course." Fletcher followed him out to the hall. "I appreciate you coming at such short notice, as the young lady was unsure of what to do. I assume you have some connection to the man?"

Quinn fumed in silence a moment, debating if he could keep his identity secret. How was this scandal to be hushed up to protect his mother and sisters, sparing them from embarrassment? That a lord was discovered insensible in a mistress' bed was not unheard of. That he was found in his *son's* mistress' bed would spread through London faster than a gale. There was no telling the harm such gossip would do to his family.

Quinn had been cuckolded by a man well past his prime—out of spite, no doubt—and although everyone would laugh at him, too, but he was more concerned for his mother.

He took Fletcher into the little-used bedchamber across the hall and closed the door. He dug into his pocket for what coin he carried and passed the lot over. "To cover expenses, your time, and any man hired to cart him back to Newberry House. How much will it take to hush this situation up?"

Fletcher took the money and tucked it away. "I cannot hide the details, and you know it."

"The man has a wife and daughters. They will be devastated by where and how he was found."

Fletcher frowned. "Was it unknown that he had a mistress?"

"It was unknown that he was sleeping with this particular one," Quinn growled. "This is not his property. It is *mine*, and he should not be here."

Fletcher's eyes almost popped out of his head. "I am not sure moving him is in the best interest of his health."

"He cannot remain here another hour," Quinn decided, and then shook his head, attempting to stifle his temper. Fletcher did not deserve to take the brunt of his anger.

"He could be taken out via the mews," Fletcher suggested as he took a step back, swallowing hard. "I will do my best, but I cannot make promises no one will see, or that he will survive the journey."

"Do it," he bit out. "Deliver him to the Rutherford House mews, not the front doors."

Fletcher swallowed. "As you wish. I'll make arrangements immediately."

Quinn nodded. If anyone found out where father had fallen ill tonight, the scandal would be enormous. Quinn would be a laughingstock. Cuckolded by his own sire—a man twice his age and three times as devious as the worst criminal sent to the colonies. How fitting that father had been struck down in the midst of such an act.

Was this—seducing his mistress—Father's punishment because Quinn refused to come to heel like the dog his old man expected him to be?

He allowed Fletcher to leave and then took a deep breath before heading out to the hall again.

He did not look into the room containing his father. Quinn trudged down the stairs, seething with anger and disgust, but stopped when he heard Adele Blakely call to him.

He clenched his jaw, and then turned slowly, viewing her with fresh eyes as she sat weeping over his father's condition. Sitting in the parlor Quinn had paid to be refurbished last year to make her happy. Hugging the robe *he'd* bought tight to her breasts...breasts his father had no doubt groped earlier that night.

He gagged, almost casting up his accounts then and there. The humiliation that he'd been so deceived in Adele's character rose thick and horrible around him.

She was faithless.

A cunning little actress. Ambitious for acclaim and attention, just as his father had claimed all along.

"I should have told you about us long before—" she whispered.

He held up one hand to prevent the flow of words. He did not want to know how long their affair had been going on. He highly doubted that Adele was sorry for deceiving him. "There's no need. Your actions present the truth I was too blind to see for myself. Was the reason you couldn't meet with me because you were always seeing him?"

"Quinn, I can explain!" she pleaded, eyes full of tears and sorrow for her situation. "You were gone, and he was kind."

"My father was not *kind*. This was entirely his doing, a means to put me in my place. Punishment. He's been at me for months to break with you. And you helped him do it! Goodbye, Mrs. Blakely. We will never speak again."

He could not forgive Adele for playing him the fool. She was not the friend he'd imagined her all these years. Not if she'd been keeping company with his father, too.

He strode out and climbed into his carriage, noting with approval that Miss Dalton was two steps behind him, and he'd not had to call her. He didn't look her in the eye; he was too humiliated, too gutted, to be in any way a civil gentleman.

"Newberry House," he called up to the driver, and the carriage rolled away.

At his side, Miss Dalton allowed him a few minutes of peace, and then stirred. "Who was she to you?"

Bile rose up in his mouth again, almost sending him flying from the carriage. He fought the sensation. As much as it pained him to reveal the truth of his distress, his secretary was too bright not to learn of the connection through her own inquiries. He'd have to tell her.

"We were friends for five years. I shared everything with her. She was my mistress. Apparently, one Ford wasn't enough for her."

Theodora's hand settled over his thigh and squeezed. Something she was prone to do quite often, he suddenly recalled. "The stupid little fool," Theodora whispered in a disapproving voice.

Quinn gritted his teeth, and as an afterthought, recklessly took her hand in his.

Theodora was kind to say otherwise, but he was the real fool here.

He had been faithful to Adele, never suspecting that she wasn't in return. But Adele had put him off so often, preferring to go her own way rather than meeting him at the halfway point, he should have suspected.

She could have been meeting with his father for years, or someone else entirely while he'd been gone without him knowing.

She was crying over Father now, rather than the future she'd thrown away with him.

Why should he fight an attraction to any woman who desired to be with him?

He laced his fingers with Theodora's, taking every scrap of comfort she offered, readying himself to face his mother and tell her the news about her unfaithful husband's latest escapade.

CHAPTER ELEVEN

NEWBERRY HOUSE INTIMIDATED Theodora on first sight as it loomed above her in the light of a half dozen lanterns. The imposing portico flanked by liveried footmen bearing lanterns made her feel very small and very, very much out of place in her drab mourning gown. She hoped no one thought her attire a bad omen for the family. She considered remaining in the carriage, but Lord Maitland held out his arm and drew her against his side as if she were not his secretary, but a close companion.

She glanced up at his face, alarmed by how still and unnatural his usually expressive features had become since she'd interrupted his dinner to share the horrible news about his father.

Her mind whirled with questions that she did not dare ask. About Amy, a sister he comforted with such sweet affection but who was not spoken of at Maitland House; about the mistress; about his father being at his mistress' home. She'd heard enough whispers that night to know the particulars of what Lord Maitland had discovered upstairs, and to become furious about it. She held her tongue though, watching in silence, observing the anguish of the man at her side, powerless to say or do anything to soothe him. It was not her place to look after Lord Maitland, but she was surprised that she wanted to.

She clung to his arm a little tighter as an old butler met them. "I must see my mother immediately," Lord Maitland explained.

The old man winced. "Lady Templeton is always abed at this hour."

"Lord Templeton has fallen gravely ill and will be brought home shortly. Have the staff prepare to receive him from the mews," Lord Maitland said so coldly, he might have been speaking of bringing home fish from the marketplace. "Have Lady Lenore roused, too. The countess shall need her cousin's comfort after I've spoken to her."

"Yes, my lord."

Lord Maitland drew her to the staircase and started up. Shadows shrouded the portraits adorning the walls and, once at the top, they strolled quietly down a long, carpeted hallway. Newberry House was very grand but at the same time seemed quite comfortable.

The viscount paused eventually to tap on a closed door then waited, eyes closed. For a change, his body was utterly without fidgets. "Mama, it is Quinn."

"Come," an older woman's voice called sleepily from within the room.

Theodora separated herself from her employer and stood back. "I'll wait here."

He nodded, opened his mouth to speak, but then disappeared inside the room without saying anything more. He'd been like that earlier. Appearing willing to talk but unable to voice his thoughts aloud.

Theodora sagged against the wall. Now that she was apart from Lord Maitland, she could breathe freely again.

"What!" Lady Templeton cried out suddenly inside the room.

Theodora straightened as footsteps marched through the room, her employer's voice a steady murmur under the sound of his mother's outraged outbursts. There was silence for a time, and then Theodora strained to hear anything at all.

An older woman burst out of a room further along the hall and hurried toward Theodora wearing a robe and a mop cap over her silver hair. "Is Lord Maitland still with Lady Templeton?"

Theodora nodded. "They're still talking."

The other woman held out her hand. "Lady Lenore Roswell. Lady Templeton's cousin. And you are?"

"Theodora Dalton. Lord Maitland's new secretary."

The other woman smiled. "A pleasure. My lady was speaking of you and her son earlier tonight."

"She was?"

The older woman nodded. "She hoped you would be a better influence on her son than his last secretary. She has missed her son, and would like to see more of him."

Theodora took the request to heart. "I shall do my best to remind him to visit her more often in the future."

"Good." Something crashed and broke inside the room, and Lenore's face fell. "Oh, she's in a vile temper over this latest scandal if she's throwing things already. I'd better go in."

The door opened, and Lord Maitland stepped out. "She is waiting for you."

The other woman said a quick goodbye and disappeared into the room. Quinn pulled the door closed but stood there, hand on the knob, his eyes closed as the women inside discussed recent events in ever-rising tones.

Concerned by his stillness, Theodora placed her hand on his chest. "My lord?"

Lady Templeton screamed out from within the room, "He will stop at nothing to humiliate us!"

Lord Maitland refocused on Theodora's face, ignoring further crashes as objects were destroyed inside Lady Templeton's bedchamber. "He will be here soon."

She drew her employer down the hall without really knowing where she was going except with a vague idea that the stairs were back in this direction. The farther they were away from Lady Templeton, the better. Some furies were not meant to be shared.

However, before they could reach the head of the staircase, Lord Maitland tugged her sideways into a room and shut the door. Theodora blinked until her eyes had adjusted to the lower light of a moonlit room. A little-used bedchamber, judging by the chill in the air and the dust covers draped over furnishings. Lord Maitland kept his back to her, his fingers pressed so hard to the wood of the door that his knuckles showed white.

Theodora had a sudden insight into what bothered her about her employer's reaction tonight. What she had noticed earlier when they'd talked. Lord Maitland's responses were not those of a concerned son.

"You hate him," she said, keeping her voice very low. "You hated him before tonight."

He sagged and slowly turned around, leaning against the door for support. His eyes were huge, too full of pain to hold for long. "Yes, I hate him," he whispered. "He made my life hell."

She moved closer and set her hands on his chest, rubbing his body soothingly, astonished by the confession but not the fact. There was little to love in a man who would behave as Lord Templeton had tonight.

Lord Maitland trembled under her touch, but it was not grief that had changed him. It was rage.

"It will be all right," she promised.

"Will it?"

Very slowly, Theodora slipped her hands up to cup his face as Amy Cabot had done earlier. Lord Maitland had previously rebuffed Theodora's romantic overtures, but in the wake of what had happened tonight, she might be excused in her bid to offer comfort.

His cheeks were hot with the evidence of his temper, and she scratched against the whiskers of his cheeks with a half-smile. Oh, this man was a challenge. One moment carefree and unaffected yet the next, brimming over with so many emotions he couldn't hope to hide them from her. He would not want platitudes or promises of a swift recovery for a man he despised. He would want facts that meant something to him.

"It has been my experience that few recover from such an affliction as the doctor described. Templeton will linger, helpless as an infant, until he dies, most likely."

Lord Maitland trembled and then grasped her elbows tightly. "I want that."

Although surprised by his venom, Theodora leaned into his embrace, using her whole body to connect with him. What kind of monster had Lord Templeton been to his son that death was preferred, anticipated, with such violent longing?

They stood together for a long while, Theodora plastered to Lord Maitland in a way that made her pulse race. She stroked his face gently, tangled her fingers in his wavy hair until he relaxed against her fully. His head dropped to rest against hers and he sighed raggedly. Comfort, however, was not to be mistaken for affection or, by any stretch of the imagination, a prelude to intimacy.

Theodora slowly drew back, cupping his cheeks again and smiling up into his face. If Lord Maitland saw his father again tonight, he would no doubt become angry. Theodora could help him by stepping between them. "A good secretary might be asked to oversee the care of his employer's family and report any developments as they occur."

"And you are an outstanding secretary," he whispered with a half-smile tugging his lips.

"The best you've ever had." Theodora caught his eye and winked, hoping further levity might be desirable at a time like this. "I shall go down and await the carriage bearing Lord Templeton and report to you any new developments after he is settled in his bedchamber. You may depend on me to keep you informed. Where will I find you when I have something to report?"

"With my mother, most likely." He shuddered and straightened from his slouch. "She will not want to sit at my father's bedside, either. She has a sitting room next to her bedchamber. Look for me there."

Theodora grasped his hand and squeezed. "I cannot imagine the pain you both feel today over such a terrible betrayal, but I promise to do all I can to lessen your cares."

He ran one finger down her cheek, causing her to shiver. "You already have."

On impulse, Theodora pressed a kiss to his cheek before she peeked out into the hall.

Lord Maitland caught Theodora's hand before she could escape. "Thank you."

She nodded and, when released, she left him quickly, hurrying downstairs to find a servant that could direct her to the rear of the house and the mews. The carriage should be arriving at any time now and she would wait amongst the household staff for Lord Templeton's arrival.

Later, when Lord Maitland had time to grapple with his own feelings, he would come and speak to his father alone. She was sure there were many things he should get off his chest before it was too late to speak his mind to the man who'd betrayed him.

She did not have very long to wait for the cart conveying Lord Templeton, and he was carried inside, still, and silent strapped on a house door with just a pillow under his head and a blanket over him. As Theodora glanced around her, it became clear there was not a damp eye among the servants of Newberry House. Lord Templeton was not likely to be missed by many here.

Once the earl was settled into his bedchamber, the evening dragged into the new day with no change in Lord Templeton's condition and nothing worthy to report each hour. He clung to life with a tenacity Theodora never expected, living many hours beyond what she had initially been told he might. During the long day, a handful of highly regarded physicians came to examine him, prod him. One had even sent a current of electricity through his left hand in a bid to stir movement, to no avail.

Only the original physician remained to monitor the patient beyond luncheon.

There was not much to do or see. The only thing that caused any reaction was mention of Lord Maitland's name in passing. Just the smallest hitch in Lord Templeton's breath denoted awareness of his surroundings.

Theodora studied the prone figure across the room as the day drew to a close. As expected, neither her employer nor Lady Templeton had visited the patient. They awaited her hourly reports in other parts of the house; their only words were of thanks for her coming.

It was nearing time for her next report too. She stood, a little stiff from her hours-long vigil, and approached the bed.

Lord Templeton met Theodora's gaze. He blinked several times.

Her heart skipped a beat at the response. "Can you hear me, my lord?"

He blinked again, then opened his mouth to speak, and a croak came out. The first sound she'd heard from him that day. It may only be that he was clearing his throat, but it was a valiant attempt to communicate. "Well done, my lord. Wait. I shall fetch your physician immediately."

Theodora flew out of the room, along the hall to where the

physician had retired to take tea in an upstairs sitting room. She tapped on the door urgently and poked her head in. "Sir, he spoke."

The door flew back so quickly she stumbled inside. Mr. Fletcher, a man of middle years and portly proportions, gaped. "Surely not."

"He made a sound, but there was no sense to it," she promised. "He tried."

Fletcher strode past her, wiping his hands on a scrap of white cloth before tossing it carelessly over his shoulder. "This I must see with my own eyes to believe it."

Fletcher examined Lord Templeton thoroughly. He checked his pulse, the feel of his hand, his face. He peeled back the man's eyes and brought a candle close.

After a few minutes more, he straightened and faced Theodora. "There's no change."

"But there was. I swear. He did try to communicate."

The man removed his glasses and polished them with a cloth from his pocket. "Are you sure you did not fall asleep and dream it?"

"No. How could I have imagined it when I was standing beside the bed?"

"Is there a problem?" Lord Maitland asked in a cold tone that made her jump nearly out of her skin for the harshness of it.

Her employer stood beyond the doorway, looking at Theodora rather than his parent and appearing every inch the bored aristocrat.

Theodora rushed toward him. "Your father spoke to me, or tried to."

"I think it highly unlikely," Fletcher protested.

Lord Maitland frowned, and the façade cracked as his lips quirked briefly into a nearly missed smile. "If Miss Dalton heard him then it was undoubtedly real. She would not offer up false news to me."

Theodora sagged, grateful for Lord Maitland's belief in her even if he must wish to believe she was so very wrong about his father. "Thank you."

He sighed. "However, it makes no difference. We're leaving, my dear."

She glanced at Templeton. The earl's eyelids fluttered as if he recognized his son's voice, but could not react to it more than with that effort. "Are you sure you don't want to say something to him?"

"No, I do not." Maitland grasped her elbow firmly and drew her out into the hall. "We have both wasted more time here than he deserves. I am going to take you home to your mother, and our lives will return to the way they were always meant to be. The countess agrees that lingering is quite unnecessary."

She glanced back at the man in the bed. Lord Templeton was still again, eyes staring across the room with no life in them whatsoever. Perhaps she had imagined an improvement. "If you're sure."

"I am. We will leave the earl in Mr. Fletcher's capable hands. A little more electricity in him might do the trick," he muttered.

Lord Maitland escorted her downstairs without another word. She still believed Lord Maitland might feel better by speaking with his tormenter one last time, but she had to admit she was very much out of her depth with him right now. He led her down to where the butler waited with hats and gloves at the ready.

"Thank you, Mr. Falstaff," she murmured to the servant whom she'd come to know a little during the day. He was a kind man who had worked for the family for decades.

"You're welcome, Miss Dalton."

"Send word when his condition changes for the worst," Maitland asked before leading her out of the house and down to his carriage.

Her employer appeared made of iron; he was utterly rigid, and she wished there was something she could do to improve his mood.

Theodora was utterly drained and feeling very low, and all for the man who'd shown her so much kindness and compassion in her time of need. She felt so very bad for Lord Maitland. Angry on his behalf, too. What a terrible way to discover your lover had thrown you over. How humiliated he must feel. She could not understand why Adele Blakely had not been more devoted to him. Theodora would have been, if given a choice.

"My parents were not a love match," Lord Maitland said suddenly, shifting awkwardly on the bench at her side. "How could they be?"

"Lady Templeton is an exceptional woman," she murmured softly. After the initial outburst in the privacy of her bedchamber, the countess had mellowed and shown unexpected strength of character in the face of a terrible situation. Theodora had been quite impressed with the older woman's composure during her brief reports. "I don't know any other lady who would have held to such self-possession under the circumstances."

Lord Maitland's hand ghosted over hers where it rested on the edge of the carriage bench seat, but he clasped his hands between his knees and leaned forward. "I want to scream," he confessed.

"Don't," she urged, concerned but full of understanding for his reaction. Men did not normally express their emotions loudly. It startled her that he was probably holding on to his temper by a mere thread. No wonder he was anxious to escape to his own home. Theodora felt very protective of him. "Not yet. There are too many ears around us now."

He turned to look at her over his shoulder. "Thank you for today."

"It was my pleasure." She rubbed his back in companionable sympathy. "It was high time I repaid you for all you've done for my mother and me. Sitting at the earl's bedside was the least I could do. You all but held me up off the ground when my father died if you recall."

"I stopped you from destroying yourself. You would have run into the fire because you loved your father so much." He shook his head. "I've never had that affection for mine."

She leaned against his side. "His loss, not yours."

His eyes glowed, and he reached out to caress her cheek in an entirely inappropriate manner for their current situation of employer and employee. Lord Maitland had turned her down days ago, but there had been several times today when his hand had sought hers discreetly. She held his gaze now and time had slipped away, captured by the speculative look in his eyes. Theodora tried not to read more into his behavior than she should, but she wondered if the loyalty he felt for Adele Blakely had ended with her betrayal.

And if it had, what he would do about it, if anything.

His hand fell away as the carriage stopped before the stairs of Maitland House. He alighted and helped her out. Together they ascended the stairs side by side without touching, stepped into the foyer, and they both sighed with relief.

In their absence, Theodora's mother had finally come down from her room and rushed to greet them.

"Mama." Theodora hurried forward and embraced her, eager for the comfort of familiar, loving arms about her. It felt so good to see Mama on her feet at last. "I hope you received my message," she whispered.

"I did. Thank you." Mother turned to Maitland. "I am so very sorry that your family has suffered this tragedy."

"Thank you." Maitland bowed formally. "If you will excuse me. It has been a difficult day."

"Of course. If there is anything I can ever do, just ask." Her mother searched his face but nodded when Maitland made no reply. She smiled nervously. "Well, good night then."

Lord Maitland took the stairs two at a time.

As soon as he was out of sight, Mama turned on her. "We've brought him bad luck."

"Nonsense." Theodora hooked her arm through her mother's and led her to the hall table. She was not going to get into a protracted discussion about curses and fate and all that. Lord Templeton had been fornicating with an actress, his son's mistress of five years, for heaven's sake.

After the long day away, the hall table was overflowing with correspondence, but she hadn't the heart to open anything. She shook her head. She had no wish to read about a new ball or dinner her employer was offered as entertainment. "We had nothing to do with the events of today, or last night, and you know it."

"Poor man. What are you going to do?"

Theodora looked up in surprise. "Me?"

"He seems very angry. He will need an outlet for that anger. Something other than using his fists would be best. You must talk to him. Calm him."

Theodora frowned. "He's not a violent man, Mama. At least, I don't believe so. He was very gentle when he broke the news to his mother."

"His mother raised him."

She remembered his gentleness with Lady Templeton all throughout what had to be the most trying of days. They were close. She was glad at least one parent loved him. The other seemed to have viewed him as competition. "Well, I for one am very glad that he does not follow in his father's footsteps."

"Maitland will assume a new title when the earl dies, he'll most likely move to grander lodgings, perhaps even to Newberry House. We should make plans to move out."

"I..." Theodora bit her lip. "I will not leave Lord Maitland at such a time, even if I could."

"Why not?"

"I like the work I do for him very much."

Mother's gaze became speculative. "What if he should bow to social expectations and replace his unconventional female secretary with his father's existing staff?"

Theodora had already met Lord Templeton's secretaries during the day—a pair of dull men who seemed genuinely eager to help her employer with anything he'd asked for. Her introduction as Quinn's secretary had been a tense moment. The men had frankly stared with barely concealed shock. She had caught one of them, the elder, smirking rudely at her behind Lord Maitland's back too.

Quinn had not noticed, or perhaps he had and found such behavior normal. It was hard to tell, given how quiet he'd been that day.

Unfortunately, Lord Maitland had appeared comfortable around the two gentlemen and had made plans to meet with them soon. It had been very plain to see the pair were organized, perhaps irreplaceable even for the soon-to-be new earl, at least at first. The rosy future she'd envisaged managing Maitland's simple affairs could very easily move out of her reach because of his elevation, and sooner than she was ready for. She might have to share her employer and defer to the other pair entirely.

She pulled a face. "Those decisions are out of my hands. All I can do is my best work." She grasped her mother's cold fingers tightly, trying to convey hope that she did not feel at that moment. "No matter what happens, we will survive, Mama. I have this month's wages, should the worst come to pass."

"Yes, you have your wages," Mama said slowly, her attention drifting to the front windows.

She chafed her mother's hand. "If Maitland doesn't want me working for him anymore, perhaps I can find another employer very quickly with his reference. He knows our situation. I cannot imagine he'd be so cruel as to toss us out on the street without cause or provocation."

"I suspect he wouldn't." Her mother forced a smile, the first one she'd shared in days. "Have you eaten?"

"Only a little, at Lady Templeton's insistence. She sends you her condolences, Mama. She had already heard about our situation before we met, and seemed very keen to know we were comfortable."

"Lady Templeton's warm reputation is well known about Town. Quite the opposite of her husband's." Mama put her arm around her back and steered her away from the study. "Come. Cook has laid out a cold supper in readiness for Lord Maitland's return, so you must have something. You appear exhausted."

"It was a difficult day," Theodora admitted as she sank into a chair while her mother began to fill à plate for her. "I've never known a stranger day, in fact. It must be hard to feel sorry for a man like Lord Templeton, given how he was found."

Her mother dropped a plate before her and poured tea. "Your message hinted at scandal."

Theodora nodded. "It could be and if that happens it will not be an easy time for Lady Templeton."

Her mother leaned closer. "That bad?"

Theodora whispered the details directly in her mother's ear in the briefest way possible.

"Oh my," mother said as she drew back. She glanced upward. "What a blow to the boy's pride."

Theodora picked at her food. There was nothing boyish about Lord Maitland. Tall, broad-shouldered, and devilishly handsome when he smiled. His mistress had been a fool to jeopardize their connection in favor of the inferior father. She was certain Maitland would be a much more agreeable lover than a man twice his age and girth could be.

She set her fork down, concern for her employer still pressing upon her. He might need a confidant. Someone to bolster his ego after today. He'd already begun to turn to her in private moments. Her mother was right that Lord Maitland was holding in so much. He would need an outlet that came without strings or expectations. Punching things would only see him hurting himself, and she couldn't bear for that to happen.

Not when there was an easier way that harmed none.

"I think I will retire early."

"That would be wise." Her mother caught her hand. "I'm sure the worst is yet to come."

Theodora hoped that wasn't true as she kissed her mother's cheek and then eyed the sideboard. "Do you think cook will mind if I take up a plate to see if Maitland will eat?"

"I would think she would be pleased," Mama said, nodding. "They're all very loyal and worried for the family. We'd be smart to do the same."

Theodora picked out a selection of meats and tarts, foods easily eaten with the fingers, and carried the plate upstairs. There was light shining beneath Maitland's door, so she tapped softly and waited until he opened it.

Maitland opened the door swiftly, regarded her and then the plate.

"You barely ate today," she reminded him, noting his bare feet and throat.

He widened the door and, despite his state of undress, gestured her inside his room. "I've never had a secretary worry for my appetite before."

"You've never employed a woman in the role before. As a whole, we are fairly observant, no matter the position we fulfill." Theodora glanced around, noting the bed covers had been rumpled already, a single tumbler half filled with amber spirits rested on the cluttered mantel, and the windows were thrown open to let in the cold. There was no table to place his meal upon. "Where would you like it?"

"On the bed will do."

Theodora set the plate on the counterpane and then crossed to the windows, intending to pull them tightly shut against the blackening sky and chill in the air. There was a bright moon tonight, and the ruins of her old home drew her attention like a magnet. She could still smell the scent of charred wood even from this distance. "It will be a cold night," she whispered.

She closed the windows and turned to face Maitland before her churning emotions could gather momentum.

"I did not notice." He stopped at the plate and picked up a sliver of ham to taste, and then continued until the plate was cleaned off. "Thank you. I was hungry after all."

Theodora moved toward him, her skin prickling with awareness. She was not the only one in pain anymore, and the night hours could be difficult. Maitland suffered but in a different way than she did. His arms would feel very good about her tonight. If he was agreeable, she might provide the same comfort to him, as well as take his mind from his troubling thoughts.

His eyes were shadowed with exhaustion, but he appeared restless, shifting his weight from foot to foot. She reached out to touch his arm to still him. "What can I do?"

"Tell me why you are really here, Theodora." He met her gaze, his expression weary, defeated, and vulnerable. "I'm not in the mood for games."

CHAPTER TWELVE

"I WANT WHAT YOU WANT," Theodora whispered, fingers sliding seductively up Quinn's arm.

Quinn craved her touch even as he worried at her motives in following him to his bedchamber at this hour. All through the day, when Quinn had felt the weight of his anger bearing down on his shoulders, Theodora's fleeting touches had quieted his mind and given him renewed strength to endure the humiliation. He did not think she was aware of how much he'd needed her today.

She lay against him, rested her chin on his chest and held his gaze in a way that seemed too intimate for so short an acquaintance. Even as he marveled at her boldness, he craved more from her. "What do you imagine I'd want?"

Her smile was immediate. "I'm here for whatever you need. To talk, or not talk. Whatever it is, just ask, and it is yours."

"I don't want to talk." What appealed to him as Theodora rubbed against him was a vastly improper use of his new secretary. But he could not use her just because he was angry and heartsick. He was wary of beginning an affair under the cloud of tonight's events, too. He curved his lips in a tight smile. "I don't want to think."

"Then don't. There is a time and place for everything. A time to be proper and a time to set aside everything just to feel."

He touched her face, unable to help himself. He'd been committed to Adele for five happy years, or so he'd always foolishly imagined them to be. In all those years, he'd never once been tempted to indulge with another woman, whereas Adele had already strayed.

What would it feel like to take another woman to bed? Would he feel guilt or self-loathing in the morning for seeking comfort from a woman who thought she still depended on him for her livelihood? Her mother appeared not to have told Theodora about the gems he kept for them. He wasn't sure why. "Is that what you did after your Daniel died? Carried on as if you were not broken inside and pleased yourself in private?"

"Yes, but not at first." She touched his face too, scratching her nails over stubble gown too long. He'd not shaved since the night before, and the ruggedness of his appearance must have appealed, since she continued to stroke his face as if she was fascinated.

Adele could never bear him looking like this. She'd have ordered him home to shave before coming back to spend a few brief hours in her bed.

Was it really so wrong if Theodora was an eager participant—nay, enthusiastic seductress—in this affair? He had not invited her to come to his room or encouraged her beyond opening the door.

She smiled, blushing a little. "Daniel was not my husband, but I was expected to mourn him, to wear black and sit quietly in the corner as if my future had ended with his life. It was unfair. Daniel may have died, but that didn't mean I had to die, too. I had my own dreams to fulfill that remain wanting still. There are desires to explore that he awakened. I was uncertain at first, but if one is cautious, and chooses the right time and partner, such selfishness can be a balm for the soul."

"Selfishness?"

"Shared selfishness is perhaps a more appropriate description in our case." She sighed. "No one ever touches me, but it is what I miss about my ill-fated engagement to Daniel. Connection. Comfort. Reassurance I am not alone, even for the length of one short hour to make love."

Would he only be allowed an hour? Rushing intimacy had never been satisfactory, in his experience. "You're not alone. You have your mother," he reminded her as her hands moved over his body. Exploring.

"It is not the same. I miss a man's passion more than I can bear at times," she whispered. As her fingers crept toward his ear to tease, Quinn shivered with anticipation. "I would like to touch you," she said, her lips parting and her breath quickening.

"I believe you already are." He grasped her shoulder, drawn to reciprocate the attention she'd lavished on him all day. She sounded very lonely and so vulnerable. He knew the feeling, but still did not like to think he'd be taking advantage. He tried one last time to draw back. "Are you sure this is wise?"

"What I want is never wise. It *is* necessary, though." Theodora unbuttoned the waistband of his trousers and then unbuttoned his shirtsleeves. "You were together a long time. Years, you said. Time spent together discussing your hopes and dreams. You're angry at her, and that is understandable, even expected."

"I imagined I'd marry her." His confession startled him. He'd never revealed that to anyone. Not even his mother knew that he was contemplating the battle he might face to make Adele his wife.

Theodora smiled tightly. "And now?"

Now he never would. Adele had revealed her deceit. Her true colors. "I don't want to imagine the woman anymore because when I do, I see my father, naked in her bed where I lay with her not three nights before."

She slipped the shirt over his head, and her hands fell to his waist. "You need a new memory to cling to, if only temporarily."

"Temporarily?"

"As I have already promised you, I have no ambitions to become a permanent part of your life. But satisfying this ache," she slipped her hand into his trousers, and discovered he'd unwittingly become aroused by her proximity and their frank talk of pleasure, "can take your mind off a troubling image."

She stroked him with the assurance he needed tonight. With skill and enthusiasm for the task of bringing him fully erect. He'd never been one to be led into dalliance, but she had a point. He couldn't think clearly with Theodora Dalton's tiny hand sliding over his skin. He wanted oblivion very much tonight.

As his trousers slid past his hips, he caught the first button on Theodora's gown and undid it. He undid each button slowly, pausing to touch every new piece of skin revealed. Although he had briefly imagined Theodora in this manner when she'd propositioned him, he'd never honestly expected to take her to his bed. But if he had, he couldn't imagine a better beginning than this. He'd made her no promises, not for money or jewels, not even for tomorrow morning.

She expected nothing from him but kindness and passion.

He dropped his lips to her shoulder and tasted her skin for the first time as he pulled the ribbons of her corset undone. Her skin was sweet and soft and warm, and very, very available. A soft little moan fell from her lips, and brought a smile to his. He cupped her breasts after her shift was tossed away and let himself feel nothing but desire.

Theodora made that very easy. She leaned into his touch, even while caressing him. She traced his chest, sliding her fingers over his muscles, teasing her fingers into his chest hair. She had taken her lip between her teeth, and her fascination with his body caused him to thicken even more.

He kissed her. He had too.

He had been captivated by her clever mouth since the moment they'd met.

Theodora wound her arms around his neck as he pulled her close against his body, and they fit together as naturally as water sliding over the hull of his ship. He loved the way she moved without a trace of awareness or awkwardness—as if they were the only two people in the world and nothing else mattered but pleasing him and herself.

He lifted her off the floor and hugged her tightly. A small squeal left her lips as his fingers lightly grazed the side of her breast.

He chuckled softly. "You are so..."

"So?"

"Provocative." He palmed her breast again, but more firmly this time. "I think that is the most unexpected thing about you."

He kissed her again, hungrily, and deeply, stroking his tongue into her mouth without restraint. Memories of Adele were pushed aside in the rush of pleasure of having Theodora Dalton in his arms.

He lowered her feet to the ground so he could frame her face with his hands. Holding her head still did not mean Theodora was in any way passive. She teased his balls, stroked his erection firmly a few times, only to stop suddenly before beginning again.

She drove him wild until he ached to be inside her, until he shook with something far better than his anger.

Quinn shoved the plate aside and eased Theodora onto the foot of the bed. As her legs parted, he ducked his head between and took a long, slow lick of her sex. Her soft whimper of pleasure was music to his ears, so he did it again. This he knew and trusted to be real.

Theodora was intoxicating and very wet. There was no chance she could fake the excitement he found and tasted.

He buried his head and feasted while Theodora shuddered and gasped, pressing up toward his lips every time he retreated for air and his sanity. He was on fire for her bold passion, torn between the need to delay to ensure her pleasure was found, and the desire to possess her for his own to forget the day and night that had passed.

He covered her with his body, beguiled by her soft curves and warm, grasping hands. He braced himself above her and slowly lowered his face to steal another kiss from her sweet lips.

A shiver raced through him at the contact of their mouths. Theodora hummed, as she did while she worked, and the tune stuck in his mind firmly and couldn't be expunged. The tune goaded him on, caused him to decide that next time he could go slower. Tonight, he wanted like he never had before.

He cradled Theodora against him and carried her up the length of the bed. When she was settled with her head upon his pillows, he held her head between his hands gently as their passion rose, tongues danced, and bodies aligned. With Theodora's fingers tracing down his spine and grasping his bottom, he knew too soon where their adventure would lead them.

Theodora was too impatient to demand less than everything he could give.

He drew back, climbed off the bed, and shoved his trousers off his legs, and then returned to Theodora's waiting arms.

She said nothing, but sought more kisses immediately and held him close as he moved into position again between her widened legs. He delayed a moment, pausing to kiss her thoroughly until she writhed beneath him.

As her legs wound around his back to pull him in, he thrust forward carefully, entering her gently but determined to lose himself, for them both to become lost in a sexual daze of passion and completion before the night turned into a new day.

Her breath shuddered past her lips as they moved against one another, grinding together silently in his bed. He pinned her arms to the mattress and thrust harder, causing her to moan aloud finally. Her back arched and her eyes fluttered shut. Quinn watched her every move, spellbound by her excitement.

Her lashes fluttered, and her eyes opened slowly. "Quinn," she whispered, at last using his given name. A slow smile formed on her lips. "You are a good-looking man. Simply gorgeous to behold...but this is a gift. My God," she gasped, straining upward as he slowed his thrusts. "Don't stop."

"I've no intention of doing that, my dear." Her praise of his looks thrilled him, as did the hunger in her eyes and words. She was about to come, and he dared not change a single thing about his technique. Her mouth opened, eyes widened, as she convulsed wildly but in utter silence beneath him.

After five years of Adele's theatrical screeching, he was taken aback by Theodora's quiet confirmation that his passion was exactly what a woman wanted. "Theodora?"

She licked her lips, chest heaving as she came down to earth again. After a while, her eyes opened, and she stared at him sleepily. "Yes."

He released her arms, fearing he'd been too rough. "Are you well?"

"Oh, indeed." She slid her fingers up his arms to his face, and she brushed his lips with them.

Still hard and eager to tease this woman, he took one digit into his mouth and sucked deeply. Theodora groaned, quivered around his cock until he released her finger. She moved, tightened her legs about his hips, forcing him to slide within her body, creating glorious friction.

"Do that to me again," she whispered.

"Which part?"

"All of it."

He thrust again, pleased with her request. He wasn't ready to come yet, and he certainly wasn't ready to end their night so soon. "If you would allow me the honor, I'd have you stay in my bed until dawn," he whispered.

"Yes!" Her smile was slow as she slid her palms down his sides. One delicately arched brow lifted. "Give me everything you are and more, please."

CHAPTER THIRTEEN

"AH, Mr. Bellington. So good to meet you. I am Lord Templeton's new secretary, Miss Theodora Dalton." Theodora held out her hand to Lord Maitland's rent collector, noting with approval the hard gleam in his eyes. They shook hands, hers almost crushed in his.

"Miss Dalton." The man's voice was like gravel, and she shivered imperceptibly. Rent collection was not for the weak of heart or the timid. She doubted Lord Maitland had ever missed a collection from one single tenant, thanks to the first impression this man made.

Bellington's stare intensified, and then his attention darted about the room. She understood his apprehension perfectly. He was utterly out of place among Lord Maitland's elegant furnishings. But then again, Bellington was not here to take tea.

Theodora adjusted the satchel on her shoulder containing the addresses and details of rents due to be collected that day. "Whenever you are ready, we may leave."

"A moment," Lord Maitland called as he rushed down the staircase toward her and Bellington.

Theodora's breath caught. She'd been hoping to avoid her employer this morning. She wished to escape the inevitable after-sex conversation. She experienced a moment of acute discomfort as Lord Maitland smiled so warmly at her that her sex throbbed eagerly in response.

Theodora returned his smile politely, hoping to maintain her usual professionalism around him. The events of last night were not easy to set aside, unfortunately. She'd been satisfied in his bed. Far more thoroughly than she'd anticipated. "Good morning, my lord."

Bellington tipped his head and mumbled out a rough, grumbled greeting to the viscount.

"Miss Dalton, I need to claim a moment of your time." The viscount regarded her gravely, and then gestured her toward the drawing room.

Theodora acceded to Lord Maitland's request reluctantly and stepped into the room. "Have I forgotten an appointment?"

"I will accompany you today."

Theodora blinked, dreading the close proximity of a carriage with a man who'd set her senses on fire. She shook her head. "I assure you, I am more than ready for the task of collecting a little money."

"Oh, I believe you." His attention flickered to Bellington, where he waited in the entrance hall. He frowned at the man. "It has been some time since I toured my properties. We shall do so together, along with your chaperone."

Theodora held back a wince. "I do not need a chaperone. I am in your carriage and will be protected by your staff. Do you not trust them to look after me?"

He clenched his jaw a moment before speaking. "Of course I do."

No, he didn't. This is exactly what Theodora had feared. Lord Maitland had an "I'm responsible for you" gleam in his eye today. She'd experienced his protectiveness on the night of the fire. To her mind, intimacy should change nothing between them. "I am on official business for you."

"This is not a negotiation you can win, Theodora," he warned. "I am coming with you."

Theodora closed her eyes as a rush of heat swept her face when another memory from last night rose in her mind. They'd done that, too—found release at exactly the same moment because he'd demanded she wait until he allowed her to let go.

However much his bossiness in the bedchamber excited her, she could not afford to be distracted by him during the day.

She smiled and curtsied, lacing her expression with extreme deference. "As you wish, my lord."

His eyes narrowed, and he held out his arm for her to take.

Theodora made a show of collecting the list of addresses from her satchel as she swept out ahead of him. "Mr. Bellington, shall we go?" An older housemaid appeared before Theodora could escape out the door. "Ah, Clare, there you are."

The woman smiled warmly, probably pleased by her unexpected outing. Escape from the drudgery of cleaning was always welcomed by any servant. Theodora could not begrudge the woman her easy day, but she could remain annoyed by Maitland's highhandedness for as long as she wanted to.

She drew the woman toward the door.

The butler held the front door open and bid them a pleasant day as they brushed past him, only to find Lord Maitland's best carriage paused before the stairs.

"Foolishness," she cried out, turning on Maitland. "Any tenants with wits and in want of funds will see the crest on the door and hide, rather than answer our knock now."

Maitland shrugged. "It's this carriage, or you remain at Maitland House."

She gritted her teeth, annoyed by yet another example of his protectiveness. There was no time to press for a change. Bellington was already looking uncomfortable, so Lord Maitland would only have himself to blame if the day's collection did not meet his expectations.

All business, she spoke to the coachman about their destinations, passing over her list of addresses and the order to visit them. When she turned for the carriage door, Lord Maitland was waiting for her.

She smiled sweetly. "My lord."

He scowled. "Time is passing, Miss Dalton."

She clambered inside, noting the housemaid and Mr. Bellington had already claimed the rear-facing seats. That meant she'd have to sit side by side with Lord Maitland on the butter-soft, sea-green, forward-facing seats. So close to and yet so far from her handsome lover.

As Lord Maitland joined them, Theodora shifted toward the far windows and did her best to ignore the way her pulse raced, the brush of his arm against her side, the memories of mutual pleasure to be found in his embrace.

She did everything to ignore his proximity.

He glanced her way, and a small smile curved his lips. "Are you well today, Miss Dalton?"

"Of course." But her cheeks blazed with heat. He must be aware she could not calm her pulse or the tingling sense of excitement she experienced around him. Why, he looked positively smug as he braced himself for a turn.

"I'm glad," he murmured, schooling his features to the bored mien of a born aristocrat. He nodded. "I should not like anything to overset your delicate sensibilities so early in our adventure. We could have many more together."

Was he talking about collecting rents, her employment, or sharing his bed again?

She thought perhaps the latter, given the way he tried not to smile. She felt almost certain that he was attempting to tease her about last night's tryst. At least their adventure in passion appeared to have put him in a jolly frame of mind.

She smiled quickly, took a steadying breath, determined to make it through the day without throwing herself at him for another bout in his arms. Aware that they were not alone, she kept her tone light. "Our adventure has only just begun, I suspect."

"That is excellent news." He brushed lint from his thigh. "I look forward to discovering what might happen by the end of the day."

"As do I, my lord." If she could have him again tonight, she'd be a delighted woman. "As do I."

Three hours later, they returned to Maitland house more or less successful. The gleaming black carriage had undoubtedly announced their arrival to the tenants, but in most cases, not their intent. Three-quarters of the rents were collected, and all of the properties had been viewed as the viscount had wished. Bellington would round up the remaining rents due.

Exhausted, she smiled for the butler's sake. "Where might I find my mother?"

"I believe Mrs. Dalton has retired to her room to rest."

"Thank you."

"We'll take tea in the drawing room," Quinn demanded.

"A tray for me in the study," she requested.

"A tray for both of us in the study it is."

Theodora risked a peek at Lord Maitland's face, a little startled that he would decide to join her so obviously. After their first teasing conversation, Lord Maitland had withdrawn from her. He'd been every bit the bored aristocrat society expected as he'd inspected his properties, which had made the time spent together in a confined space awkward at times. She had no idea what he thought of the way she'd handled the business of collecting the rents, or of last night's tryst now. However, she couldn't very well insist he go elsewhere in his own house to have his refreshments.

Theodora slipped up the stairs, relieved to return to the quiet of her work desk. She set down her satchel, extracted the collected funds and set them aside on Lord Maitland's desk to be recounted and secured in his safe. When she turned about, Lord Maitland was a foot behind her.

"The Gerrard Street property has a window broken on the upper floor. Have it fixed, Dalton."

She dodged around him to reach her desk, made a note of his wishes, and straightened, expecting more orders.

Lord Maitland's hands swept up her arms from behind, instead.

She shivered. "My lord?"

"Do you have any idea how frustrating it is to watch you at work?"

Theodora licked her lips and glanced over her shoulder, very distracted by what his hands were doing. "I'm only doing my job."

"Too well. I've never felt so unnecessary before."

She turned fully at his ridiculous remark. "Come now."

"Come?" The corner of his lip lifted into a half smile. "That's what I want *you* to do. Immediately, if possible." He eased her backward until her thighs pressed against her table. "Sit."

"My lord, I don't think—"

He covered her lips with his fingers. "That is what I want. Don't think about anything. I want you to feel."

Theodora was rendered mute by the heat in his gaze. He perched her on the table edge and drew her skirts up to her knees.

She should stop him. Anyone could come in and find them. However, a quick glance toward the door revealed it was already closed, giving them privacy.

She licked her lips.

Lord Maitland traced patterns on her thighs until she wanted to part her legs and agree.

"Tea will be here soon, but I'm famished right now. Let me feast?"

"No."

His jaw clenched. "Why?"

"Mixing business with pleasure is a bad idea."

His brow furrowed. "I didn't need your pity."

"What?"

He turned away abruptly and moved to his desk. He took the rent money and stashed it away in his wall safe without bothering to confirm the amount was as expected. "Last night. I didn't need you to pretend."

He busied himself with property reports, looking down at the desk instead of at her.

"Oh, no. No, no, no." She bounced off the table, lowering her skirts then moving closer to him. "Quinn, that was not what last night was about."

He shrugged.

"Dear God, what a dim-witted thing to suggest that I might pity you."

He frowned, jaw clenching.

Against her better judgment, she put her hand on his arm. He was rigid again. Concerned, Theodora shook him. "I enjoyed last night. I needed it. Perhaps you took pity on *me*?"

He rolled his eyes. "Hardly. I seem to recall you giving as good as you got. Several times, in fact."

A flush of heat swept her face again as she whispered, "We enjoyed being together last night. But there is a time and place for everything. I am here to work. I would not like to lose the good opinion of the staff if we were caught in an indiscreet moment. Do you want someone to find me draped over the desk, panting because you excite me so well?"

"No, but I like the idea of you panting for me." His lips twitched. "Tonight then?"

She met his gaze, and her quim pulsed in anticipation of him kissing her sex again. She most definitely wanted him to. "Yes. Please."

"Eight o'clock."

"After eight. Once the house has settled down, I will come to your room again."

He set his hand to her hip and his fingers closed over her body. Even that excited her unbearably. "That will be an eternity," he said.

"For both of us, but pleasure must wait until the perfect moment, when we will not be interrupted."

He leaned close, close enough that his lips brushed her ear. "I've been thinking of your legs wrapped around my hips all day. Damned fine daydream, I must say, but nothing will compare to the fact of it later."

"And I thought of your hands on me, of you being deep inside me all day, too," Theodora confessed, her voice husky with need. "But it's not something anyone else needs to know we are thinking about, is it?"

"I suppose not," he agreed reluctantly. He smiled suddenly. "I'll make you burn for me by nightfall. However will we keep our hands off each other, my dear?"

"I assure you, you already have achieved your goal of making me burn for a repeat performance. Stop gloating. You already won me over."

"I take a great deal of pleasure from that admission," he whispered as his fingers drifted from her hip to squeeze her bottom. "And I will wring a great deal of pleasure from your body later. As much as you can take, in fact."

"Quiet now, my lord," she pleaded. "If you don't stop talking of pleasures soon, you will distract me so much that I might commit you to attending the wrong gatherings."

"I wouldn't want that," he admitted with a wince.

Theodora escaped him and returned to her desk, aware that her body throbbed in earnest now, and she was already anticipating hours of uninterrupted play at the mercy of Lord Maitland's very great lust.

A servant tapped on the door the next moment and slipped into the room. "Lady Templeton has arrived, my lord."

"I'll be with her in a moment." Quinn moved closer to Theodora once they were alone again. "I guess that's how I'll survive the afternoon. Nothing cools a man's ardor faster than having his mama come to call. I'd better go see what she wants."

He stole a kiss before he left her though, a long one, with the brush of his tongue in her mouth that took her breath away yet again and made her wish it wasn't necessary to let him go.

CHAPTER FOURTEEN

QUINN TUGGED ON HIS CRAVAT, bitterly disappointed by
the interruption. Damn, but his mother had the very worst timing
imaginable sometimes. He'd been so close to achieving his goal of
diverting Theodora from work that afternoon. She had been more
than a little excited by their conversation. Her eyes had so filled with
lust, he'd barely held back. But she was right. He had to be responsible. He didn't want anyone to know about their intimacy. He didn't
want there to be a reason for them to stop.

He found the Countess of Templeton standing in his drawing
room, dressed in a pretty blue day gown that brought out the
mischief in her eyes. Quinn kissed his mother's cheek when it was
offered. "What are you doing here, Mama?"

"I am escaping the bleak despair of Newberry House. It is intol-
erable, and I've driven poor Lenore to leave London already," she
said with a weary sigh. "I couldn't stand to remain there alone
another moment, so I came to see you instead."

He gazed upon his mother's miserable face, largely unsurprised
by the news that Cousin Lenore had cut her visit short due to
Father's illness, and then kissed the top of her silvered hair. He and

mama were of the same mind with regards to Templeton. It was very hard to weep over his father's illness. "Tea?"

"Please, and your company, too," she begged. "Have you been keeping busy?"

Quinn was happy to oblige her, and sat next to her on the chaise. Mama rarely demanded his company so directly. "I've been reviewing the properties I own. I've only just returned, in fact."

"I wish I'd known. I might have enjoyed coming with you."

He laughed softly. "Mama, you hate scrambling in and out of carriages all day long."

"I could have watched from inside," Mama protested before sighing. "But you're right. I would have hated waiting."

Quinn reached over and squeezed his mother's hand. "He will get better, or he won't, when he decides."

She closed her eyes. "I know."

"And there is nothing you can do," he assured her. "No good will come from upsetting yourself."

"I know that too." She sighed and turned her face away. "I went to see him this morning."

"Mama," Quinn protested. "You know he cannot answer you."

"I told him how I feel about him now." She sucked in a sharp breath before continuing. "I wanted him to know the pain and humiliation he's caused me cannot be forgiven. What he did to you with that woman was disgusting."

Quinn hugged his mother tightly against him. "I hardly think about it, and nor should you."

"How did you stop? I close my eyes and imagine him..."

How had he curbed his anger? He'd allowed Theodora to divert him.

"I bury myself in work." He considered how to help his mother, and smiled. "Perhaps you'd like to join me upstairs in my study while we discuss rent day collections?"

"That is exactly what I need. Serious conversation that has nothing to do with ailments or medicinals. I am quite lost on the topic." Mama beamed at him and stood. "How is that woman you hired working out? Such an unconventional arrangement you have with her. Lenore was quite impressed with her manners, and so was I. What was her name again?"

Ah, this must be the true purpose of the visit. Mother had probably memorized Theodora's name, and everything else she knew about his secretary so far, but still wanted more information. Mother had likely come to interrogate Theodora about her still being here, and when she'd be leaving. The prospect of that wasn't desirable. Not after last night. "Her name is Miss Theodora Dalton. She's managing me very well."

"Someone needs to."

He smiled. "But I do have one favor to ask of you before we go up."

"Anything."

"When Mr. Dalton died, he had his wife's necklace about his own neck." Mama gasped. "The stones were recovered, but when I tried to return them to Mrs. Dalton, she became quite upset and would not take them back."

"Oh," Mother whispered. "I do understand why she wouldn't."

"I've put them away for safekeeping. I suppose I must wait for Mrs. Dalton to ask for them back, but the thing is, I don't believe she told her daughter they are wealthy still."

"Do you fear to distress the daughter with the news of where the stones were found?"

"I do indeed." Quinn scratched his head. "Her mother took the news very hard, bursting into tears again, and hasn't spoken very much at all since. However, Miss Dalton is a very different sort of female to her mother."

"She doesn't like to cry," Mama mused. "She seemed quite bookish and unemotional to me."

"She is emotional but dislikes anyone to see her that way, I think," Quinn confessed. "I'd like for us not to be the reason she would become upset."

Mama stretched up and patted his cheek. "I do understand. I will say nothing of the stones or her leaving because they do have funds. If I have the chance, I will see if I can get Mrs. Dalton to talk about her situation a little."

"Gently, Mama."

"Of course. I am always the soul of discretion, and compassionate."

Having Mother's help would be a blessing. Quinn was a little out of his depth when it came to an inconsolable loss like Mrs. Dalton had suffered. "Come upstairs with me. Miss Dalton was working when I came down. Perhaps her mother has joined her there."

He sent the butler off to amend the order for tea being delivered upstairs to his study and took his mother's arm to lead her up the staircase. He hoped Theodora did not mind the interruption.

He knocked on the doorframe before entering the study, noting Theodora had been frowning at a journal on her desk before looking up and smiling warmly. That smile slipped a little as his mother came into view, and she hurried to her feet.

"Miss Dalton, I'm sure you remember Lady Templeton."

Theodora hastily curtsied. "My lady."

"Ah, there you are at last." Mama hurried across the room and took Theodora's hands in hers. She leaned forward and kissed both his secretary's cheeks with rather startling familiarity. Mama drew back, grinning. "He's not dead yet, if that is why you frown so."

Theodora visibly relaxed, even as she extracted her hands. "That is good news."

"I know. Black does not become me." Mama tilted her head to the side, assessing Theodora with a sly expression. "On you, however, it is a rather arresting color."

Theodora glanced Quinn's way. "Ah, thank you. Mama and I have only a few simple gowns we need. Lord Maitland has been very generous to pay for them."

"Well, since the alternative is having you running around in a state of undress, I can understand why." The corner of Mama's lips quirked up. "Although, being a man, he may not mind that sort of thing."

Theodora inclined her head. "Of course."

Quinn was impressed that Theodora wasn't blushing already. Mama really did like to tease family and their friends. "Why don't you sit, Mother."

"Oh, very well. Miss Dalton, come sit by me." Since Mama caught Theodora's elbow and dragged her before Quinn's desk, Theodora was given no choice in the matter. "You've done something different with this room," Mama noted, glancing about the chamber, and giving a nod of approval. "Much better. Now, tell me how your mother does, my dear girl. I was so hoping to make her acquaintance today."

Subtlety was not always his mother's stock in trade.

Theodora smiled quickly. "I am afraid Mama is not in good spirits again this afternoon and has returned to her bedchamber to rest."

Mama reached for Theodora's hand. "They were a love match, I understand?"

"They were." Theodora's smile grew brittle. "So in each other's pocket, they carried each other's handkerchiefs quite often."

Mama's smile dimmed as Theodora clenched her jaw and her eyes grew bright with unshed tears. He gave his mother a warning look. She'd promised not to upset Theodora.

Mama patted Theodora's hand. "That must have been lovely. I remember my parents only a little now. Lenore is the only family I have left to connect me to the past."

This time Theodora squeezed Mama's hand, and Quinn was quite touched. "Family holds us together. You have the love of your daughters to sustain you, I understand."

"Indeed."

"And a few undeserving sons, too, I suspect," Quinn threw in to make them laugh.

His levity had the desired effect, and Mother wagged her finger at him. "Impudent sons, too." She wiggled her fingers toward Theodora's desk. "What were you doing over there, Miss Dalton, before I interrupted you?"

Theodora glanced Quinn's way, a question in her eyes.

"There's no point keeping secrets from my mother. She's here for the distraction of sticking her nose into other people's business. Currently, mine will do."

"You see!" Mama cried out. "Impertinent, wretched child."

He grinned when Theodora laughed out loud.

"Hardly a child, my lady," Theodora suggested, with a quick smile for him. "I was attempting to create a reference book for Lord Maitland. A journal of sorts, to hold important events he should never forget. Birthdays, marriages, and the like. They can be quite invaluable for someone with as large a family as yours. I was just leafing through a previous appointment book of his to see what I can find written in there."

"How clever of you. My son always forgets someone."

"I was away for many occasions, Mama, and the dates did not stick in my mind."

"But your career in the navy is over now, and you are back where you belong in society. The family needs you," she promised. Mama turned to Theodora again. "Perhaps I could assist you and fill in any gaps."

Theodora nodded. "I should not like to impose, but your help would make the task go much more smoothly. Thank you."

With a new pursuit to distract her attention, Mama shifted into the chair beside Theodora's desk, and they began to natter amongst themselves without his participation.

After a time, he cleared his throat. "So, you've no wish for *my* conversation now, Mama?"

Mama shooed him away. "Oh, you can go back to whatever you were doing before I arrived."

No chance of that. He'd been seducing Theodora, but revealing that to his mother wasn't in his best interests. Not if he didn't want to be lectured on the perils of unwise romantic pursuits. He was feeling too good without Mama getting in his ear and ruining his mood with her dire warnings.

The problem with Theodora—and it was his problem alone, and not hers—was that she was too pretty and clever to be viewed as an ordinary, dull secretary. She was nothing like his last one. Quinn *was* better organized. He knew where to find his important papers. What had once seemed an insurmountable task, coming to grips with his affairs after a prolonged absence and loss of a valuable employee, had been managed by a mere slip of a woman in a few short days.

A determined, unorthodox, and exciting woman that she was.

Since he was no longer needed, Quinn returned to his desk to make notes on the repairs he wished completed on his properties, even as he kept an eye on the informality developing between his secretary and mother. Having them become better acquainted hadn't ever occurred to him as a possibility.

"My dear, it was a lucky day when my son took you in," Mama noted, beaming at the woman across from her.

Quinn jerked his head up. What the devil was Mama doing, saying such a thing? It wasn't luck. Mama knew that.

Theodora sighed, straightening the papers before her. "It was the worst day of my life, my lady. I don't know how I survived it, or why. My only regret is that I may never learn how the fire started."

"It was an unfortunate accident, my dear." Mama leaned forward. "Everyone who matters believes it was. No matter how careful we are, there is always a chance tragedy will strike down someone close to us."

"I know but still, what was said afterward..." Theodora started.

"Were the ramblings of a dying man," Quinn interjected quickly. "You and your mother were lucky to have escaped at all. No one believes otherwise, I swear to you."

Mother caught Theodora's hand. "Nothing can change what happened. You can only look to the future. That is reason enough to be glad to have you here. Many men would have turned you away, but I raised my son to look for the potential in everyone. This is exactly the place you and your mother need to be right now. He would never push you out until you were ready or take advantage."

Oh, hell. Quinn was most definitely taking advantage, but then again, so was Theodora taking advantage of him. They were using each other to feel better. To forget the pain in their hearts.

He didn't want anything to upset the applecart.

He leaned back in his chair, listening without comment as their chatter veered to her mother and their future travels.

"In time, I will have sufficient funds to move on," Theodora promised.

"Now, you must not rush things on that score," his mother advised. "If I might offer some advice, allow your mama time to grieve before making serious decisions about where you will live next. This will be a lonely time for her. Do not make it worse by tearing her away from familiar surroundings."

Quinn marveled at his mother. She had neatly presented a very compelling reason for Theodora and her mother to stay on here. She had made it sound like the most natural thing in the world for the two ladies to remain as his houseguests indefinitely. He'd cheer, if he wouldn't have had to then explain why he did so to his own mother.

"I suppose I could remain in London a while longer than strictly necessary," Theodora said slowly, "but I'm afraid Lord Maitland only employed me on trial. I may have no choice in the matter but to move on."

"The trial is over," he said, butting in. "The position is yours for as long as you want it, Miss Dalton."

Quinn received the most beautiful smile in return for his statement. It seemed Theodora was hoping he'd offer permanence. But it was alarming that the smile was mirrored on his mother's face, too, when she looked at him, one brow raised expectantly.

He stood, feeling decidedly exposed. He did not want his mother considering his employment of Theodora Dalton too closely. "If you ladies will excuse me, I must speak with the stable master."

"Of course. Would you mind if I remain for dinner?" Mama asked. "Newberry House is quite dreary at night without Lenore."

"I'll inform the housekeeper to set an extra place," he agreed, concerned that his mother was grasping at any excuse not to be alone.

"Perhaps by then, Mrs. Dalton might be persuaded to join us," Mama remarked. "I long to hear of her travels abroad."

"Mama is fascinated by other people's travels," he reassured Theodora as he stood to leave. He stopped by his mother's chair and winked. Theodora would have seen, but he had to do something to thank Mama. With her help, he'd have Mrs. Dalton's gems returned in no time, and the future decided eventually. "I'll make a point of inviting Mrs. Dalton down to meet you, and after dinner, I will escort you home, too."

CHAPTER FIFTEEN

THEODORA SLIPPED QUIETLY into her mother's bedchamber the next morning and watched her at work beside the bed. "What are you doing?"

"Packing," Mama murmured, as she continued to fuss with the few things scattered across the counterpane with only the briefest of glances in Theodora's direction. "The housekeeper was kind enough to loan me a small trunk of Lord Maitland's to keep our salvaged possession in. There's not a lot of my life with your father left, is there?"

"No." Theodora closed the door behind her, heart heavy when her mother brushed at her eyes. She was weeping again. She had thought Lady Templeton's company last night had cheered her up, but apparently the countess' effect was short lived, despite being such an overwhelming character. Dwelling on their loss was only going to make Mama cry harder, but Theodora could understand her need to have the few things they'd gathered from their old life close by. "Why don't you place them about your room? Make it feel like home?"

"Because, at some point, we will have our own home again.

Listening to Lady Templeton talk about her daughter's upcoming season made me realize I mustn't become too comfortable here." She sighed and pressed her fingers to the counterpane. "A lady can suffer delusions that maid service six times a day is perfectly natural and that lifting a finger is completely unnecessary. Lord Maitland has been so kind, so certain that I need do nothing, that I'm starting to feel uncomfortable about it. He has a sister who will need his escort and protection soon for her season. I don't wish to forget my place. I don't live here. I am homeless but not without means, thank heavens."

"What do you mean, you have *means*?"

Mother sank onto the bed. "Do you recall your father was going to have the clasp on my necklace repaired before he died?"

"Yes. He was so tardy at doing so that I had threatened to send Mr. Small to do the errand for him."

"I didn't know how to tell you before today, but it seems your father hadn't forgotten his promise to me. He was wearing the necklace when he died. The gems were found when his body was prepared for burial."

Theodora's eyes burned suddenly, and she covered her face as she burst into tears.

She'd believed recovering financially would take the rest of her life. She had struggled to hide her despair of ever being settled again behind false bravado. She'd thought she'd have to work forever, but that wasn't the case. "Oh, Papa."

Her mother's arms wrapped around her as she sobbed. But relief had already turned to guilt. She'd rather have her father back than the money, but they needed the money the sale of the gems would bring to live. They could travel in comfort back to India, buy land and prosper there. Mama could have her own servants again. As many as she liked, too.

Theodora pushed back from her mother, wiping her eyes. "Why didn't you tell me before now?"

Her mother was crying, too. "I couldn't speak of it. I couldn't think of them without remembering the day your father gave them to me."

Theodora hugged her mother quickly. "He was so happy to see you wearing them."

"And so was I."

"Where are they?"

"I don't know. Lord Maitland tried to give them back to me after the funeral, but I refused him."

"He kept them?"

"I suppose he put them away in his safe somewhere."

"They are not there," Theodora said out loud. "I know the contents of his safe inside and out."

Her mother drew back to stare at her. "You shouldn't snoop."

"Rent day," Theodora promised. "You should ask him for the necklace again."

"It's not a necklace anymore. The stones are best left with him for now, until I decide what to do."

Theodora led her mother to the window seat and pressed her down on the soft cushions. "You could sell the necklace. Mr. Peabody on Bond Street would give you a fair deal."

"I suppose I will have to consider it. Your father told me the gems were very fine."

"Only the best for you," Theodora promised as she held her mother's hand. "If we exchanged some of the gems, we would have a little money to spend and we could live anywhere we liked. We could return to India now."

Her mother nodded slowly. "The moment we returned to England, you wanted to turn back."

"That is true," Theodora said quickly. She did not want to rush her mother into any decision, but she was excited again. There was so much to do if they would travel again. "Home has always been where we made it. Do you remember when we first arrived in India? Months at sea, suffering the worst of the confinement, only to face a strange city and such heat as we'd never felt before. We both looked at each other, knowing life there would take a great deal of adjustment. This is no different."

"I like it here."

"Living in England?" Theodora's smile faltered as her mother nodded. "You want to stay?"

"I like the peace of familiar surroundings and customs," she murmured.

"I suppose we could stay awhile." Mother remaining in England without her had never occurred to Theodora. She couldn't leave her parent at such a time...or ever, she suspected.

Her mother's face fell. "Without your father, I don't know what to do with myself. Lady Templeton suggested I remain here, but Lord Maitland's kindness reminds me of all I've lost. I miss your father. I miss the life we had together."

Theodora caught her mother in a tight hug. "Oh, Mama. I miss him too."

When her mother began to cry softly, Theodora held her until she stopped. She'd become so busy with her new position that she had forgotten Mama had next to nothing to do with her days. The hours must seem very long with so little to occupy her mind.

Eventually, Mama quieted and drew back. "What can I do? I don't have callers or call on friends while we're in mourning. No one has come around to inquire about us since the night of the fire, have they?"

"I'm sure they simply don't have our new directions," Theodora suggested, unsure if that was true or not. Someone should have been concerned enough to call by now. "Should you like me to write to our friends and let everyone know where we are, and that we suffered no harm?"

Her mother nodded slowly. "I had not thought of that. People used to come and see your father all the time, and at all hours."

"I know." She thought a moment, unsure of what to suggest. "Perhaps someone we know will call today. Shall we go downstairs together and see?"

"I don't want to watch you toiling over the viscount's papers again."

"I am sure that is dull for you," Theodora murmured apologetically. What fascinated Theodora about business and finance had always bored her mother. "How about instead, we take tea outside? I noticed a small table and chairs in the walled courtyard at the back of the house that no one seems to use. I'm sure Lord Maitland won't mind if we make it our own for a little while."

"I'd like that."

Mama hurried to wipe her tears away, and together they headed toward the main staircase. As they reached the head of it, they heard Lord Maitland in conversation with someone in his study. She had not known he was meeting with anyone today. Curious, Theodora listened carefully.

"You know you are a very pretty lady," he said, chuckling softly. "Come here, my dear."

Theodora grimaced. Flirting with another woman in the study? Where she worked? Theodora would put an end to that sort of nonsense immediately. She entered the room without knocking.

"Ah, there you are, Dalton," Lord Maitland exclaimed. "I was just about to send for you."

"Were you?" Theodora looked about, but there was only Lord Maitland occupying the space.

"Come meet my new friend," he begged, gesturing her urgently toward the high-backed chair nearest him.

Theodora rounded the seat—and saw a small black puppy had been placed on the cushion, and it was chewing the brim of Lord Maitland's hat.

"It's a dog."

"Very clever of you to notice," he said, laughing. "I found this little waif near the stables, and since she was in danger of being trampled, I thought to save her."

Theodora wasn't fond of dogs, having been nipped by them as a child too often, but her mother had always doted on them. "Mother, come and see what Lord Maitland found outside today," Theodora called.

Her mother came in unsmiling, but brightened immediately when she saw the black pup slobbering all over Lord Maitland's hat. "Oh," she cried out. "You shouldn't let her do that," she chided the viscount.

The man merely smiled. "Do you know about dogs, Mrs. Dalton?"

"I do indeed. I haven't had one for a long time." Mama reached for the pup and scooped it up against her chest. The pup licked her face excitedly, and she laughed. "What a darling little creature. Her coat is so soft. Is she yours?"

"I think she might prefer to be *yours*," Quinn suggested, scratching the pup behind the ears. "I had a groom bathe some of the dirt out of her coat but there's likely more than a house pet should have still there. She's a bit of a lightweight, too. Someone needs to care for her. Would you like her, madam?"

"I would take very good care of her, my lord." Mama stifled a sniff and then pressed a kiss to the dog's wriggling head. "Thank you."

"She'll need a name if she's to stay in the house," he suggested next.

All of her attention focused on the excited pup, Mama nodded. "Soot. Yes, that is a good name for her."

Lord Maitland threw Theodora a pleased smile, and her heart melted. He'd done just the right thing to cheer her mother up. How clever of him to realize Mama needed something special to distract her from grief, too. "Thank you," she mouthed to him.

He winked and then stepped to her mother's side. "I'm sure you and Soot will become the best of friends in no time," he murmured before leaving them. "The walled courtyard is just the place for her to play."

CHAPTER SIXTEEN

QUINN STARTLED FROM A DEEP, dreamless sleep at the unwelcome sound of pounding on the front door and Mrs. Dalton's new pup launching into an excited bout of barking. Blinking sleep from his eyes, he stretched his arm out across the bed, expecting to encounter Theodora, only to find he was alone, and her side of the bed was cold.

He sighed that she was gone too soon. He smoothed his bed quickly so it would not appear he'd had company during the night and sat up. He hadn't felt Theodora leave him, but he would see her soon enough. There was a lingering fragrance of Theodora's perfume in the room, and he breathed it deeply. Contentment trickled through him, and he fought the feeling.

He had the perfect arrangement, but should not grow used to it. Theodora was a remarkable lover and a dedicated secretary, too. He was glad she'd found her way to his bed. She was the perfect distraction. His thoughts did not linger on Adele or her betrayal once he had Theodora in his arms. His anger at his father had faded only a little. He had been used by people he trusted, and he had survived the pain because of Theodora.

On reflection, he'd lost little from his life in parting ways with Adele Blakely's, but he'd gained clarity.

Love and lust were quite different, and he only needed one in his life. Lust was simpler. Desire, when fulfilled so thoroughly, as his affair with Theodora proved, was enough.

He climbed out of bed feeling well rested, despite the fleeting moments of sleep he'd snatched between bouts of lovemaking last night, to open a window and take in the view outside.

As often happened, his eyes were drawn to the desolation across from his home. The Daltons' residence had been reduced to nothing more than blacked brick and crumbling timbers.

Despite that tragedy, he was content in a way he'd never experienced before. There was nothing more he wanted in his life but for this secretive arrangement to continue for as long as possible. And when it did end, as he was sure it would, there were plenty of other women in London willing to invite him to their beds, he suspected.

A knock sounded on his door, breaking him from his thoughts. He snatched up a silk banyan and threw it over his nakedness, ready to face the challenges of a new day. "Come."

Rodmell poked his head into the room, the sad expression on his face warning Quinn wasn't going to like what he heard next. "My lord, forgive me for waking you, but a servant has come from Newberry House."

A chill swept him that his father might have recovered. "What is it?"

"Lord Templeton has passed during the night," Rodmell told him. "Lady Templeton has asked for you to come immediately."

Quinn struggled with his feelings, relieved, and unsettled by the sensation of satisfaction. "Please inform Miss Dalton of the situation, and tell her the dinner she was organizing must be delayed. Thank you, Rodmell."

The door pulled closed slowly, and the air burst from Quinn's lungs.

When he'd first awoken, he'd thought he couldn't be happier. But he was.

The bloody tyrant was no more.

CHAPTER SEVENTEEN

FUNERALS WERE UNBEARABLE, even for someone so unloved. They brought Theodora's grief too near the surface.

Theodora's father had been laid to rest without pomp or ceremony in a simple grave last week, but she couldn't bear to glance in that direction yet. The quiet service for her beloved father was in stark contrast to today's ostentatious display for a man disdained by his son.

Today, Lord Templeton's body had been consigned to an impressive mausoleum in the same cemetery where her father rested. No expense had been spared to prove the earl's importance in society, even in death. A trio of child mourners had followed the carriage bearing the mahogany coffin trimmed with gold in advance of a dozen professional mourners. There might be a few true mourners following behind, she suspected—navy officials and titled lords of his acquaintance—but not too many.

Theodora shifted in the darkened carriage parked at the edge of the cemetery; keeping an eye on the silent and straight-backed figure of her employer as he listened to the vicar of St. George's send up prayers and whatnot for the late earl's passing. She was too far away to hear clearly what was said of Quinn's father, though she thought perhaps only a little of it could be true. Quinn had yet to say anything nice about the late Lord Templeton, but she'd been left in no doubt he was not missed.

A little shiver raced along her limbs as she considered Quinn overlong. She admired his honesty with her. She admired the rest of him very much indeed. They rarely spoke of the hours they spent in each other's arms at night anymore, and that seemed to suit them both perfectly. Theodora worked diligently during the day, a model of propriety and calm efficiency, but her nights were full of wild abandon atop his comfortably large and soft bed.

Theodora brushed her thumb across her bottom lip as lust caught her in its grip yet again. Quinn was very inventive, had a stamina she'd learned to crave. Their affair had begun as a balm for his anger, but he expected so little in return it concerned her. She could not shake the feeling that his experience with the actress Adele Blakely had somehow hardened his heart against truly enjoying himself.

Did he trust her?

She thought he might not.

She shook off her disappointment as she noted the mourners turning away from the grave, solemn and with little conversation for each other. The Duke of Rutherford had not made the journey to London for the burial. By all accounts, the duke had taken the death of his eldest son and heir very badly. The bulk of the family had gathered at Newberry Park around the duke, and only a few of the men of the family attended the funeral today. Theodora suspected they'd come not out of respect for the late Lord Templeton, but to support Quinn.

She returned her attention to him, a dark figure bundled up in black against the chill of a bleak day. He nodded to many but as he made his way back to his carriage with his head down, she could see he was lost in thought. She wished there was some way to take away all of his pain beyond what she'd already done for him.

She made room for him as he joined her in the carriage, but he took the opposite seat instead of sitting at her side, as he'd taken to doing.

He placed his dark hat carefully beside him before speaking. "It's done."

"Yes."

She braced herself as the carriage moved off, gaining speed as it turned into the traffic that teamed toward the capital.

Quinn stretched out one leg to brace himself against her bench seat. "I will be moving into Newberry House tonight."

She'd expected it but still questioned him. "Why so soon?"

"I am a Templeton now. I must be seen to take the reins."

He sounded so bleak, so unsteady, that her heart lurched in sympathy for him. It was clear to Theodora he'd not yearned for the responsibilities that came from his elevation to earl. However, they could not be avoided or passed on to another, as Quinn's right of succession had been clear. There would be much to do and become familiar with in the coming months.

"I can join you in the morning."

"I don't think you should come."

She leaned forward, her heart taking a leap almost out of her chest at the idea she'd outlived her usefulness to him. She was finally beginning to find her way as his secretary. To understand his moods and whims too. "Why not?"

A deep frown marred his brow, and he paused a long moment before answering. "In my home, my staff know the history of why you are there. They understand how much you've lost, and see how hard you have worked to keep your mind off that loss. At Newberry House, others might see you as less than you are. I will not tolerate anyone treating you or your mother unfavorably."

She truly admired Quinn Ford for his protective habits. She also loved being in his arms, where decisions about the future were kept at bay.

They both knew she need not be his secretary although they'd never discussed it once. Her mother had funds to make their every wish come true, if she ever asked for the gems to be returned to her. They could stay behind or leave to settle in their own home at any time they wished. But she felt, deep down in her bones, that remaining at Quinn's side was what she was meant to do right now.

"I am your secretary, and that is all anyone needs to know about me," she said briskly.

His gaze pierced her with a questioning glance. "That's not strictly true. You do have other options."

She smiled quickly. "Mother told me about the gems."

His breath rushed out. "And?"

"She refuses to discuss any future use of them yet. She does not wish to leave England, so I am stuck as I am. Money or not, I would prefer to spend my days being employed in a useful manner."

He nodded slowly. "And what of the other business between us? Someone might suspect our intimate connection if you are spotted leaving my new chambers in the mornings," he said, frowning.

A chill swept her. Quinn thought of bedding her as a matter of business? She fought not to show any distress at such an impersonal label for the hours they'd spent comforting each other. "What is there to suspect? I will work as diligently as ever."

"I don't want..." He smiled tightly. "I would not like my family to become difficult about you. You don't yet know their ways."

"For heaven's sake, I'm not going to tell anyone we've slept together."

"Who slept?" he quipped, but his brief moment of levity faded fast as he frowned again.

She studied his face, wondering what else he wasn't telling her.

Did he regret the nights they'd spent in his bed? Did he want her to stop visiting his room now that he was an earl? She couldn't quite bring herself to ask that question, so she chuckled softly in response to his quip.

He sighed heavily. "My father was difficult in life. In death, I expect his affairs to be no different," he confessed. "I have to assess his estate, judge what debts he holds over others, and decide what to pursue or forgive. I must curry favor with offended acquaintances. Take up unfinished tasks, however unpleasant they might be."

"I am your secretary, Quinn. I am not afraid of long hours or unsettling discoveries," she promised him. "Let me do what you have employed me to do. Let me help you. That is all I want."

He let out a tortured sigh.

"What truly bothers you?"

"I'm afraid of what we'll find." His expression grew pained. "He's tainted my life."

"I would never hold you responsible for your father's actions. I know now that you're nothing like him."

"But many will believe I am." He glanced her way, jaw clenching briefly. "Did you see Mr. Cushing approach me after the funeral? He insists on coming to see me. I have a sense that whatever it is he has to say will be unpleasant, and affects me particularly. My fear is that my father will have committed me to some mad scheme meant to extend his power, and now my own."

"Many fathers scheme to better their children's expectations. Usually, they mean the best for their sons and daughters." Theodora gasped when Quinn winced, realizing at once what he was really concerned about. "Has your father committed you to a marriage?"

"I don't believe so."

The air rushed from Theodora's lungs suddenly. Her relief was immediate and acute. She did not have to give up Quinn for that future yet. But it was understandable for him to worry about the possibility. Theodora understood his mood better now, even as her own heart pinched with fear that his father might just have been the sort to bind him into an unbreakable marriage contract and not warn him. "Your father did not confide in you?"

"Never. Father snapped out orders and expected me to come to heel," Quinn replied, swishing his hand as if he held something.

A chill swept over her skin. "How did he do that?"

"Not now, love," he whispered, closing his eyes, and blocking Theodora out of his thoughts.

Theodora wanted to understand this man. To know why Lord Templeton provoked such hatred from his eldest son. Templeton had not been spoken of fondly by anyone within Theodora's hearing, and his seduction of Quinn's mistress showed a distinct lack of morals. "Why not talk about it now? It is just us alone. I would like to better understand how you feel about him."

He sighed, eyes flashing open and pinning her with an angry stare. "When I was a little lad, not more than eight years old, I fell off my horse far from home. I broke my arm. My father was with me, and no one else. I remember turning to him in agony...and him turning away. He told me to be a man and bear the discomfort in silence. He used his riding crop across my backside to get me to remount my horse immediately. I remember thinking he must hate me."

"Oh, Quinn. That is horrible. How could he?"

"He didn't hate me. As I aged, I realized I was a commodity he meant to use for his own gain, as he tried to use my younger brothers and cousins at times, too. None of us got off lightly. Mary, I fear, suffered the most at his hands."

"Your sister?" Theodora still did not understand why the young woman was not spoken of more openly, but she had the worst feeling about what they did not say. Questions burned her tongue. "What happened to Mary?"

He paled, glancing away. "I do not know, but I fear some situation he placed Mary in meant death was her only escape."

"She…" Theodora could barely speak the words. "She killed herself?"

At his curt nod, her stomach roiled. No wonder Quinn had been so insistent that she accept her father's death was an accident. No wonder the staff refused to speak of her passing to anyone. They were *afraid* to speak of it, none more so than Quinn appeared to be now.

He moved restlessly, fingers worrying at his coat edge. "What happened to Mary could have been avoided if I'd not been so wrapped up in myself and my efforts to thwart our father at every turn."

"Surely you cannot blame yourself?" He said nothing to that, but she saw signs of guilt writ large on his face. He *did* blame himself. "Quinn, you are not responsible for everyone's happiness."

"I grew to hate him, especially so since her passing for the way he brushed aside her death without a proper investigation. I've done as much as I can to protect my remaining siblings, all the while secretly wishing all manner of indignities upon him. I suppose knowing he was so desperate to prove himself my better by seducing my former mistress is as much revenge as I could ever have."

"He suffered," she promised him, certain that Lord Templeton had been aware of what was going on around him, even if no one else believed her, until the very end of his life. "For a man who liked to be in control, his helplessness would have been agony."

Quinn's smile was tight. "There is little comfort in that, since any knowledge of Mary's last days died with him."

Theodora grew very still, watching Quinn. The jolly viscount was gone, replaced by a man who would become bitter if not turned aside from that path.

She looked out the window, thinking hard. Some men were

cruel, and it was a bleak relationship she could hardly comprehend between father and son. Quinn Ford had so many admirable qualities—devotion to family, compassion for those in need. His father should have been so proud of him, instead of always finding Quinn wanting.

She could not allow this man to become trapped by hate. She would not allow Quinn to push her away in his time of need. "Work has taken my mind off my father's death, and so it will for you, too." She smiled brightly. "Whatever comes, you can confide in me if you need to. I would never tell anyone."

"Adele said that too." He set his head back against the squabs. "And all the while, she was playing me false. She had her own agenda, to advance her career through our connection and, when that wasn't enough, she likely applied to my father for his support, too."

"My only concern is being of help to you. You have done so much for my mother and me. It would be impossible to repay you unless you take me with you. I want to be of use more than anything. I think I have been so far."

He studied her, and then his eyes skimmed her dark mourning gown, coming to rest on her breasts. Her pulse kicked up speed, and she brought her hand to her chest. Mourning gowns could never be considered pretty, but when alone, Quinn had a way of watching her that made her think he looked beyond them to what lie beneath.

His lips quirked a little on one side. "You have. More than you know."

She smiled shyly. "I'm glad."

He leaned forward suddenly, placing his hand firmly on her knee. His touch was insistent as he pushed her gown between her thighs in his quest to reach her quim. Her breath caught as he succeeded, and skimmed her sex with firm pressure until she was panting with want and aching to lift her skirts for him.

"I always want you like this," he whispered.

She breathed deeply, holding on to her rules by a mere thread. Quinn was so hard to rebuff. He made her almost angry with herself that she had so little control around him. Theodora would almost break her own rules just to make love to him during the day, to ease the yearning that never seemed to go away.

"I feel the same, but..." Reluctantly, Theodora covered his wandering hand with hers and removed it from between her legs. "Forgive me."

He scowled fiercely at being denied. "You'd better come with me to Newberry House *tonight*," he said.

Theodora smiled broadly, considering it a victory to have achieved her goal to stay with him. "I can be ready."

He caught her smile and frowned again. "Better bring your mother and Soot, too. They'll be your chaperones during the day to allay wagging tongues."

"And the nights?" Theodora let her attention drift to his groin, and couldn't help but notice a decidedly flattering bulge had formed there.

His eyes caught hers, and they softened slightly. "The nights will be decided by your invitation."

"Come to me tonight," she whispered, anticipation rippling over her skin. They'd never made love in her bedchamber before. She had always gone to him. But with mother preoccupied with her puppy, she depended less on Theodora for company.

"Not tonight. There will likely be too many servants running about," he suggested. "I would like to visit you the next night, when we are settled into Newberry House, if you are agreeable."

So long to wait, but she supposed it couldn't be helped. Theodora nodded quickly. "I will speak to Mama about the necessity of the move and make sure the transition is smooth. I promise you'll hardly notice her or Soot underfoot."

"As long as everyone else notices her presence as your chaperone, I will be content," Quinn said with a wry smile. "Appearances matter very much at a time like this."

At last, they were of the same mind. "Indeed they do, my dear man."

CHAPTER EIGHTEEN

"YOU LOOK LIKE HELL, TEMPLETON," Captain William Ford exclaimed as he strode into the drawing room.

Quinn smiled for his cousin's sake and held out his hand while repressing the urge to glance around for his father on hearing the title mentioned aloud. He feared it might take a very long while to grow used to being referred to as Templeton rather than Lord Maitland. "Thank you, William. It's good to see a friendly face, even with the sarcastic tongue you have in your head."

"I'm honest, and family, so must always be forgiven." William sidestepped his outstretched hand and embraced him. Quinn's back was pounded, and then he was released and stared at. William held him by the shoulders, his face full of concern. "I'd offer my condolences if they were necessary," he said, knowing sympathy for the loss was the last thing Quinn wanted.

He shrugged. "You know my feelings so well."

"I should. You've bent my ear enough over the years about how shoddily Templeton treated you." William took a chair, accepted a cup of coffee from a footman when offered, and leaned back comfortably. "Things will be better now. For everyone."

Quinn hoped so. Every waking moment seemed a dream, a nightmare. He was grateful for the focus Theodora encouraged during the day. He took heed of her example and worked harder than ever, rather than fretting over his new responsibilities and all he must do for the good of the family. Last night, though, his first night in his new bed at Newberry House, Quinn had trouble sleeping because she was not near to talk to. He had not expected to miss her when she was only a few doors away down the hall.

"As long as I can make sense of what he's done, it will be."

"What do you mean?"

William knew how to keep secrets. He had always taken Quinn's side in any argument, so he felt no concern opening up to him now. "A Mr. Cushing spoke to me immediately after the burial. Do you know him?"

William nodded. "I've heard the name before."

"He's expected this morning. Wants to discuss an important matter of business that cannot wait. Since I have no connection with him beyond sharing a dinner with him a few weeks ago, it must be something my father had a hand in."

"A sticky hand, no doubt. He was always looking for a way to feather his nest, driving a hard bargain that suited his purpose more than the greater good." William made a face, which made the scar he'd received in battle rather more frightening than usual. "Cushing is quick in coming to you so soon after the funeral. Whatever it is must be very important to him."

He frowned, glancing toward the door. He was on edge today. Out of place in Newberry House, with its gilt-edged furniture and tiny silk pillows. He much preferred the rustic nature of Maitland House, but Mother had asked him to move, and at such a time, he could not refuse her. "Which makes me all the more worried about what the situation might be. What do you remember of him?"

"Not a bad chap, well connected in trade of course. If I recall correctly, your father introduced us the year before my injury. Been in your father's pocket this last year or more, I imagine. He has a few daughters, one of an age to come out soon if memory serves." William's eyes narrowed further, and then he rolled his eyes. "Matchmaking from the grave?"

Quinn considered Cushing's anxiety, his urgency to speak in private as soon as possible, and feared the worst for their meeting. Marriage was utterly out of the question. Father had known his views on arranged alliances. He'd only marry for love. He was convinced that was the only way to be happy with a wife. He'd been as firm on the subject as it was possible to be.

And yet he couldn't shake the feeling that his father had committed him to some foolish scheme anyway.

"Shall I stay?" William offered.

"I'd appreciate it." William could be trusted to hold his tongue, and his support might be needed if Cushing proved difficult. Quinn would not agree to marry anyone his father had picked out for him. "If you've nothing else to do, that is."

"Certainly I can stay. I warned Matilda I might visit with you for a while. She knows I'm the sensible, levelheaded one, and you're the emotional one."

"Emotional?"

William leaned forward, lowering his voice. "You *were* the one who recklessly dove off a cliff after Mary when she drowned herself."

"You were right behind me, if I recall."

"I swam out from the shore, not dive from the cliff top. We're lucky we didn't bury two bodies that day," William ground out.

Many thought William a cold man, but Quinn had seen through his facade of restraint long ago. William felt too deeply to bear to show it sometimes. William and Theodora had that in common, except for the anger. Even though Quinn had been grieving over losing Mary, William had torn strips off Quinn later in privacy about that reckless dive. "We were both desperate."

"It was a shock to all of us to lose her like that." William sat back, worrying at his lower lip. "Perhaps, now that your father is out of the way, we can finally put the matter to rest."

"Father denied any involvement in her death, but the topic came up recently, and I thought he acted very guilty. Of course, he fell ill before I could discover more, and is dead now, so what he knew died with him." Quinn glanced toward the study that was now his. "I'll have to look elsewhere for answers, if there are any to be had."

"I've already told you all I know, but do you need my help?"

He considered William's suggestion seriously. Whatever had happened before Mary had died must have been terrible. The fewer people who learned the details, the better. However, there was one person who might approach his problem with clearer eyes. He'd already begun to seek Theodora's opinion on many things, including how women viewed romantic situations. Sharing his concerns with Theodora would require that he trust her with a very dark moment in his past. It was a risk he wasn't sure he should take with his family's reputation yet. "No, but thank you."

The door creaked open and Falstaff, the Newberry House butler, slid through the gap. "My apologies for the intrusion. Mr. Cushing has arrived earlier than his appointment. What should I do?"

"Send him in," Quinn told the butler.

Quinn stood, smoothing his waistcoat as Mr. Cushing strode into the room a moment later. The man was of middle years, ruddy complexion, but not smiling. He steered his daughter Genevieve into the room on his arm, a girl Quinn had found quite timid and, well...dull.

William gave him a warning glance, and he restrained his smile of welcome a bit more.

Quinn shook hands with Cushing and nodded politely to the daughter. "Sir. Welcome."

"Thank you for seeing us, Lord Templeton. And Captain Ford, I did not expect to see you today."

"So I see," William stated coldly.

Cushing swallowed. "Yes, well. May I present my daughter, Genevieve, to you, Captain?"

William nodded politely to the young woman, even as Quinn noted her hands were shaking. She clutched them to her stomach rather than offer them. Was she ill or terrified of William's looks? The wound William had barely survived in battle made many ladies of their acquaintance decidedly uncomfortable.

"Please do sit down," he said, speaking to Genevieve. He was not prepared to have the young woman faint today. "Would you care for tea?"

The young woman shook her head quickly and glanced toward the door as it closed. Quinn was rather glad she did not want to be there. It meant he had a chance to turn the matter to his benefit without hurting her feelings.

Rather than draw out the tension, Quinn got straight to the point and addressed her father. "You said the matter was urgent. How may I be of assistance?"

"I won't pay," Cushing blurted. "Not unless you marry her first."

It was almost comical that he had expected such a scene that morning, but he found nothing to smile about. William seemed to agree, as he drawled, "Marry whom?"

"My daughter, of course," Cushing ground out as he gestured to the girl on the verge of fainting.

Quinn ignored the mention of marriage to Genevieve and worried about the bill instead. He kept his attention on Mr. Cushing. "You mentioned a debt. Forgive me for my ignorance. I am still unaware of many of my father's financial entanglements."

The fellow dug into his pocket and procured a well-folded scrap of paper. When he passed it over, Quinn smoothed it out and read very quickly. Five thousand pounds lost at Faro and owed to the Templeton estate. The repayment of such a large amount was no small matter. It was enough to bankrupt a business and ruin a family. Damn his father for this!

That Cushing attempted to delay the repayment by offering up his daughter suggested the amount could very well be more than could be repaid at all.

Acid burned in his stomach at the inexcusable situation he'd been placed in. It was not Quinn's way to gamble with the livelihood of others, and he would never take advantage of desperation over money. "This debt is forgiven."

He stood, moved to a desk, and scrawled his signature across the promissory note, marking it as paid in full. He could bear the loss of that money better than he would tolerate a marriage begun under these circumstances.

When he passed over the paper, Mr. Cushing stared at him in shock. "That was five thousand pounds," the man whispered.

"I am not my father. I will not be bribed to take a wife." He turned to Genevieve and inclined his head. "No slight intended, my lady. I am sure you would make someone else a perfectly suitable spouse. But not me. I wish you all the best for an enjoyable season."

"None taken, my lord. Thank you." Her eyes glowed with sudden happiness, and she cast a quick glance at her father as she smothered a laugh of relief. She met Quinn's gaze again, and beamed, no longer the timid mouse he'd first met. "Thank you so very much indeed," she gushed, her relief obvious that he would not fall in with her father's suggestion that he marry her. They were both spared a bad decision by him forgiving that debt.

Cushing was pale, but at his daughter's urging, eventually spoke. "Thank you."

"My pleasure. I do hope you can enjoy the coming season far better now without that nonsense over your head."

"We most assuredly will, my lord. Father will never gamble so recklessly again," Genevieve promised, still beaming with happiness. She was quite transformed.

He escorted them as far as the drawing room doors and then closed them firmly.

No sooner were they gone than William barked out a short laugh.

Quinn scowled at him. "Shut up."

"Oh my! You should have seen Cushing's face fall when you turned away. He wanted that marriage very badly, even if his daughter did not."

"He'd probably been planning for it, expecting I'd agree just to get the money back. Thank heavens for the war. If not for my own income, I might have had to consider it," he admitted.

"Cushing probably thought you'd be heartsick over the loss of the mad bastard." William frowned and dug into the seat behind him, only to drag out a riding crop—one of the many that had belonged to his father. William flexed it between his hands, testing the strength of the wood. "Now this is a fine thing to discover today."

Quinn went cold at the sight of the object of his most recent punishment.

He snatched it from William's hands despite his protest and snapped it in half over his knee. "Mad bastard. That is too kind a term for him." He tossed the broken pieces into the fire and watched them blacken and burn. "Good riddance."

William, who knew the manner of his father's previous punishments, moved beside him, and squeezed his shoulder. "Yes, good riddance indeed."

Quinn smiled tightly. "That's most probably only the first caller with such news I can expect to receive in the next few weeks."

"Oh yes, there are plenty more schemes being plotted to see you cornered into a marriage," William warned. "Miss Cushing seemed pretty enough, but didn't tempt you to instantly fall to your knees and declare your undying love?"

William's ridiculous question made him laugh, and the tightness of his chest eased. "Not in the slightest."

"Cousin Rothwell's wife is rumored to have a good eye for matches, and can be counted on to send the girl in the right direction instead of in yours, if you want her help." His expression changed, growing puzzled. "Speaking of direction, did you have someone in mind for yourself to marry? I'm sure Aunt Pen would be only too happy to help foster a connection that led to marriage, if that's what you do want."

Quinn's thoughts turned to Theodora Dalton so fast, he was surprised at himself. What he had with her was good, but he'd not wish to alter their current arrangement. A wife was a complication he didn't want to deal with yet. "No, there is no one."

"Well, whoever you choose eventually, I do hope she possesses a backbone. She'll be the next Duchess of Rutherford. Your mama and Aunt Pen will eat her for lunch if she's not up to snuff for the challenge."

"I'm sure whoever I choose will more than meet their high standards." Actually, he couldn't wait for Aunt Pen and Theodora Dalton to meet. Quinn held back a laugh, imagining Theodora and his aunt battling over which of his social engagements were more important for him to attend. He'd always valued his aunt's advice, knowing she wanted nothing from him in return but his respect, however, Theodora had quite a number of opinions of her own, too, that she was sure to voice. The two could likely clash quite often.

Oh, those meetings would indeed be fun to watch. He'd sit on the sidelines trying to determine which woman loved him more. Except...love had no part in his arrangement with Theodora. If he were to get married, the woman would have to love him without question.

He shook his head before he began to speculate the depth of Theodora's emotions where he was concerned. His own were clear right now. He was not in love, and lived from day to day. "She'll have a backbone, shin bones and—"

"A very tidy pair of breasts?" William suggested as he made his hands form the shape of groping a pair.

His thoughts returned to Theodora's eager little body, and how well they came together in his bed.

Yet he could not easily forget her remarks on that first day in his home. She'd boldly tried to seduce him as a means to gaining employment. She was not sweet, possibly quite devious in her methods of obtaining what she wanted in life. He couldn't say what her ambitions were now, but she claimed marriage to him wasn't one of her goals.

Quinn threw a pillow at his cousin. "Stop that. Are you not supposed to be a dull and sensible married man by now?"

His cousin set his hands behind his head and leaned back, smiling. "Married, but not without the imagination of what's important to all gentlemen of sense."

Quinn studied William closely. Crusty William had seemed to settle into marriage well, even forsaking his club and friends for the quiet of home life with Matilda, a former maid. Father had been livid about William's marriage. "Are you suggesting you've thought about bedding other women?"

William's smile dropped in an instant as the pillow sailed across the room and hit Quinn in the head. "Of course not! A man can never keep a wife and mistress happy at the same time and remain happy himself. Better to love your mistress enough to make an honest woman of her than juggle two without caring for either," he growled.

"I say," Quinn said, surprised by William's vehemence. "Steady on."

"I nearly made that mistake," William admitted in a quieter voice. He smiled then. "But I am happier now than I ever hoped to be."

"Please, you are sickening." He threw the pillow back at his cousin. "Whoever thought you would be happily landlocked and spouting nonsense about matrimonial bliss?"

"No one, I expect. That is why I enjoy claiming to be pleased with my situation so often. It unsettles everyone when I smile." William threw the pillow back at his head. "Do you feel better now, or shall we break out the swords next?"

Quinn sat the pretty silk pillow on his knee, contemplating the question. "No need for further violence. I will survive."

"You're not alone," William promised. "You'll never be alone. Our family, all of the branches, only want the best for you and the estate."

Quinn grinned at his cousin. "So does that mean the family can expect to have the pleasure of your company more often? My sisters wrote to say they were quite taken with your wife when you visited Newberry Park at Christmas."

"Perhaps," William said, straightening his spine. "Matilda is still quite shy of everyone."

"She has no reason to be concerned. Eventually, given enough time and my sisters' unfortunate influence, she'll be just like the rest of them. Opinionated. Unruly."

William rubbed a hand over his scar. "I like Matilda just the way she is, so perhaps we will not visit often."

"People will change. A timid mouse might one day become a lioness."

William frowned. "That would not suit my temperament."

"Don't worry about it. I'm sure you will adjust." Quinn smirked.

"I am positive Matilda will come into her own in due time. Heaven help you then."

"I think we should talk about a marriage for you again," William teased, making an obvious attempt to change the subject.

"Nothing can be done in pursuit of a lady while the family grieves, even if I had someone in mind."

"I doubt mourning would stop you if you set your heart on someone," William mused, then helped himself to another cup of coffee. "How long will you mourn?"

"Three months." He sighed. "There is Louisa to consider."

"Yes, Louisa and her third season," William said, with his own heavy sigh. "I'm beginning to wonder if she'll ever tie the knot."

"She'll marry eventually, or she won't." Quinn tapped his fingers on the pillow. "I'm not truly concerned by my sister's lack of interest in finding a husband that suits her. Unlike father, I will support any decision she makes. I will not control her friendships at the expense of her dreams. I will give her the chance to make the most important decision of her life in her own time."

And if deciding on as short a period of family mourning as possible helped, it was all for the better.

"You're wiser than your father already," William promised. "As for you, you'll find someone to love soon enough with that attitude. Women will come running to stake a claim on your tender heart."

Quinn felt no rush to gain a wife, but planning how to continue his affair with Theodora in this house, without being noticed, required delicacy and perfect timing on his part. He threw the pillow at his cousin one last time. "Put a cork in it, William. You really are becoming unbearable."

CHAPTER NINETEEN

A SCRATCH at the door alerted Theodora to her lover's arrival. It was late, and the house had been quiet for some time. She was just giving up hope of seeing Quinn tonight when she heard him outside her door. The move from Maitland House to Newberry House had exhausted her; her last glimpse of the ruins of her former home had brought her grief closer to the surface than she cared to admit.

Catching sight of Quinn in a dark silk banyan and bare feet banished the tension she'd been fighting since coming up to her new bedchamber. She held out her arms, beckoning him closer. Excitement rippled up her spine as he locked the door behind him and hurried to join her.

His lips were hungry as they settled over hers and soothed her as nothing else could.

They did not speak. There was no need. They both were well aware of why he'd come and what Theodora wanted from Quinn tonight.

Quinn's kiss was exactly as she remembered, but fiercer somehow. Hungrier. As if he was filled with the same desperation she felt after one night of abstinence. Twisting away, Theodora ripped the tie to her robe undone, and he did the same. Given they were both naked beneath, Theodora did not wait to push her body against his, gasping a little at the contact of his hot skin against hers.

He slid his hands down her back, beneath the robe, then lifted her up. "Mine," he taunted.

Theodora curled her legs about Quinn's waist and tightened her grip on him. "All mine, too."

The smile on his face at her claim took her breath away, but she had no time to respond. He backed her against the bedpost, and her lust increased another notch as he kissed her quite desperately.

Quinn's passion was what she desired in a man. A little rough, but only in a good way. She curled her arms around his head as they kissed, finding new ways to inflame him with her tongue and lips. She gripped his hair and tugged his head to the side to expose his neck.

Theodora settled her lips to his throat and kissed him there until he gasped. She nipped the firm column of his throat, not enough to bruise, lavished kisses on his jaw, and flicked his earlobe with the tip of her tongue until he was moaning. She finished with a firmer bite to the tip of his chin and met his wild gaze.

"Vixen," he whispered. "You'll pay for that."

"Promises, promises," she teased.

He moved around the bed and dumped her onto the sheets. She gazed up at him as he stripped off his robe completely and reached forward to grasp her hips. He flipped her over onto her stomach before she could protest she wasn't done admiring him. He dragged her to the edge of the bed until her feet touched the floor. "There's but one thing to do with a woman like you."

She lifted her chest and twisted to look over her shoulder, trying to see his face. "And that is?"

"Have you, until you beg me to stop," he whispered roughly against the back of her neck.

She caught his eye. "That could take all night," she mused.

"I have a plan," he countered, skimming his hands down her sides until he reached her hips. He slid one hand beneath her and covered her sex. "I intend to spend a great deal of effort tonight, filling you, bringing us pleasure to make up for what we were denied last night."

"Good." He parted her folds as he explained his wicked plan in great detail. When he slid his fingers over her clit, she shuddered and squirmed against him. "Please, Quinn."

He slid his fingers from her clitoris and thrust into her, again and again.

She groaned loudly. "I need you."

Quinn widened her legs, and soon he was sliding in and out of her eager body. She gasped each time he reached his limit and whimpered when he withdrew. His fingers covered her clitoris again, and he made love to her until Theodora couldn't hold back. She came too quickly, jerking on his cock and against his fingers.

He slipped away, turned her over, and surged back inside her before she could catch her breath.

She opened her eyes as Quinn started to move above her again. "My apologies for my unseemly haste," she whispered.

"Don't be." He cupped her cheek briefly, and his expression became serious. "You can never wait to have me, and I'd never deny you. Yours is the most honest passion I've ever experienced."

Theodora shivered. What they shared was so much more than she'd expected. Her experiences in Quinn's arms far outweighed the desire she'd experienced with her former betrothed, Daniel. It felt briefly disloyal to admit it, but she was having trouble remembering what had made her betrothed special enough to have almost married him. She seemed to have more in common with Quinn, both in and out of bed.

"I'm always honest when it comes to my appreciation of your technique," she said.

Theodora closed her eyes to savor the moment. She was well and truly over the first love of her life. She had grown beyond that infatuation and moved on to a love affair that gave her everything she'd ever wanted—passion and respect and unending challenges.

Quinn ran his hands along her thighs, and then pushed them high into the air. Theodora opened her eyes again as he curled his fingers around her ankles to thrust slowly in and out of her body.

Theodora smiled at his restraint. Now that her first rush of pleasure had passed, she would admire him, appreciate him, tease him, and tempt him in ways he couldn't resist. He seemed most responsive to praise. "You are a devil in bed," she whispered.

"I was thinking the same about you." He buried himself deep and then chuckled. "I've made a pact with the devil."

"For good, not evil," she promised, then used her own body strength to move against him when he remained still. It may be brazen, but time was too short. One day he'd have enough of her, and fall in love with someone else.

Quinn caught her hips tightly as she set her bare feet against his skin, one on his chest, the other over his shoulder in a bid to still her. However, with the additional leverage, she could rotate on him no matter what he attempted. "I'm very good for you," Theodora promised.

Those few little movements brought a wicked gleam to his eyes. An expression Theodora had grown to love seeing on his face. Everyone enjoyed a good romp between the sheets, whether they admitted to it or not. Thankfully, she had Quinn for now.

"I should have known you couldn't be passive," he murmured, his lips curving into a deep smile. "To be honest, I'm glad we're in bed together again. It would have been hell working beside you if I couldn't have this too."

He thrust hard and withdrew, then repeated the pattern as her breath whooshed out of her lungs from the sheer joy of being so well used. Pleasure built as he continued to hammer her body harder than ever. She put her fingers on her clitoris and let his thrusts jolt her fingers against the hard bud of her sex until she was moaning out loud.

Her body was flushed with heat and sweat when he turned her again, so she lay on her side while he was still buried deep. He moved her to the angle he wanted, held her top leg up, her hand trapped between her legs and thrust very slowly.

"Wait for me," Quinn demanded.

Theodora jerked her hand away from her quim, but it was too late. She lost her control over her arousal and came anyway. She turned her face into the bedding just in time to muffle a scream.

Above her, Quinn stilled and then, by the short, abrupt thrusts, she knew he was about to join her in bliss.

CHAPTER TWENTY

QUINN LAY ON HIS SIDE, watching Theodora sleep. He'd exhausted her, and his lips curled in pleasure that he could. When it came to lovemaking, Theodora was very physical. She liked what he liked, which seemed to be any position he wanted to bend her into. She liked to tease him with bold conversation. They were well matched indeed, and yet it was always Theodora who collapsed first. He'd never known such honesty in a lover. Never taken so much pleasure in a woman's desire.

Despite their poor beginning, Theodora appeared made for his pleasure.

Quinn studied Theodora's face in repose. In the light of the new day, she was breathtaking. Pure and yet so very wicked at heart. Gentle and yet fierce. She made every moment together an event, a necessity for his soul. He could hardly believe he'd turned her down once. He wouldn't ever be so foolish again.

He moved a curl of her dark hair from the pillow and lay it gently across her exposed breast. He grasped another carefully, so as not to wake her, delighting in the texture of the dark strands between his fingers, and added it to the first. She was a strange and fascinating creature. He had no regrets they'd become lovers. He did things to her he'd never have attempted with Adele in the past, which made him reconsider how deeply he'd cared for his former mistress.

To be honest, he'd never actually felt like this before. Every glimpse of Theodora's body filled him with anticipation. Every conversation with her revealed an odd symmetry of thought. He did not fool himself that she agreed with him on every subject, but what they had discussed was done with enough friendly banter and intelligence to her logic to have him looking forward to their next conversation, and even disagreements...not that they'd had any yet.

She'd become deeply involved in his affairs, his properties and investments, his ambitions to live on his own terms. She made making sense of his father's affairs feel less overwhelming.

He'd grown so accustomed to sharing everything with her that it seemed disloyal not to turn to her for advice. He considered again whether she might help him solve the puzzle of Mary's last days. He could explain what he knew of Mary and see if she concluded anything beyond his own thoughts.

"There's always a sheet to cover me with," Theodora grumbled sleepily after he added another curl over her breast.

"But then I'd be denied the view of the rest of your delicious body," he whispered, teasing his fingers over her soft belly until she squirmed. He wished they could remain like this until morning came, but he had a valet who would come to "wake" him in his own room shortly. He had to return there soon.

He stole a kiss, and Theodora lifted her face for more. He obliged, kissing her softly, teasing her awake. Quinn moved over her, propping himself on his arms and knees to lose himself in her delicious scent yet again. It was almost more than he could bear to pull away and not continue exploring their mutual passion. "I must be going. It is almost six."

She peeked around the room with one eye open and groaned softly. "You woke me up just to tell me you were going? In truth, I didn't expect you to stay so long."

Neither had he, but when their last pleasure had ended, he'd wrapped Theodora in his arms and dozed longer than normal. She was very soft and seemed very willing to be held. Something he adored about her. It was also an intimacy Adele had never allowed him to indulge in often, he suddenly remembered. She hadn't liked him to see her at anything but her best looks, either.

He ran his hand over Theodora's tangled dark locks fondly. "I dislike slinking off in the dark like a thief," he murmured as he considered his last relationship. He'd not particularly liked the terms struck between himself and Adele that only allowed him three nights a week in her bed at most. Most often it had been once a week because she claimed to be committed elsewhere.

Father, of course, had been among her other engagements.

He was glad to be rid of her, in truth.

So far, Theodora had never denied him a moment in her company, although he'd never asked for more beyond their beds. He should like to dance with her one day, though. He was eager to learn what she thought of his friends too.

He dropped his lips to her breast and teased her until the bud pebbled, then he drew the peak deeper into his mouth. He feasted on her lightly until she caught his head and held him there with firm pressure. Theodora had full breasts, ones perfectly shaped for his hands and lips to devour. He could easily spend an hour making love to one if he could bear to leave the rest of her body alone for that long. Quinn drew her firmly against him, cupping her back and then sliding his hand down to her rear. He tilted her hips up until she pressed her quim against his belly, and she gasped softly before grinding her sex harder into him.

There was one thing he absolutely knew about Theodora Dalton

—she was always eager for pleasure. She always welcomed him with open arms.

Her fingers tightened and then she tousled his hair. "It seems I must forgive you, since you are waking me with such lovely kisses."

Reluctantly, he drew back from her breast. He had arranged to meet a friend this morning in pursuit of information about Mary's final days. He couldn't be late. "Kisses that must stop, if I'm to return to my room unnoticed."

"Sadly true. I was just beginning to feel warm all over." She pulled a face, not a pout but an expression of acceptance. Adele would have complained about him abandoning her and sulked, denying him her bed until he'd bought her a pretty trinket to make her smile once more.

He kissed Theodora's lips quickly. Theodora was a sensible woman. It was unfortunate that they could not play together in bed all day and get away without it being noticed. "Hold that thought until tonight, or if you dare, you may finish this morning without me, and we will start anew later."

She smiled slowly. "If you are certain you must go, I suppose I have no choice but to please myself."

"I am sorry I cannot stay."

She peeked beneath the sheets toward his erection. "I know."

He smiled and rolled out of bed. As was often the case, he felt very energetic after being with Theodora. Quinn found his banyan, slipped it on, and spent a moment gazing upon a very tousled Theodora. Her hands moved beneath the sheet, sliding down her body. She widened her legs a little and raised her knees.

Vixen! She was going to take him up on his suggestion while he was still in the room! What he wouldn't give to stay and watch her make love to herself.

"Until later," he whispered.

He hurried out, giving his erection a stern warning to subside. If he stayed, he might be tempted to stay with Theodora forever. An idea that was slowly beginning to become appealing.

He was inside his chamber less than five minutes before Rodmell arrived, arms full of riding clothes. He was out to the stables fifteen minutes later.

Once Quinn had regained his appreciation of firm land beneath him, and lost his sea legs, he preferred to be out in the fresh morning air each day on his favorite horse, Locket, riding with old friends in Hyde Park. He pushed Locket to a trot to reach the prearranged meeting place as quickly as possible.

Lord Deacon was already waiting on a restless mount, but had unexpected company in the Duke of Calder at his side. He galloped to join them. He was late, and apologized for making Lord Deacon wait and then turned toward Lord Calder, a man a little older than him but quite a prankster. "Good morning, Calder. What brings you out of your bed at this ungodly hour?"

"Good news. I've found a bride," Calder said, beaming from ear to ear.

Quinn blinked, and then pressed his hand to his chest. "You? Married? The world is about to come to an end."

"That's what I said," Deacon added glumly.

"We'll be married by the end of the month."

"Well then. Congratulations." Quinn maneuvered his horse so he could shake Calder's hand. Calder would have chosen very well. A woman with a large dowry and impeccable connections were needed when an estate had fallen on hard times, as his had. "I'll tell my secretary to accept the invitation immediately once it arrives."

"Good, for I should like the pair of you to stand up with me."

Quinn's horse pranced. "It would be an honor. Now, do tell me about your bride. Who is she?"

"You don't need to know yet."

Deacon scowled. "There's the rub. He won't say who she is. Means to surprise us all, he says."

"What?"

Deacon slumped in his saddle. "I ask you, how is a man supposed to pick a wife if there is every chance he pursues the hand of a woman who's already off the marriage market and won't say a word about it?"

"You would never suit my lady, Deacon, and I am most definitely keeping her away from the likes of you, Templeton," Calder promised, then laughed.

"Afraid she'll throw you over for an inferior title?" Quinn joked.

"Or perhaps I am merely afraid she'll take a look at my friends and become hysterical and run." Calder quirked one haughty brow and then laughed. "I am not giving society a chance to gossip about my choice of bride until the very hour we're to marry."

Quinn exchanged a long glance with Deacon, but saw his confusion too easily at Calder's plan. It was highly unusual, and not at all like Calder to be secretive. "You're not marrying the baker's daughter, the one on Bond Street that you always flirt with, are you?"

"She's a fine wench," Deacon murmured, with a touch of reverence in his voice. "Her sugared buns bring me back to her shop again and again," he promised.

"No, not her." Calder laughed heartily at that. "My lips are sealed until the ceremony. You'll have to wait like everyone else to find out her identity."

Quinn shook his head. Calder was the most outspoken of his circle of friends. It would be a miracle if he didn't give away his own secret before the appointed hour. "This ought to be very interesting," Quinn conceded.

"I think so too." Calder's grin widened. "Now all we need do is see the two of you similarly well matched."

Quinn pulled a face. The only woman he wanted in his life was

Theodora, and he had her already. "Perhaps we should concentrate on finding Lord Deacon a wife first."

"That's a good idea. He's become rather maudlin about everyone else getting wed before him." Calder turned his mount about. "By the way, Templeton, I'm sorry to have missed the dinner for your sister. I don't recall receiving an invitation in the mail."

"Invitations were not sent, in the end," Quinn confessed. "It seemed imprudent timing, given my father's illness."

Calder expression softened. "Ghastly business with your father."

Quinn stiffened. So far, his friends had been kind and not spoken of Father and Adele Blakely being lovers. He did not want to discuss the matter, either. He looked away rather than respond.

"She would understand the need to delay for a happier occasion," Deacon promised.

"Possibly," Quinn murmured.

Deacon tapped his boot with his riding crop suddenly, forcing Quinn to spin about. The man stared at him, one eyebrow rising in question. He smiled, and then his expression turned sly. "She always liked Calder, though I don't see why she should have. Nothing to recommend him but his lofty title."

"She was a good sport, wasn't she?" Calder said, but then his grin returned. "Although you might be right about her taste. What she saw in Deacon and that other fellow I'll never understand."

"Her choice of friends was occasionally questionable. She should never have befriended me, I know," Deacon moaned.

Mary had always been a staunch supporter of Lord Deacon, always suggesting Deacon would love this or that entertainment. Inviting him home to the family estate in Essex for a few weeks every summer until her death. Quinn had not thought Mary wrong about Deacon, but he'd not noticed she'd favored anyone else in that way. "What other fellow are you talking about?"

Calder blinked. "You know, the one she was a bit smitten with."

Quinn's heart sped up a little. "No, I don't think so. Do you, Deacon?"

"Name was…" Deacon scratched his head, then shrugged. "Damned if I can remember."

Quinn clenched his hands around the reins, his pulse racing. "Try very hard to remember. It could be important."

Deacon's lips drew into a thin line. "What does it matter?"

"It may seem unimportant to you, but I still want to know who my sister was speaking with back then."

"Romeo," Calder exclaimed suddenly. "I remember teasing Mary that we would all have to call her Juliet one day."

Quinn recalled no one by that name. "Romeo?"

"Romeo…" Calder looked at Deacon. "Come on, man. Surely you remember him better than I? He had a house near yours, didn't he? He wore a wide-brimmed hat with a ribbon wrapped around and little feathers at the front. We used to laugh about it being rather silly when he strutted off to his employment, as we were only just returning home from the night before's revels."

"What did he do?"

"I can't recall that I ever knew," Calder said, shaking his head. "We used to make up so much nonsense to tease your sister with that I don't think I'd trust my memory now."

Deacon closed his eyes briefly, and then he sighed. "Roman, not Romeo. Roman Gently. A clerk. Are we going to ride?"

"Indeed we are," Quinn promised, but he was racking his brain trying to place Roman Gently in his sister's life. Mary had no business being involved with a lowly clerk. He was fairly certain his father and grandfather had never employed anyone by that name in London, either. He would do well to ask Theodora if she recalled reading the name anywhere in his father's papers.

CHAPTER TWENTY-ONE

"ARE YOU FINISHED FOR THE DAY?" Theodora glanced at the ornate clock on the mantel, and then at the late Lord Templeton's two secretaries, who were on the point of leaving the room. Mr. Kemp and Mr. Sever were sticklers for punctuality and routine, which Theodora grudgingly approved of, even if they were leaving too early in her opinion.

Mr. Kemp, the elder of the pair, nodded. "Our workday ended at three o'clock. It is quarter past the hour now."

"Oh, I see." Theodora exchanged a glance with her mother, who had kept them all quiet company from her spot by the window all day, leaving only long enough for Soot to be walked when she needed to go out. "Very well. Well, good night, Mr. Kemp and Mr. Sever."

She reached for another file and flipped open the cover to read the first sheet. It was a contract to purchase a property in St. James and, according to the note, no income was derived from the tenant for the last six months. She frowned at it, wondering who the late earl had liked enough to allow them to live there rent-free. The late Lord Templeton was hardly known for his charity.

Sever turned back at the door. "You're not done?"

"No, and not for several hours, I expect." Theodora copied the particulars of the property into a small notebook, ready to pass along to Quinn when he had time to investigate the anomaly. She'd begun keeping records of her own as soon as she'd uncovered a dozen odd things among the late earl's papers. "I will see you both in the morning."

There was a lengthy silence after their departure before Mama spoke. "I think you just put two grown men to shame. It is not a good idea to alienate secretaries who would replace you."

"I know, but I learned early that to work meant I must toil harder than any man. Besides, the late Lord Templeton's affairs are rather complicated. If I kept to their hours, I might never understand before my hair was streaked with gray."

Her mother stood and drew close. "Just don't stare at that chicken scratching pretending to be handwriting for too long. You've barely glanced out the window today."

Theodora sat back immediately and glanced up at the ceiling, then left and right, with only her eyes. If she worked for too long in one stretch, her vision had the troubling habit of becoming blurred by the end of the evening. "Thank you for reminding me."

She stood and stretched, moving to the front windows to peer out. "Another carriage is leaving."

Soot began to bark and whine when the door opened behind her.

Her employer slipped into the room, frowning as he shut the door behind him to keep Mama's dog from running off into other parts of the house.

"Captain William Ford called again and stayed a while," Quinn advised after greeting the dog. He joined Theodora at the window.

Theodora smiled at her employer but noted he wore an unusually guarded expression. "The captain is your cousin, is he not?"

"First cousin," Quinn nodded, drawing near. "We are close."

Theodora returned to the desk, sidestepped the enthusiastic puppy who wanted her to play, and drew out her personal journal. She made a note for herself to learn everything she could about Captain William Ford. Quinn relied on memory in general, but with his added responsibilities, there likely would be a great many small matters unintentionally forgotten. Family affection should not be a casualty of his elevation.

He followed her, his fingers discreetly skimming her arm, out of sight of her mother. "How are you surviving here?"

Her senses tingled. Lusting after her employer wasn't the done thing, but she had to admit it was a splendid way to pass the time. Quinn's presence always put her in a good mood. "Very well, although I think Mama found today very dull."

"Not dull at all. I've had the advantage of watching two grown men try to make sense of my daughter. I don't think they've ever seen a woman so interested in legal documents before."

"I'm glad one of us is." He sighed, moved to a sideboard. "That is what my future will be. Dull and tedious paperwork and parliamentary debate for years on end."

"Fascinating." Theodora crossed the room and immediately took the decanter from his hand. "Don't drink from this one. Move the five books to the right on the bookshelf beside you. I believe your father kept the best brandy stashed away, out of sight of visitors."

Quinn grunted and shifted to the side. He moved the fake books aside and uncovered a decanter that matched the ones on display. "Typical of him. How did you discover this little secret?"

"Mr. Kemp sampled a glass from there after luncheon, and made certain to hide it again as I returned. He then pretended to top up his glass from one of the displayed bottles, and I concluded he wanted to try to keep it a secret still."

"He will underestimate you at his own peril, my dear." He

smiled suddenly. Quinn moved the good brandy to the sideboard and switched the previously displayed one into the secret hiding place. He glanced her way, eyes dancing with mirth. "A little fun."

Theodora nodded encouragingly, glad to see a spark of mischief in her employer's eyes. He might be an earl now, but there was no reason he needed to be serious all the time. He shouldn't have to change his nature. She liked him just as he was. "Here, my lord, come and look at this."

"If there is nothing else, my lord, Theodora, I should like to retire upstairs for a while," Mama interrupted, Soot tucked firmly under her arm.

Theodora smiled at her mother, pleased she'd remained downstairs so long. She had taken Quinn's request very seriously to act as chaperone, and to be visible about doing so, until now. "Of course, thank you for your company today, Mama."

"Yes, thank you, Mrs. Dalton. I am sorry to have forced you into company during your mourning period."

"I do understand."

She left, speaking to Soot about rest time, using the servant's entrance to move through the house instead of the main stairs.

Quinn drew another circle on Theodora's upper arm. "Is she all right? Is she comfortable?"

"Yes, I think so. Soot has cheered Mama considerably, and I am glad she ventures from her room. She even conversed a little with Mr. Sever after luncheon."

"I hoped as much," he whispered. Quinn continued to tease her arm, gently skimming her skin the way he would often do at night when they lay sated in each other's arms. There were still many hours until she would retire to bed, and she was suddenly restless. She should not think about intimacy so early in the afternoon.

"Now," Theodora said, flourishing her journal before him. She discussed the day's findings, her concerns that needed investigation, and waited for his response.

Quinn's teasing touch fell away as he pointed to the St. James property. "I have a recollection of him directing his driver there a few months ago, as I left his carriage, but I'm not aware of who lives there."

"Ah," Theodora said carefully. She drew a breath, prepared to broach a delicate subject that had been on her mind the last few days. "I know this is an awkward topic but...what is to be done about mistresses? Did he have any that you know of? Do you wish to continue supporting your father's, and your own, too?"

"There were no bequests left to any in my father's will." Quinn sighed. "Damn him for making me decide about them."

She suspected Quinn would most likely pledge them some financial support or offer other help. She hoped his tender heart would not be too generous, though. "What did you do about Adele Blakely?"

"Nothing." He turned back to the brandy and poured another glass for himself.

"She is currently living in your property, rent-free, and unencumbered by contract to you," Theodora said quietly as she followed him. "If she takes up with another man, will you allow her to remain on your property?"

"No." He raised his eyes skyward. "Why are you, of all people, forcing me to talk about her?"

Because she couldn't stop herself. She did not like the idea of that woman living in Quinn's home after what she'd done to him. "Isn't it my job, as your secretary, to remind you of such matters and carry out your instructions? Even the unpleasant ones?"

Quinn lowered his face, searching hers. "You would have no trouble in speaking with her on my behalf, would you?"

Frankly, Theodora was dying to catch another glimpse of that fool again. She'd love nothing more than to give the actress a piece of her mind for her behavior. "None at all."

"There's nothing for you to worry about. Now I know Adele never cared about me, I find I am unable to summon the energy to see her again. She's been replaced."

Theodora leaned back, offended by Quinn's description of the current situation. "I did not replace her. I'm not your mistress."

He cupped her cheek, skimming his fingers into her hair to angle her face up toward his. He leaned closer, biting his lower lip as desire filled his eyes. "Aren't you?"

"Never a mistress." Theodora caught his wrist when his eyes widened, and she pulled his hand away from her face before he went too far. Anyone could burst in and see them together. Lady Templeton, for example, rarely knocked on doors before she opened them. No one would believe his caress innocent, which it certainly wasn't. "I do not ask for jewels or gifts. I do not expect to be seen on your arm or to be entertained by you. I remain your secretary and temporary lover. Nothing more lasting than that exists between us."

He stepped back, eyes narrowing, jaw clenching. For a horrifying second, Theodora saw that her words had hurt his feelings, but he quickly masked it, adopting an aristocratic hauteur so utterly wrong for him.

But the pleasure they'd shared in each other's arms required no tawdry label. She hoped he understood the limits she placed upon their relationship were for the best possible reason. If he paid her for sex, the entire act of intimacy became a business transaction between them. A matter of commerce, rather than the pleasure it had always been. "My lord?"

A muscle ticked in his jaw before he spoke again. "As you wish."

"I think it is best to keep our relationship on a professional footing as much as possible. Now, about the mistresses." Theodora wouldn't be giving a scheming tart two shillings more than necessary to make her go away. "They need to be dealt with soon."

"Very well." He smiled suddenly and Theodora grew warm all over. He went to his desk and wrote a few lines on a piece of parchment before handing it to her. "But first I have another matter that requires your expertise, my dear. I want you to find out if my family had any dealings with a man by the name of Roman Gently. This is an address in London where he might have lived for a while and his occupation too if that helps."

She'd never heard or read the name before. "Who is he?"

"I've not the faintest idea." He gestured to the room. "See if you can find him among all this, and question my father's secretaries, too."

"Of course."

He bent to press a lingering kiss to her cheek and whispered, "Mother expects me in the drawing room now, but I'll return as soon as I can, or we can talk tonight in bed."

Theodora watched him stride away, and then reluctantly returned to her work.

CHAPTER TWENTY-TWO

QUINN ACCEPTED Rodmell's help to don a black waistcoat. He was beginning to loathe mourning attire already, as well as the hushed atmosphere that had taken over Newberry House since his father's death. Usually, there was chatter to be heard in the halls as servants went about their tasks. Lately, he'd heard very little banter. "Is all well this morning?"

"More or less, my lord." Rodmell fetched his pocket watch and held it out. "The housekeeper is in a mood, though."

"What about?"

"It's Miss Dalton, I am afraid."

"What has the woman done to upset the applecart?"

"She seems to be dismissing the maids before they can do their work, my lord."

He sighed. "I never thought a day would come when a maid would complain about having no work to do, but here we are."

"Neither would I," Rodmell agreed. "They only want to make the bed, but Miss Dalton has already done the work by the time they arrive, more often than not. There's a rumor going around that she doesn't sleep."

Quinn colored a little. Theodora had slept alone last night—and would for some time to come, he'd decided yesterday after their illuminating little talk.

Hearing Theodora explain how she viewed their affair had surprised him initially. But that surprise had soon turned to annoyance. Did she not understand how rare their connection was? They had such delightful symmetry of body at night that he'd begun to feel there was more between them. One that boded well for a happy future. But if she would cast aside their growing closeness, too, by claiming it could not be lasting and hiding behind a professional relationship.

She was deluding herself.

Quinn intended to show her the error of her thinking. After their discussion, he'd decided the best path to take was to restrain his private affections and return to their original arrangement of employer and employee for a while. She could continue to work for him, he would provide accommodation for her, and her mother, as promised without question. When Mrs. Dalton decided she was ready to live on her own terms again, he would wish them well.

Theodora was very nearly the perfect woman in his opinion.

But not if she couldn't see where their arrangement was leading them together. "I'm sure she sleeps. Anything else worries the staff about her?"

"She keeps such odd hours."

"I know. Please make everyone aware—quietly, mind you—that it's Miss Dalton's way to cope with losing her father. She will mourn him a full year, I suspect, or perhaps more." He glanced at the mantel clock. He was dragging his feet today, and that was unlike him. He wanted to spend less time alone with Theodora, to make her miss him. The trouble was, he yearned to see her already, and it was not even eleven o'clock in the morning. "I assume Miss Dalton's hard at work already."

"No, my lord. Miss Dalton has gone out. I spoke to her earlier as she waited for the carriage. It was before ten o'clock, and she marched out with her satchel under her arm. She hasn't returned yet."

"What the devil is she doing going out so early?" He knew of no business that would take her out today. It must be a personal errand, but he couldn't remember her mentioning one yesterday. "Did her mother go with her?"

"No, my lord," Rodmell advised, his expression disapproving.

"No chaperone?"

"No, my lord."

Quinn was not happy to know Theodora had gone out without a chaperone when he'd expressly asked her to have one with her at all times since she'd moved to Newberry House to prevent gossip.

Theodora had always been rather more independent than his previous secretaries, and he hoped she'd left him a note or some such small crumb on his desk to let him know she had at least thought of him once before running off. "Did you by chance hear where she asked to be taken first?"

"There was one address I heard," Rodmell said. "Wellington Street."

Quinn blinked in surprise that Theodora would have any business in that street. His former mistress lived there.

Quinn groaned suddenly, remembering yesterday's conversation about mistresses. He had hoped Theodora would forget all about Adele Blakely. He certainly had.

Theodora had no business traipsing off to call on his former mistress, but he knew that was exactly the errand she'd gone on that morning on his behalf. Was Theodora the worst secretary he'd ever had? Oh, she was dedicated and organized and a hundred other descriptions he could easily name if he had all day. But he should never have let her believe that a professional relationship was all he wanted. She did not seem to realize former mistresses and current lovers should never know each other.

Once his coat was in place, he held out his arm for the mourning ribbon to be tied around his upper arm. He'd utterly underestimated Theodora's desire to manage every aspect of his life. He'd seen the subtle signs of possessiveness she'd tried to hide and winced. Theodora had no reason to be concerned that Adele Blakely held any power over him after her betrayal.

He could care less about Adele Blakely's future. He didn't want to see his former mistress again. And now Theodora may have forced his hand by going to call upon her.

"Have my carriage brought round."

Rodmell met his gaze. "Miss Dalton has your town carriage, my lord."

He rolled his eyes. "A horse then, Rodmell, or my grandfather's second-best town carriage will do at a pinch."

"As you wish." Rodmell hurried off, leaving Quinn to finish dressing, and then Quinn strode to the front of the house after Theodora.

CHAPTER TWENTY-THREE

THEODORA STEPPED out from behind the servant to view Quinn Ford's former mistress properly. Last time they'd met, or almost met, Adele Blakely had been covered in a robe best suited for the bedchamber and had been weeping copious tears.

Without them, she was pretty, in the way most actresses seemed to be—pale-skinned, long flowing hair to match, adopting a dramatic pose to appear artless to the casual observer, low-cut gown to accentuate her overflowing figure.

Theodora was less than impressed.

"Mrs. Blakely?"

The actress glanced beyond Theodora in confusion. "Who are you?"

Clearly, Adele Blakely had been expecting "Dalton" to be a gentleman caller. "Miss Dalton, Lord Templeton's secretary."

The woman startled, hand covering her lips. "He's assumed the title already."

"Of course." Theodora sat, although she was not invited to do so. This home belonged to Quinn, and his investments and properties were her responsibility. She took in the pleasant room the woman was occupying freely. The room was charming, light, and spacious. It would do very well for a small family in need of a home for the coming season.

Theodora was already drafting an advertisement offering it for lease in her head when Adele spoke. "How is he?"

"Extremely busy, which is why I am here to complete the arrangements."

"What arrangements?"

Theodora smiled. "Are you really so foolish as to think you could continue living in his home after bedding his father?"

"I can explain."

"I'm sure you can, and if I had time and interest, I could listen. Lord Templeton's interest in you ended the night his father was found naked in your bed. A discovery, I'm sure you can understand now, that brought him great personal pain."

The woman sobbed, but her eyes were suspiciously dry. "I never meant to hurt him."

Theodora wasn't moved at all by her false weeping. The little fool knew exactly what she was doing by sleeping with both the father and the son.

Theodora opened her satchel and drew out the deal she had written up last night before she'd gone to bed alone. "Lord Templeton never had a written contract with you, but given your history offers one last generous payment to help you move on. Sign this."

The woman scanned the sheet, her eyes wide by the end. "This is outrageous!"

Actually, Theodora believed it was more than the actress deserved, after what she'd done. Theodora had factored in the length of Adele Blakely's association with Quinn, and his protective nature. The sum should ensure Adele Blakely was able to live and possibly thrive for years without a protector, so long as she kept her expenses on the conservative side. "The late Lord Templeton has a wife, two living daughters and three sons. His lordship is extraordinarily fond of his mother, as you should already know. Do you think he will make you a better offer after the humiliation you dealt them both?"

Mrs. Blakely gaped.

"I don't think so either," Theodora confided. "Sign."

Mrs. Blakely wet her lips. "I want to speak with him. I deserve that."

"You deserve nothing, in my honest opinion," Theodora warned. "If Lord Templeton had wanted to speak with you, he would have already come."

Adele licked her lips again, her eyes hardening. "He will come if you convince him I'll hurt myself if he abandons me."

Theodora was taken aback a moment. "Madam, such a blatantly false claim would never sway him."

"You don't know him like I do." Adele snatched up a letter opener from her writing desk and held it over the inside of her wrist threateningly. "He'll come. He won't let me destroy myself as Mary did."

Theodora smiled, pretending she knew nothing about the death of Quinn's sister. "Mary?"

"Yes, his sister. She killed herself. I could too if he will not meet with me!"

Anger rose in Theodora, beyond anything she'd ever felt before for another living soul. Adele Blakely wasn't done finding new ways to hurt Quinn apparently. "You conniving little slut. How dare you think to torture him with your lies?"

"He told me about her himself." Adele's eyes gleamed with triumph. "He told me everything about the day he lost his younger sister."

And Theodora would bet a thousand elephant's that Adele would use her knowledge to strike back at Quinn if she did not get what she wanted from him. Theodora couldn't bear for him to be so poorly treated.

"I know nothing of that," she lied. "And I'm sure no one will believe you no matter how theatrically you perform." Theodora set her satchel aside and perched at the edge of her chair. The woman had to be stopped. Here and now. Although bile rose up in her throat, she knew blackmail could never be surrendered to. "But do go on. Do it now. Show me you're serious in your threat. Prove that you cannot live without him if you believe that will gain you sympathy. Go on, hurt yourself."

Adele moved her hand a bit but did not cut into her skin. She chewed her lip and hesitated.

Theodora smiled slowly. "You don't care about him at all, do you? How could you? You care only for yourself and your selfish ambitions."

She snatched back the agreement and shredded it into little, tiny pieces as Adele gasped with the first real emotion she'd shown that day. "I rescind the offer. And make no mistake it was my offer and not his. You have until Thursday to leave this house, and don't think I won't have you tossed out in your unmentionables if you do not comply."

"Wait!"

"Why should I give you another moment of my precious time?" Theodora raised a brow. "You threaten emotional torture of the worst sort for Templeton if you do not get your way. He doesn't deserve a woman like you in his life. I'm glad you showed your true colors. You disgust me. You disgust *him*, too."

She collected her satchel and walked out, certain that Adele's threat to take her own life was an empty one. She might be there Thursday at nightfall, but Theodora did have connections that would help the woman move out to temporary lodgings, by force if necessary. Theodora might resume negotiations, but she would never offer this woman as much as she just had.

The coachman, John, was already waiting beside the door with the steps down. "St. James next."

"Right you are, Miss Dalton." The coachman glanced into the carriage. "My lord, if that suits."

"No, it does not," Quinn answered from within.

Theodora scowled. The servants would obey Quinn without question. "Move the carriage, John," she ground out, still angry with what she'd just heard. "Take us anywhere that isn't here immediately."

She climbed into the carriage, and tossed her satchel onto the seat opposite the earl. She met Quinn's eyes reluctantly across the carriage as the carriage rocked with the weight of the grooms reclaiming their perches.

They stared at each other a long moment in silence. How could Adele Blakely think she had any right to blackmail Quinn?

"Very well." Quinn opened the hatch to the coachman. "St. James, John. At a slow pace, if you please," Quinn called.

Theodora forced herself to calm her temper. "What are you doing here?" she asked softly.

"This is my carriage." He tugged on his waistcoat as he sat up straighter. "Do you often forget that you are in my employ, Miss Dalton?"

He was stiff and cold, and not at all the man she'd come to care for. "Of course I don't."

Theodora longed to reach for him, but hesitated. Quinn had not come to her room last night, and to see him outside his former mistress' home made her anxious for reasons she did not care to examine too closely. She'd had the most wretched sleep as a result of his absence from her bed and had woken up out of sorts. She'd missed him very much.

He crossed his legs, turning his body away from hers in the carriage and addressed his next remarks to the window. "I'm not sure that you do. I'm sure you will agree that I am a man who would expect his wishes complied with. All of them. I told you, in no uncertain terms, what I expected from you."

"Well, I've dealt with Adele Blakely already."

"I could care less about that woman. I'm talking about your foolish decision to come out without a proper chaperone."

She gaped at him in surprise. "The maids had other duties, and my mother is too delicate for the discussion I've just endured." She ground her teeth. "You're well rid of that grasping shrew, I promise you."

"Spouting opinions like that to any other employer would get you dismissed from your post immediately. I have been very lenient, but a line must be drawn. You will always have the company of a maid, or you will remain at home. And it is not your business *what* I do about my mistresses," his brow rose high, "nor will you be involved in the negotiations should I take on a new one."

A new one? He wouldn't dare. She glared at him. "You may do as you like, as always, my lord. As will I."

His jaw clenched. "Were you born stubborn, or did you make yourself this way?"

Theodora shrugged, turning to look out the window herself. "I was born this way," she said, allowing her words to drip with sarcasm. "I suppose you would have me different. Missish and quiet. Shall I defer to you as if I'm incapable of making any decisions for the position you hired me to fulfill?"

Quinn leaned forward, resting his arms on his strong thighs, but Theodora wouldn't look at him. "Most men find managing tendencies a most undesirable quality in a female."

Theodora sucked in a sharp breath, suddenly furious at him. After all they had shared, he suddenly didn't like the way she thought or acted? She couldn't speak for the anger coursing through her veins. Well, if he was done with her, she was most definitely done with him. She would speak to mother tonight and—

Quinn laughed suddenly. "Most men, but not all. If you truly wish to work in the position of a secretary to others, you might try to curb your managing tendencies a little in the future. I would have dismissed Sever and Kemp for going against my wishes as you have today."

Theodora sat up a little straighter, but noted he'd said "would" rather than "will". "My father never complained if it was to his benefit."

"He was a very indulgent father then. What did your father's employees make of you? Was Mr. Small jealous that you had such free rein in your father's affairs?"

"I've no idea that he might have been." She glanced toward Quinn, astonished that even in the midst of an argument he was smiling at her. "He was a good man. He was supportive and generous with his time when my fiancé died."

He recoiled suddenly, looking at her with alarm. "Just how much time did he generously bestow upon you?"

"Oh, it wasn't like that between us. Heavens no," she qualified. "No."

"And yet by your own admission, you see no harm in seeking comfort where you like."

"Within reason. Small was only ever a friend. I would never seduce a servant in my home."

Quinn glanced away. "As I have done."

"That is not what I meant."

His brows rose. "But that is what has happened between us. You share my bed but refuse to be my mistress. You act as if you're my secretary, my servant, in effect, for all that you don't act like any I've employed before. What we have done together in private is considered quite wrong in certain circles, you know."

"I don't believe that there is anything wrong with what we—"

"I know your feelings on the matter. You've been very clear indeed on how you view this," Quinn waved his hand, "whatever this *was* between us."

She stared at him, trying to figure him out. "Was?"

He nodded curtly without meeting her gaze. "We're in St. James, now. What was the house number?"

Theodora told him and dug into her satchel as the carriage slowed. But her heart currently resided in her shoes. Was Quinn saying they were done with each other because she wouldn't replace his last mistress? She swallowed to wet her suddenly dry mouth. "I have the description here. Five bedrooms, portico front with fanlight above, half basement, and a complement of four permanent staff. Doorman, cook, maid, and footman."

She glanced at Quinn as the carriage stopped directly before the townhouse and waited for some reaction. Quinn wouldn't look at her. She swallowed the lump in her throat. She'd gone too far in her zeal to manage his affairs. But after meeting his former mistress, and discovering her true nature, she could hardly regret anything she'd done that day. She would save Quinn from that woman if it was the last service she ever did for him.

She looked at the house and tried to put her feelings for Quinn aside. Doing that was quite difficult she found. She didn't want to give up Quinn if she didn't have to. She looked at the house, rather than think of a life lived without him.

It was a pretty house, distinguished. The neoclassical detailing on the façade made it seem quite grand. She cleared her throat to get Quinn's attention. "Did you hear me, my lord?"

"Yes. Bedrooms, basement, servants," he said in a bored tone, moving his face closer to the window as he peered out. "Much the same as all the rest in this neighborhood, most likely."

Theodora glanced at the house just as a wigged gentleman answered the groom's knock and received Theodora's calling card. The man nodded, agreeing to give her entry, and they got out. Quinn was still staring in the wrong direction, though, once he stood on the footpath.

"The house is this way, my lord."

"It cannot be," Quinn exclaimed, taking a few steps in the wrong direction.

"Lord Templeton," Theodora called. "Are you coming with me or not?"

He met her gaze briefly and looked away, frowning fiercely. "Usually, yes."

Theodora blushed and dropped her chin, skin tingling at how quickly her thoughts turned to intimacy with him.

He hurried to join her, caught her elbow in a firm grip and practically dragged her to the front door. "It seems a pleasant prospect."

"Indeed it does." Grateful for his renewed interest in the house, and for his touch again, she smiled quickly. "You don't have to come with me. I am capable of assessing the situation on my own."

"No, I came this far. I'm coming inside with you." He caught her elbow and steered her toward the steps. "You mentioned your meeting with Mrs. Blakely went poorly. You were angry."

Such an understatement. "She understands her options are limited," Theodora said firmly, hoping not to have to reveal the whole of their conversation. "I have asked her to exit the property by Thursday."

"Good. Good."

His grip fell away as they stopped inside the entrance hall.

The doorman appeared at a loss when he stared at her, clutching her card in his gloved hands. Theodora smiled warmly, hoping to win the fellow over quickly. "We would like to inspect the house?"

He glanced at the card, then at Quinn, who was peeking out the front windows.

Her employer returned. "I am the late Lord Templeton's eldest son, formerly Captain Quinn Ford. Now the earl. I'm here to decide what to do with the house I've inherited from my father."

The man sighed. "It's unoccupied, my lord."

He glanced past the servant. "So, there is no one presently living here?"

The man nodded vigorously. "Myself and two other servants."

"Excellent. If you don't mind, we will show ourselves around."

The man stepped back. "I'll wait here in case I can be of any further assistance."

Quinn gestured for Theodora to lead the way. She passed him to look around. The rooms were sparsely decorated and had few personal possessions scattered about. Most of the furniture had white covers spread over them to keep out the dust. She peeked under a few, noting the furniture was first-rate.

The staircase was steep to an upper floor of four rooms, but only one held a bed. The bed was made, but Theodora would wager it had seen recent use, given the poor job done of straightening it. There were a comb and soap at the washbasin, a spare cravat already pressed to perfection inside a tall cupboard.

"Such a large bed for such an empty house," she commented.

Quinn had paused at the door, one arm resting against the door-frame, and his gaze was speculative. "My father slept here on occasion."

Theodora winced. Quinn was always happier when his father was not part of their conversation. "What makes you say that?"

"Look at that ridiculous bed. Father refused to sleep in any bed smaller than eight feet square. He probably met his lovers here."

"He's owned this dwelling for some time." Theodora remembered the details from the deed of ownership. "A decade or more. Does your mother know about this place?"

"Probably. Mother has never been squeamish when it came to dealing with the other women in my father's life. You two have much in common in that regard."

Theodora bit her lip, unsure if she was being complimented or warned off. "Is she aware of who Mrs. Cabot is to you?"

"Oh, yes." He studied her, and then a slow smile spread across his face at last. "Mother shops at Cabot Haberdashery every week when she's in London. The poor girl will never escape Mother. Be warned, you could face the same future."

She struggled not to smile at that prospect. She liked Lady Templeton very much. She even thought she understood her a little. Lady Templeton adored her son, and would do anything to ensure his happiness. "Surely not."

"I've seen enough. Let's go out."

"Yes, lets."

Once in the carriage and underway, Quinn pulled down the curtains on all the windows until only a little light illuminated the space. "Did you discover anything about Roman Gently yet?"

"I'm afraid not. There was nothing in your father's last diary."

"Look back further. As far back as eighteen eleven, perhaps."

"Eleven?" She pulled a face, cursing her premature tidying. "Those diaries and some other papers were sent up to the attics yesterday. I'll have to fetch them back."

"Send someone to fetch them for you." He studied her a moment. "You would do well to make use of the servants, Theodora."

"But I know exactly where they are. It will take only ten minutes to fetch them myself."

He sighed. "You'll be the death of me."

"I only want to make your life easier, Quinn," she whispered, knowing it was true.

"Do you still?"

"Yes, of course. Haven't I achieved more than you ever expected of me?"

"More than I ever knew I wanted." He suddenly snatched Theodora off the bench and deposited her on his lap. "I will miss you."

"I'm not going anywhere yet," she warned, feeling a slight catch in her breath. Did she really have to stop working for him? Stop seeing him at night? "I was thinking—"

Her attempt at conversation was cut off as his lips sealed firmly over hers. He kissed her thoroughly for several minutes. "You are always thinking. It's very distracting to have such a clever creature within arm's reach and not touch you," he whispered as they drew apart.

She smiled quickly, tunneling her fingers into his hair. "I feel the same."

"Thank God," Quinn whispered as he nibbled her neck.

"Are you sure this is wise?" she asked as they headed west. "I have other errands to run today."

He kissed her soundly and then pressed his head to hers. "Let it go, Theodora. We're going home now and the next time you go out you will take your mother or a maid as chaperone."

Quinn's kisses turned teasing. He took her earlobe between his lips and bit lightly.

"Yes, Quinn." Theodora squirmed on Quinn's lap. "But surely..."

His fingers slid across her chest, and he cupped her breast again. "How can you think at a time like this?"

"I'm trying very hard to overcome your allure," she said dryly, but her body was already responding to his assault on her senses. She did like the way he made love to her, and she had missed him.

"I'm very hard with want for you." He pushed her hand between them, where his erection hid. "Tell me you would prefer to play today, instead of pouring over dull papers in the study."

She drew back, holding him firmly by the hair, tempted for the first time ever to be recklessly irresponsible. There was a lot at stake if she gave in to him. Her reputation. His, too. He might also imagine every day might be spent like this, which it couldn't. However much that might appeal, she shouldn't plan any sort of future. "Tonight."

He groaned softly and kissed her neck. "Spoilsport," he grumbled.

After a few minutes of his ardent nibbling, Theodora reluctantly slipped off his lap to straighten her gown, hoping it was not crushed too badly and would not be noticed when she stepped out. She felt much too excited for the daylight hours. People might notice the hot flush of her cheeks, too.

Quinn ran a hand through his hair to straighten it. He sat back, accepting the need to wait until nightfall with only the smallest outward appearance of disappointment. "Since I cannot convince you to play wicked games with me today, I'll be going on after I drop you off at Newberry House."

"To where?"

"To visit Mr. and Mrs. Cabot at their home."

She smiled warmly. "I liked them."

"Good. Good." He nodded. "I don't know when I'll return. It could be late if the Cabot's invite me to stay for dinner."

She nodded, understanding that family, even a half-sister, was important to him. Still, she was a little disappointed that she might not see him again today. She thought a moment, and then whispered. "I'll miss you."

His eyes widened, and then he wagged a finger at her as the

carriage stopped. "That is exactly the sort of thing that makes me doubt my sanity at keeping you as my secretary. Do enjoy your afternoon shuffling through old papers, my dear."

Although the grooms were waiting at the door, she smiled brightly at Quinn. Whatever had been troubling him before was clearly no longer an issue between them. "I always do, my dear Lord Templeton."

CHAPTER TWENTY-FOUR

"I WANTED to see for myself that you are not upset," Quinn promised as he greeted Amy Cabot in her front hall of her residence on Brick Street.

Amy squeezed his fingers briefly and then pressed her hands to her stomach. "I'm fine, Quinn. Truly. But it is so very good of you to call again. I know how busy you must be now."

"Never too busy to see you." He glanced around, looking for her husband. "Has Cabot left you alone again while he tends the shop?"

"He is always there at this hour, and I do not mind. I have important visitors. Won't you please come and meet them?"

Quinn considered declining, but Amy looked too excited about her visitors to risk disappointing her. "I'd be very happy to meet your friends indeed," he said quickly. Running Mr. Banks to ground would have to wait another half hour. "Lead the way."

He followed Amy into the rear of the property—and came to a standstill.

His sister Lady Sally Hastings had made herself at home on a window seat, and smiled warmly at him as he stood there in shock. "There you are at last," she said.

Quinn spared a glance for Amy, who was grinning madly now.

"Ambush," he complained, though he wasn't truly put out. He wagged his finger at Amy and then strode across the room to greet Sally with a hug. "Sister dear? When the devil did you get to London?"

"An hour or so ago. Since you were not at Newberry House, and Mama was not to be found either, I decided to pay Mrs. Cabot a call."

He set Sally free and took in her appearance, cheeks flush with color, eyes glowing with happiness. She appeared radiant, despite her wearing a gown of mourning colors. "Without your husband? I had hoped you were enjoying a retired married life at Newberry Park."

"I am indeed, and I'd never travel without him." She laughed and glanced toward another doorway. "Felix has just gone to fetch a drink from Cabot's book room."

At the mention of his name, Felix Hastings appeared, two glasses in hand and a ready smile gracing his face. The smile annoyed Quinn. His new brother-in-law looked positively smug these days. "Thought I heard a surly voice. Hello, Templeton."

"Hastings."

"Good to see you, dear brother-in-law, and married life, for your information, is entirely what I'd hoped it could be, and more besides. Oh, here, this is for you," Hastings said as he held out the second glass to Quinn.

Sally blushed. "Quinn knows full well how happy we are, darling. He's just teasing."

Quinn took the drink he was offered but set it aside for a moment. "Also making sure the unpleasantness of the broken engagement was worth her putting up with you."

Sally shook her head. "Lord Ellicott took the break very well, all things considered. We nodded to each other the last time our paths crossed. He really is the only one who has the right to be upset with me. It is everyone else who stirs up talk and discord when I'm in London. I know how lucky I am to have Felix. I wouldn't change anything to be proper again. Being a wife is simply too much fun."

Amy, her brow puckering as she glanced between them, sat forward. "Sally and I have been comparing notes on our husbands' early-morning temperaments and finding many commonalities."

"Don't tell me what they're like in the morning after sharing your beds." Quinn put his hands over his ears, and both women laughed at him, as he'd hoped they would. There were some things he really did not need to hear. He lowered his hands slowly and addressed Sally. "Why come to London now of all times?"

Sally stood and approached him and set her hand on his chest. "Just to see if all was well with you. I know you write, but..."

"I'm fine. Every day is an improvement," he promised her. But he folded his sister into his arms again and held her a moment, knowing that she felt differently about their father than he did. She had been his favorite daughter. Probably because she'd never been punished by him. "How's Grandfather? And Louisa?"

"Louisa is well. She promised me she would write every day while we were gone."

Quinn took a chair. "I'm pleased to know it. And you? How are you coping?"

"I am not sure." She frowned. "I was glad to get away from Grandfather, actually. Seeing him grieving so hard is painful to me, knowing better now what Father has done in the past. What he did to humiliate you and Mother was inexcusable, but I suppose it wasn't the first time he's been unfaithful."

Quinn was so taken aback by Sally's remark that he could say nothing at first. It was perhaps the first time in his memory that his sister had criticized their father to him. He was pleased, too. Mama had put up with a great deal of humiliation over the years, and Sally had never noticed. Amy Cabot's existence, his affairs, and his involvement with Adele Blakely were undeniable proof of a weak, grasping character.

"It is good to see you again," he said, brushing her cheek with his fingers. "For whatever reason that brought you to London. How long are you staying?"

"We have not decided. But I was hoping to leave knowing we can have everyone home in Essex for a few weeks soon."

"Why?"

"Louisa was to have a season, and now we must decide what to do about her."

"There is nothing to decide. Louisa will spend what remains of the spring in London and enjoy the season as already planned."

"Barely three months in mourning? People will talk," Hastings warned.

"Three months is too long for the likes of him," Quinn promised. "Louisa will do very well without Father scaring off the gentlemen she likes best. She'll have me at her side almost every moment."

"If you're sure we can manage the gossip, then very well. I would not feel right if we harmed Louisa's chances in anyway," Sally agreed.

"To have a successful season, we must all be out in society. I'll speak to my secretary and make sure I have no commitments that month besides those required for Louisa's benefit."

"Speaking of your secretary?" Sally started with one brow arched playfully high. "How are you lucky enough to employ not only a competent assistant, but an attractive woman for the post?"

"It wasn't luck." He filled them in on the particulars of the night Theodora's father had died, but left off explaining they had become lovers since. There were some things his family did not need to know about. He mentioned her mother, and the dog he'd given the older woman in the hopes of jollying her spirits. "Miss Dalton is extremely dedicated. Claims work takes her mind off her troubles, and that seems to be true. She also has a mind like a steel trap for details, and I have no complaints."

"Well, it is very unconventional of you, and very kind to shelter her mother, too. You know my opinion on the intelligence of women and what we are capable of. Our choices are hardly ever our own." She leaned over and punched his shoulder like a man would. "You've made me so very proud."

"I live to please the women of the family," he exclaimed, although it was hardly an exaggeration. Someone had to put them first when his father never had.

He took up his drink as Sally and Amy chatted about the plight of women who fall on hard times, and how few go out of their way to offer real solutions, watching the bonds of affection grow between the two sisters as they discussed mutual interests with great animation. Amy was the product of his father's sordid affairs, but he—and Sally, too, it seemed—could care less about her past. Amy had suffered more than anyone in the family, and if he had his way, she never would again.

Hastings lured him away to Cabot's adjacent book room to refill their glasses. "Female secretary? I swear, I don't know why I'm surprised by your good luck."

A beautiful, contrary woman, whose eyes flashed with fire when she was thwarted. He could get used to getting in Theodora's way occasionally. "Have you not become used to us by now? We never do anything in line with convention."

The man's gaze strayed to the doorway beyond which his wife sat, a contemplative smile hovering on his lips. "I have a lifetime to learn."

"Do it quickly and brace yourself. Sally is bound to shock us all again soon." He glanced at his pocket watch. Time was passing, and as much as he'd like to remain to talk for the afternoon, he should leave. "Or perhaps it will be Louisa's turn next to upset the applecart."

Hastings turned, his expression serious. "Has there been any word of Jennings and my ship?"

"Please remember you gave up your ship for marriage of your own free will, and no, I've heard nothing at all of the *Selfridge*, Fredrick, *or* Captain Jennings." Quinn shook his head at the desperate mission his father had sent Jennings on to find Quinn's brother Fredrick months ago. "I'm still well connected, keeping my ears open. There's been no news."

"They've been gone so long." Hastings took a sip of his brandy. "I should never have allowed Jennings to replace me. I should have gone after Fredrick myself when your father asked me too."

He pointed toward the door. "And have my sister miserable again. Have you both miserable. You made the right decision. Jennings is a fine sailor. No matter what, he's a survivor, too. Have faith in him."

Hastings wasn't won over and continued to brood, staring into his drink as he grappled with the feeling of helplessness.

Quinn understood the feeling too well. "How is Rutherford, really?"

"Silent unless Louisa is with him. The day we heard about your father, he retired to his apartment and only let Mr. Morgan attend him. A lot of the fight went out of him that day." Hastings winced. "Truth be told, I was a little worried about coming to London so soon, but Lord Cameron came to call and has promised to stay for a few days, and make a little too much noise to gain the old man's attention."

"He's good at that."

Hastings leaned against Cabot's desk. "Now, tell me what I can do for you?"

"For me?"

"You seem preoccupied."

"Of course I'm preoccupied. I've just become an earl."

"You know what I mean." Hastings nudged him. "I thought you'd be happier. I know I am," Hastings said with a wry smile. Hastings had run afoul of his father's ambitions too in the past.

"I *am* happy," he said quietly. "But there is something I need to investigate. I am afraid I cannot stay long."

"Oh? Sounds very serious."

"It could be." If he was correct, and not imagining what he'd seen that morning, it could have a great impact on someone he cared about very much. "I think I might have seen someone who was dead today."

When Quinn finished explaining himself, Hasting's helped him escape the Cabot home in search of answers.

CHAPTER TWENTY-FIVE

THE CARRIAGE DIPPED as Mr. Banks joined Quinn inside the dim interior at last. "Thank you for seeing me at such short notice," Quinn began immediately.

"Your message claimed the matter was important, so here I am." Banks sat his hat on the empty seat beside him.

"It could very well be," Quinn promised. He tapped the roof and the carriage lurched forward. He'd given orders that they circle around until his discussion was done. "It is about the night of the Dalton fire."

"You know the fire was ruled an accident, my lord. It is unfortunate the rumors began, and I've done all I can to quash them. But Mrs. Dalton has a fortune in gems. I'm not sure there is anything else I can do for them."

"What of the other man I told you about?"

"The fellow you claimed to have died that night, too?" The investigator shrugged. "I've found no trace of his body."

Quinn grunted. "You're sure?"

"I had seven of my best men scour all the usual places anatomists hide bodies or take them. They found nothing."

Quinn thought he might know why that was. "Mr. Small was in the house the night of the fire, and he got out, although he suffered burns. I saw his suffering and injury with my own eyes. I saw what appeared to be his death."

"Appeared to be?" Banks sat up straighter, eyes widening. "Are you saying he did not die?"

"I'm not convinced he did now, although it seemed a very convincing death at the time." Quinn leaned forward. "I believe I saw Mr. Dennis Small on the street today, here in London."

"I say. Where was this?"

"St. James, outside a property I inherited from my father." Quinn had realized, almost too late, that a man in a wide-brimmed hat and coat had been following his carriage on the other side of the street for quite some time, and had seemed familiar to him. Except the fellow shouldn't have been since he was supposed to be dead. It might have been merely a trick of the eye or his imagination, but he would swear he'd seen the late Mr. Dennis Small in St. James today.

"A chance sighting from a distance, perhaps? Are you sure it was him and not his twin?"

"No. Dennis Small had no family, as far as I know. But I am not certain it was him, which is why I wished to speak with you immediately." He shook his head. That brief moment of surprise and recognition troubled him greatly. "You've been looking for a body when the man might be walking around whole and hearty."

Quinn had only had one good long glimpse of the man's face—a familiar fresh burn pinking his right cheek—before the fellow had turned away. Small had suffered an identical burn. He'd disappeared as soon as Theodora had called out to Quinn and when he'd turned back, the fellow had already disappeared.

"A fellow with a new burn to the side of his face, one that matched my recollection of Mr. Small from the night of the fire, followed my carriage for several blocks, and then rushed away when

Miss Dalton stepped out onto the street. He was watching me, or he was watching *her*. The ladies describe him as a harmless enough fellow, but what if they were deceived in his character? What if I was, too, about his demise? If Small knowingly acted to convince us of his death, there must be a reason for doing so."

Banks whistled. "That's very disturbing."

If Dennis Small was actually alive, was it possible that trouble lay ahead? The fellow had been following Quinn's carriage. If Quinn hadn't imagined the sighting, and Mr. Dennis Small had indeed survived the fire, he had a bad feeling that Mr. Dalton's death might not be the accident he wanted it to be. "I need to know if Mr. Small is alive or not. I need to see his body—alive or a corpse."

"Small's surviving the fire would have changed the focus of my investigation somewhat from the very beginning."

"You said yourself Dalton was alive when the fire reached him. He might have gotten out, you said. But what if he couldn't? What if he was prevented from seeking safety by Small for some reason, and the man suffered those burns not as a result of bravery, but from malicious intent? Those gems found on Mr. Dalton could have been motive enough for murder."

Banks' eyes narrowed with suspicion. "That would mean Miss Dalton's suspicions were correct after all. That the fire was not an accident by her father. And it *was* Small who'd claimed Dalton had started the fire with his last breath."

"Indeed, he was the only person who could have known the truth. Perhaps it all comes back to this Small fellow. But no matter what the case may be, I must know that Miss Dalton and her mother will always be safe once they leave my protection."

"Of course, of course. I completely agree. Two women are no match for a murderer, if that is what this Mr. Small turns out to be. And they are wealthy, which could make them a target for unscrupulous scoundrels."

"Exactly. If Small is alive, if he learns about the recovery of the gems, he might increase his interest in the Dalton women. He may already know about the stones, and may be watching for a way to reach them."

"I'll redirect my investigation immediately," Banks promised. "Have your servants remain on guard."

"I will." Quinn asked to be returned to Mr. Banks' place of business, and then handed over a handful of coins. "For the extra runners you might want to hire."

"Thank you," Banks said. "I'll send daily reports from now on."

"Directly to my hand, and to no one else. Not even to my secretaries. I do not wish to alarm the women of the household."

"Of course." Mr. Banks departed quickly, a pleasing haste in his steps.

Quinn had the carriage return him home, and was surprised to see an acquaintance of his mothers on the verge of departing. Lady Berkley was a woman best avoided, so he made to pass her by with just the barest nod of greeting, but the viscountess' next words stopped him in his tracks.

"I understand congratulations are in order."

His elevation to earl was not a subject he wished to crow about. "Hardly," he replied coldly. He hurried inside to prevent further conversation with the woman.

Once safely there, he was confronted by his mother pacing the entrance hall. Given she was worrying her lips, something she rarely did, he immediately tensed. "Mama, why are you looking like you have bad news to share with me?"

"Oh, dear. Well." Mama stared at him imploringly. "I'm afraid I've gone and put my foot in it rather badly."

He ushered his mother into the study and shut the door. Only Theodora was at her desk at this hour, nearly hidden behind piles of paperwork. "How?"

"Well, Lady Berkley came to call, as you likely saw. You know how much I detest her. We came out the same year, married the same month, and had the same number of offspring more or less. Every year, our friends are forced to choose between attending my ball or hers, because she somehow always holds hers on the very same night as mine."

Quinn nodded, well aware of the rivalry between the women. It was a nasty little competition between women who could have been friends and allies, if not for their stubbornness. "Go on."

"We were talking about how my event would not happen this year, because of your father, and she was looking very smug, and one thing led to another and...I don't quite know how she got the better of me."

"What did you say to her?"

Mother lifted her gaze to the ceiling as if seeking divine intervention. "I told her you were engaged to be married."

"Mother!" He took a pace back, stunned. Behind him, Theodora gasped, too. He heard her stand and start shuffling papers as if she meant to flee the room. Quinn would, too, if the situation were not so dire and involved him. "How could you do this to me?"

"I am angry about this, too," Mother complained, beseeching him with bright, tear-filled eyes. "I am so sorry! She was so obviously pleased about the timing of your father's death. And then she told me her son had won the hand of Lord Corby's daughter, who you know I've always adored, and I just blurted it out."

He clenched his jaw to hold back a sailor's curse his mother had never approved of. He took a moment to rein in his temper. "Who did you say I am engaged to?"

"Now, Quinn, darling—"

"Mother. The name," he snapped. "And it better not be that squeaking mouse Father wanted me to marry last month. I've finally gotten rid of *her* father."

Theodora fled toward the door.

"Well, I did not say a name exactly, but..." Mother's attention followed Theodora.

He stared at her in shock. "How could you allow Lady Berkley to leave believing that I am engaged to Miss Dalton?"

Theodora gasped as her hand fell away from the doorknob. "Why *me*?"

Mother shook her head quickly, and then stretched imploringly for Theodora to come take her hand. "I am so sorry, my dear!"

Quinn's heart began to beat very fast at the idea of being married to Theodora. It wasn't panic that stirred his emotions, though. It was longing and excitement. "Mother, I am very cross with you. You will have to call on Lady Berkley immediately and renounce your statement."

"You will make a liar out of me?"

"Mother, you *are* a liar," he said crossly, keeping an eye on Theodora's face. He was rather relieved that she did not seem offended by the idea of marriage to him. At least not yet.

"But Quinn, if I deny it, all everyone will talk about is my state of mind. They will say your father's death drove me to delusions." Mother turned away, walked a few steps, and sagged into the nearest chair. "I've been trying so hard to look everyone in the eye after what he did. I'm always worried someone knows where he fell ill and who he was with. What she was to you," she whispered. "I'm afraid I've made things ten times worse now."

She sniffed and then dropped her head into her hands.

Quinn moved to her side, squatted down next to her chair. "Mother, if I do not correct Lady Berkley now, she will gossip, and what then happens to Theodora's reputation when the lie is revealed, as it must surely be? Her presence will be questioned, rather too coarsely for my taste."

"I could do it," Theodora said quietly behind him. "I could be engaged to you."

He swiveled around to stare at her. Yes, she knew him well enough to play the part of a besotted bride, but this was too much. "Don't even think of going along with this nonsense."

Theodora beckoned him to follow her across the room, and he did so, unable to predict her next words. She stopped by the far window, a frown marring her pretty features. "There is no reason to further embarrass your mother," Theodora whispered quickly. "I am here, and we already assumed people would misunderstand you hiring a woman as your secretary."

"This is grossly unfair to you," he complained. "Mother needs to correct her mistake."

"And she will, or we will, eventually." Theodora winced. "From what I can tell, Lady Templeton has suffered a great deal at your father's hands, everyone has, and I will not have it on my conscience that I helped her lose the respect she deserves. I cannot imagine what she must be feeling right now. I have met Lady Berkley before, and she's a spiteful, mean old biddy. She will lash your mother from morning to night for weeks to come, should the truth come out. You don't want that."

"But you're more than happy to pretend that you like me enough to marry?"

"I do like you." Her shoulder lifted as she shrugged. "If we went along with it for a little while, what's the harm? So much less than what could happen. Let society think what they like for now, and later, after a time, I can go away, and your mother can simply say we did not suit after all."

He considered the matter. It was asking a lot of Theodora to play along with this charade, just to help his mother save face. "No."

He turned back to his mother.

"Quinn, you know me," Theodora began as she caught his upper arm. "I would never insist you go through with the engagement. Let your mother save face with this small lie. Any gossip later on will blow over very quickly."

Of all the women he'd known, only Theodora could convincingly play the part of his betrothed. They were already intimately involved. His real problem lay in her insistence that she would never expect to marry him. "Don't you think it would feel odd to play at being betrothed to each other?"

"Not really." Her lips lifted into a soft smile. "I've been engaged before and know what is required of a proper engagement."

"I'm not sure I'd be convincing," he warned.

Theodora's brows drew together in a frown. "It would help to explain why Mother and I are still here, when we should have already found a new home for ourselves. No one believes a woman could be competent as a secretary, or enjoy the work as much I do."

He caught her fingers. "Fools."

"This will not be the disaster you fear," Theodora promised. "We make a good team already, don't we?"

A shiver of desire swept over him. If Theodora was really his betrothed, there were any number of small indiscretions they could share and be forgiven for. He could also keep an eye on her better, too. If Small was the fiend he feared, and watching them even now, Theodora could be his next target.

Unwittingly, Mother had ensured Theodora's safety.

"So, we are engaged?"

Theodora's eyes lit up with pleasure as she smiled at him. "Indeed."

He smiled, liking the idea very much. "Shall I go down on one knee, too?"

Her eyes widened. "That is perhaps overplaying your part."

"It would be expected if we were in love."

"But we are not in love," Theodora promised.

"Are you sure you're not a little in love with me?" Confident his mother could not see what he did, Quinn lifted Theodora's hand to his lips. At the last moment, though, he placed the tips of her ink-stained fingers against his lips.

Theodora gasped softly as he kissed several of them.

"Being engaged could be very enjoyable for us," Quinn whispered against her fingers. "But being married could be better."

Theodora gently pulled her hand back. "Just remember this is a temporary engagement."

Not if *he* had any say in the matter.

Now that the moment presented itself, he knew Theodora should be his wife. No other would do. He liked her. His mother seemed to like her, too. He could also hand over the estate affairs to her if she wanted control of them, without a qualm. Or they could do everything together.

"I'll do my best to remember this is all meant to be pretend, but I make you no promises I always will." He turned about to face the room.

His mother was watching them, worrying her lower lip. "Well? What did you decide?"

"We are engaged," he announced.

His mother beamed at both of them. "I knew you would understand."

"Later, we will unravel the mess that you've made of our lives," Quinn warned her. "I will expect your full support and participation to make this situation convincing."

Her smile fell.

"Lady Templeton," Theodora began, stepping around him.

"Yes, dear," Mother replied, another bright smile bursting over her lips. "And my name is Maggie when we are alone."

"Maggie, there is just one small matter to discuss."

Quinn frowned, wondering what might be bothering his betrothed now.

Theodora turned to him. "Would you excuse us a moment, my lord? I need to have a private conversation with your mother if you do not mind."

That seemed ominous. He nodded slowly. "Don't yell too loudly at Mama, my dear," Quinn advised.

He left the room, but instead of retreating entirely, he lingered on the other side of the door to listen. Quinn thought it a good idea to know how Theodora and his mother spoke to each other when he wasn't around. He eased as close to the gap in the doors as he dared to listen.

"...have the truth between us," Theodora was saying in a firm voice. "Lady Berkley did not goad you to do this, did she? You announced an engagement for a reason you will not reveal to your son. What is it?"

Quinn gaped in the telling silence.

"You are as perceptive as your mother has always claimed," his mother complained.

What was this? Quinn moved his eye to the crack between the doors and peered through.

Theodora was standing over his mother, hands on hips. "Do not change the subject, Maggie dearest. I am very cross with you right now."

He almost laughed at how his mother pretended to cower. Theodora just stood there waiting.

"Clever women like you are always a pleasure to deal with," mother exclaimed after a moment, then sat up straight again. "But we'll rub along together quite well, I suspect. That is why I chose you for this endeavor."

"The reason—and no more delay with flattering me!"

Quinn had never heard Theodora so angry before. She was cold and unforgiving. He couldn't be more impressed. Mother had ruled the roost for a long time. Many women gave way to her immediately, but not Theodora Dalton apparently.

"Oh, very well," mother grumbled. "We are in mourning, and then the season will begin. Louisa will have her chance to charm the gentlemen, and my son will be back among the *ton* where he belongs. It worries me that my son will be the Duke of Rutherford sooner than we ever planned for. I cannot have him make a mistake at such a time that might see him matched with an unsuitable woman."

"I doubt he would make such a mistake and marry the wrong woman."

"I am not so sure of that. Quinn's long-term friendship with that mistress he had is proof that he's just like every other man."

"That woman underestimated his appeal. I've already seen to it that she never bothers him again."

"Did you now? Well, that is well done of you." Mother beamed. "A betrothal will take him off the marriage mart before the season even begins..."

"...and allow him to make the right choice at a time of his choosing," Theodora finished.

"Exactly."

There was a long pause, and Theodora's hands slid off her hips. "So, you are using me."

"Well, yes. I hope you don't greatly mind the part you must play in all this." Mother fell silent a long moment. "Never think I would deliberately entrap anyone I care about into a loveless marriage such as I had?"

"I would never agree to that," Theodora promised. "Neither would he, I believe. I am surprised he is willing to go along with such a lie."

He was going along with it because marriage to Theodora was

what he wanted in the end. He'd settle for a temporary understanding, and a real engagement—complete with a proposal, flowers, and loving whatnots—would come when he was sure Theodora's feelings for him were reciprocated.

"My son is imminently sensible and very forgiving. Patient, too." There was another long pause, and Quinn strained to hear anything. "All I want is for him to marry someone he loves."

"As do I." He pondered what Theodora wanted for her future as she began to pace the room. "I want your promise that you will not make any arrangements for a marriage to actually take place. No new gowns ordered. No inquiries sent to the church. If you do anything that commits either one of us to actually marry, I shall call the whole thing off immediately and let you drown in your embarrassment. Do we understand each other?"

"Absolutely, my dear. You and I will get along famously, don't you agree?"

"Oh, absolutely."

Quinn smiled widely and backed away, delighted with what he'd heard so far. A fake engagement engineered by his mother should have been alarming, but he should have known Theodora was more than a match for his mother's own managing tendencies.

She would indeed be the perfect wife for him one day. Just as soon as she realized she was already part of his family.

CHAPTER TWENTY-SIX

"I HAD a thousand things to do tonight," Theodora whispered as she smiled at the footmen still lining the sides of the dining room. The six servants were waiting for everyone to retire to another room so they could clear the dishes from the formal dinner she'd just shared with her faux betrothed.

"Work can wait long enough for us to share a meal, surely," Quinn murmured, as he strode along at her side.

She glanced at him, and then toward Lady Templeton. "That is, word for word, exactly what she said to me earlier."

Quinn smiled quickly. "Did you never dine with Daniel when you were engaged?"

"Of course I did."

"Then this is no different," Quinn promised as he linked their arms together.

He was probably right, but being suddenly engaged today, and being paraded about the house on Quinn's arm like this, made her acutely conscious of her shortcomings. Her hair had been hurriedly redressed for dinner because she hadn't noticed the late hour, and the only gowns she had to wear were dark and rather dreary creations. Dining formally amid the splendor of Lord Rutherford's dining room had made her rather uncomfortable. She was in mourning and, given this engagement wasn't real, it was difficult to feel anything but an imposter.

"Lord Templeton, might I have a word in private," her mother asked him suddenly.

"Of course," he said, a slightly worried expression dawning on his face.

"It won't take long. Perhaps we could go in there." Mama gestured to the drawing room, and they disappeared, leaving Theodora and Lady Templeton behind.

"I wonder what that is about?" she asked the countess.

"I've no idea." Lady Templeton replied, glancing up at the incessant barking made by her mother's tiny companion somewhere above them. "She's very pleased about the engagement. I told her everything, of course, and she agreed it was a sensible precaution all round to protect your reputation."

Theodora winced inwardly. Mama hadn't actually been pleased to hear that she'd agreed to a false engagement with Quinn. Mother had asked Theodora if she'd lost her mind entirely. Only after assuring her of the temporary nature of the engagement, the necessity of sparing Lady Templeton embarrassment, and their mutual agreement to end it once the season was well underway, had mother ceased protesting.

But she had reminded Theodora that once the engagement ended, they would have to move away immediately.

Quinn and Mama returned, quiet and unsmiling. "I am ready now," Mama promised Lady Templeton.

"Mrs. Dalton and I are going to read together in the upstairs parlor tonight," Lady Templeton explained, looping their arms together. "Would you care to join us, Miss Dalton?"

Theodora shook her head quickly. Despite the engagement, she was still Quinn's secretary at heart. She couldn't let herself forget what she was here to accomplish. "I have a few matters left to finish up today."

Lady Templeton sighed, but her mother nodded. "I thought you might say that. Don't work too late, and I will see you in the morning." Mother kissed her cheek, and then quickly followed the countess to the staircase.

They all heard Soot barking and whining again.

"Soot has become quite worked up in your absence," Lady Templeton remarked to her mother as they began their assent.

"She's not used to being left alone yet."

"Well, it's early days. When Soot is a little older and grown more sedate, perhaps she could join us in the dining room," Lady Templeton suggested.

"But not today," Mother warned. "She's much too fond of tugging on the hems of our gowns to make her company tolerable in a dining room."

"Exactly," Lady Templeton said with another sigh. "At this rate, you'll need new gowns purchased before the season starts. A pity your daughter denied me the perfect excuse. I so want us to organize the perfect wedding for them."

"Never mind that for now."

The pair disappeared, and Theodora glanced at Quinn. "Should we be concerned at how well that pair are getting along?"

"Probably, but let's put that off until tomorrow, or even later. Today has been eventful enough." He steered her toward the study by taking her elbow, and then shut the door behind them. The room was lovely and quiet—and the click of the lock quite noticeable. The room was quite free of the other two secretaries, thankfully. Theodora sighed and dropped her shawl onto a chair. She had grown to love spending time alone in this room with Quinn at night.

"What did my mother ask you?"

"For the gems to be returned." He sighed. "I will deliver them later."

Theodora felt a chill sweep her skin. If mother had asked for the gems, she was ready to face the future. They could leave, purchase a home of their own, and Theodora might never have reason to see Quinn again. "I have the dinner arrangements ready for you to look over, if you have an interest in looking at them now," she told him rather than think of that.

"Indeed, I do wish to see them. There will need to be further changes made," Quinn warned.

"Oh?" Theodora handed her papers over, biting her lip as he moved to his desk, spread them out, and he studied the seating order she'd decided upon for his guests. She had believed she'd thought of everything. "What changes are needed?"

"Lord's Calder and Deacon cannot sit together for any dinner," he said. "If they do, the dinner will last until the next night. The pair can talk for hours without pause. You will need a seat at the table, too, remember, and please add another chair and place setting here," he said, pointing to her sketch of the dining room.

"I—"

"Everyone would expect my betrothed to join me for dinner," he said, smiling as he picked up the menu and perused her choices for the courses.

"Yes, of course." She studied the seating plan, a little worried. The right place for her to sit of course would be beside her betrothed, but what about the empty chair he asked for? She reached for the guest list and compared the list to the chairs available. "We're one guest name short for the number of places now. Who is missing?"

"The guest of honor."

"Who is that?"

He sighed as he studied the papers. "This is my sister Mary's birthday dinner."

Theodora gaped at him, eyes filling with tears. "You're holding a dinner for her?"

"I do so every year."

Theodora cupped Quinn's cheek impulsively, heart bursting with unexpected adoration. "What a good brother you are."

"Too little, too late." He bent to kiss her, and despite them being in the study, she allowed it.

His kiss was sweet and gentle, and somewhat briefer than she found she wanted by the end. They drew apart to finalize the arrangements, and she was rather excited she would now see the fruits of her efforts at the dinner for such an important person in his life.

Quinn's arm stole around her back. "What else is there to do tonight?"

"I was thinking about the St. James property. What shall you do with it?"

"Before I say anything on the subject, do you have an idea already?"

"I think you should make it available to lease for the season."

"It is barely furnished but for the one bed."

"A day or two will take care of any shortcomings in the decor," she promised. "I have taken the liberty of drafting an advertisement for a short-term lease, if you approve, and one for the property on Wellington Street, too. What did you want to do with the place?"

"Lease them both." He grinned. "We agree on that."

She grinned back widely. "A very sensible pair we are."

"Was there anything else?"

"Only a few years' worth of papers to pour over."

"They'll still be there tomorrow." His lips settled at the top of her spine, and a delightful thrill swept through her as he kissed her neck.

"Quinn," she whispered.

"Shh," he warned. He unbuttoned her gown a bit, and then he swept his hands around her body to cup her breasts beneath the gaping gown. "How do you like being engaged to me so far?"

"Very well, even if it's only pretend." He continued to tug at the buttons until her gown hung loose and was in danger of sliding down her arms.

"We've never pretended to like each other." He slid one hand down her body under the gown, forcing it to fall to her hips. He cupped her quim firmly. "I want to taste you. Right here, right now. Over our desk."

Theodora shivered. She would like that very much. "Your desk," she murmured, trying to collect the papers he'd spread about them before they were completely muddled.

"You can't be my secretary anymore." He pulled the pins from her hair and buried his face in the fallen locks.

Theodora spun around to stare at him, clutching the papers to her chest. "Why can't I work?"

"We're engaged now, and things must be different between us if we're to portray a legitimate engagement." His lips bussed her cheek softly as he took the papers and set them aside on the chair. "But I never said you couldn't do the work, my dear."

"Then—"

"Shh," he whispered again. "Can't you tell I'm trying to make love to my betrothed very quietly so no one finds out?"

He drew her hard against him. He was warm, impatient, and very aroused. She stared up at him as he bent to kiss her lips, eyes locked on hers. They kissed, staring at each other, and then Theodora closed her eyes. She was overwhelmed by him, and just as aroused as he appeared to be.

He lifted her onto the desktop, raised her skirts and widened her legs to stand between them. He cupped her face as he kissed her languidly. Throwing caution to the wind, Theodora lifted her fingers to his waistcoat and began to unbutton him.

He threw off his coat and waistcoat.

Theodora wrapped her arms around him, pressing her face to his white shirt as he tackled the laces of her stays. "What if someone comes?"

"The door is locked, and my mother made it very clear that she'd not return downstairs again tonight."

"They trust us to be alone together and behave."

"Their mistake, but I won't ever correct them." He lowered her bodice and teased the skin of her upper back with his fingertips. "I know what I want."

"What?"

"Just you, as you are now."

A smile curved her lips as Quinn proved how much he desired her, with his hands and with his lips. She eased back against the tabletop, using her hands and elbows to slow her fall as he pushed her gently down. Although she knew this was reckless, a very stupid thing to do, she couldn't deny him or herself another moment or two of pleasure.

Cool air brushed over her upper thighs, and she closed her eyes. Quinn kissed her breasts languidly until she was panting, and then worked his way down her body toward her thighs. He eased her legs wider apart, and then he was kissing her quim, devastating her senses, tasting the evidence of her desire for him.

He buried his face there, and Theodora arched her back, succumbing to the intensity of her own excitement. There was nothing she wouldn't do for this. No sin she would deny him, just so long as she could feel this way forever.

Quinn groaned, and she lifted her head to watch him. He was

lapping at her quim with firm strokes, eyes closed, loving her the way he did best. She stretched to cup his head, and he moaned again, right at the heart of her pleasure. Her body quivered, and then when he sucked on her clitoris, she cried out—much too loudly not to be misunderstood by anyone passing the door.

She slapped her hand over her mouth, staring at Quinn's grinning face as he moved to cover her. "Now that was a shriek worth waiting for," he promised as he joined with her.

Her body pulsed around him, and he ground down on her as another burst of pleasure swamped her. He was moving when she opened her eyes; his were fierce as he loved her hard.

She grasped his upper arms tightly and lifted her knees high to bracket his body.

Quinn came to a stop, pressed deep inside her body.

"Don't stop," she whispered.

"I never want to," he confessed, and closed his eyes. "You've always felt so good in my arms."

The last was whispered, and Theodora thrilled to hear it. "I'm yours, Quinn. Don't stop loving me."

"Never," he promised.

CHAPTER TWENTY-SEVEN

QUINN DEVOTED himself to the business of being an earl over the next few days, keeping those who would seek his company for their own gain at a distance, and his friends close. The gossip that he was off the market spread quickly and was met with considerable shock, much to his amusement.

There were a great many he met who claimed an acquaintance that had never existed, in a futile attempt to catch a glimpse of Theodora, who remained hard at work in the study and unavailable to meet with any callers.

Her reticence to socialize had the opposite effect than intended, though.

Their engagement became something of a quest for many matrons, who covertly attempted to determine if it was real or not by rather obvious means. A great many unmarried daughters were suddenly being introduced to him when he went out. He tried to keep his errands to a minimum to avoid the inevitable questioning.

Being at home had advantages he enjoyed.

Theodora was always there.

He could kiss her during the day, which she barely protested if he made it clear they wouldn't be interrupted. He attuned his hours of work to align with hers, and rejoiced when the secretaries he'd inherited left them alone.

But his sister and new husband remained in London and expected his company, too. They believed Mama's explanation that the engagement was false. Little did they know he was all too ready to make Theodora his wife, and if they suspected, they kept their thoughts well hidden.

"How did we bear it?" he asked of Felix Hastings as they rode through Hyde Park together early one morning, skirting women with no sense of self-preservation as they boldly approached on foot, waving handkerchiefs to get his attention. "How did we avoid marriage-minded misses for so long?"

"We were at sea, and the rakish reputations we encouraged made mothers rather protective of their offspring. I would say your carefully cultivated reputation as a rogue has been utterly discarded by all and sundry now."

He grunted at that, casting a sour eye on Hastings, who rode through the park with a welcoming smile for everyone they met. Despite his marriage to Sally, Hastings continued to draw attention wherever he went, too. He seemed to relish his notoriety, while still revealing how much he adored his wife in every conversation.

"Are we going to ride, or talk about why you felt the need to drag me from my wife's arms so early?" Hastings reined in, looking around them. "There's no one in sight to hear us now. You look like a man with the weight of the world on your shoulders. Has there been any news of that man you thought you saw?"

"None yet." He sighed. "Maybe I imagined it."

Banks reported daily that he had no new information about Dennis Small. Quinn was starting to feel foolish. Thank heavens he'd never spoken of his suspicions to Theodora. Revealing his doubts had been decidedly unnecessary.

"Then what?"

He needed a friend to unburden himself too, and Hastings seemed the most qualified, having recently braved the alter. "It is about Theodora."

"Miss Dalton?"

"I need your counsel." He nodded. "She could be perfect."

Hastings laughed. "There is no such thing as a perfect woman, unless you are speaking of my own darling wife."

"You know what Mother has done to me."

"Bound you to a sticky situation to help her save face." Quinn nodded. "Very awkward, too. Sally is livid with Mother, and quite worried that you agreed to such a scheme. A false engagement could become an embarrassment."

Quinn adjusted his grip on the reins. "I'm not upset with Mother. Not really. It suits me very well to be engaged right now. But I must admit, I am worried about Theodora's motives for agreeing to it."

Hastings sat forward, resting his hand on one knee. He looked very comfortable in the saddle now, when he'd never been born to it like Quinn, or even Sally. "This is all your mother's doing. I've had some experience with her ways. A little tear here and there, and everyone bends over backward to make her happy. She convinced Miss Dalton to play along, and you must never let her forget it, or next time it could be a permanent marriage you face."

"I am taking full advantage of Mother's actions."

Hastings laughed. "Helping to spread the rumors of your engagement, are you?"

"Yes. This situation with Theodora is vastly more complicated than even Mother knows."

Hastings frowned. "How so?"

"I met Theodora when her home was destroyed, and because

they had nothing, she and her mother moved in with me at my invitation."

"I knew that. Very charitable of you."

"The very first night, my connection to Theodora became more than I ever intended."

Hastings' eyes widened. "Are you saying you slept with her?"

"I could have. I turned her down the first time she offered to warm my bed."

Hastings' horse pranced a bit, and he had to work at calming the beast for a few minutes before speaking again.

"First time?" Hastings squinted at him. "Let me get this straight. Your new female secretary—a remarkably clever, managing beauty—actually wanted to warm your bed, and you said *no* to her?"

"It was the night of the fire. She wasn't thinking straight."

Hastings took a moment digest that. "I see, and now it seems you could become leg-shackled, you've developed a conscience about her. The fire was...weeks ago, yes?"

"She came to me again the night my father died, and I was very angry. Her comfort took my mind off what Father and Adele had done, how little they cared. I thought, 'what harm can it do?'" He winced. "I didn't say no that night...or ever again."

He did not tell Hastings that he'd loved every moment of that first night with Theodora, and the ones that followed. He thought Hastings might realize soon enough.

Hastings scowled. "So, you feel honor bound to really offer for her?"

"No. And yes. Let me explain further," he said quickly, then revealed all his mother had done, and Theodora's private response to her actions.

"Dear God. She's every bit as cunning as your mother," Hastings whispered. "A good choice for a happy home life if it ever turned into a real marriage."

Quinn thought so, too. He'd always known that the woman he married had to be able to stand her ground in a family like his. "I like her. I like her quite a bit more than I have let on to her. Mother's mistake actually pleases me."

Hastings took only a moment to understand. "You're in love with her."

He nodded. "I think so. The idea of never seeing Theodora each day is unpleasant. I feel very protective of her, and proud of how she's dealt with the loss of her father. She is quite without equal."

"That is love," Hastings said quietly, eyes dancing with amusement at last. "I'm happy for you. Sally will be livid not to have seen it before I tell her when we get home."

"Do not tell Sally anything. Not yet."

"I'm not very good at keeping secrets from my wife. I actually promised I never would."

"There may be nothing to tell in the end." Quinn sighed. "Theodora has promised me many times that she has no interest in becoming a permanent part of my life, and repeated that conviction on the day this false engagement began. She's never admitted to warmer feelings toward me beyond enjoying a good bedding. I'm not sure whether to hope or not."

"Probably wise." Hastings nodded. "She's not an emotional creature like my Sally, or the rest of your family, for that matter. You'll have a job to convince her you're worth the inconvenience of keeping around outside the bedroom if pleasure is all she wants you for."

"I know that, but how? Theodora is a remarkably capable woman. She doesn't really need me, but I need *her*. Honestly, she could manage the estate business entirely without my involvement, and I dread the day she decides she's had enough."

"Perhaps you should let her know you consider her your equal, and a partner already, and don't mind it in the least that she's smarter than you are," Hastings added, grinning. He sobered a moment later. "You have a lot on your plate managing this family, and more to come most likely down the years. You'll be the next Duke of Rutherford much sooner than anyone imagined, not that I wish ill on the duke. Whoever you marry needs to be capable of running Newberry Park with you one day, too," Hastings warned unnecessarily. "For all her positive qualities, your Theodora seems a bit stubborn to me. The trick will be convincing her that the challenges of binding her life to yours appeals. If you want her, I suggest you hold nothing back. Tell her how you feel, and even if she disagrees and still wants to end the engagement, hold fast, and wait for her to come around. If she loves you, she will. Sally had given up on me, I think, but I won her back at the very last moment."

"Father kept you away from Sally quite deliberately. There is nothing like that standing in my way." Quinn smiled quickly. "When did you become so wise, anyway?"

"I've always known what I wanted. I needed Sally's love, but your father got in between us for so long. Asking for her love again was not without a great risk of rejection."

"I know." Sally had been days away from marriage, he'd later heard. "I'm glad things turned out well for you both. You make my sister very happy. You gave up everything so she could continue to live at Newberry Park."

"I set aside the distractions that were in the way to winning her back," Hastings promised. "That is what you must do."

Quinn had no great distractions that he could think of immediately. He had no mistress now—Theodora had dealt with Adele. There were no pursuits that took him beyond England or his estates. He was bound to the family, though. They depended on him to make their lives run smoothly. He would not let them down.

He had already made room for Theodora, but waited on her to realize it, too.

CHAPTER TWENTY-EIGHT

"AS YOU SEE, they are quite fine," Theodora said, shifting the gems about on the velvet cushion with her fingertip. Behind her in the shop, the proprietor's two sons were commenting on the pretty lasses walking past on their way to somewhere else.

Mr. Walter Brown, a man Theodora had met before in her father's business dealings, nodded sagely. "Aye, they are still as fine as the day your late father brought them to me for setting. A shame the gold didn't survive the heat, but it would have melted right off the stones."

Theodora shuddered. She did not like to think about the heat melting the gold of the necklace, because the same had happened to her father's skin in that fire.

Brown set the small magnification glass aside, returned the gem to the pile, and set his hands on the display counter. He thought in silence for a long time, and Theodora knew better than to interrupt. Negotiations required delicacy and patience if a good result was to be reached.

Eventually, he raised his head. "What did you want for half of them?"

Selling half now, half at a later date, although not her original query, was a perfectly sensible outcome, as far as Theodora was concerned. Their value as a whole would have been well beyond Mr. Brown's reach, but half was a good compromise and more than affordable for him. If they could settle on a decent price for half today, Brown might seek her out if he needed more of these same stones in the future.

And by that time, their value could only have increased.

Mama had expressed a wish for a quick settlement, so Theodora suggested a higher sum than she really wanted as payment for half the stones and waited to see what Mr. Brown said in return.

Mama wanted money to quietly purchase a little home somewhere beyond the busyness of London. She wanted the purchase completed well before the false engagement to Lord Templeton ended, so they had somewhere to go immediately.

Mr. Brown scowled, and made a counteroffer of a sum far below their fair worth.

She shook her head, and they began to haggle over the price in earnest.

Theodora had extensive experience at wringing the last shilling from her opponents in negotiations, and although Mr. Brown underestimated her intelligence at first, he soon discovered her his equal by offering an amount that was both reasonable and fair.

"Done," she exclaimed.

"Done," he said, gazing at her with admiration. "You are your father's daughter indeed."

For the first time, Theodora didn't feel the pinch of tears at the mention of her father. He'd taught her the ropes of managing business negotiations, and it was fortunate for Mama that he had. Mama had no head for business, and had chosen to remain behind in the carriage outside. A fact for which she was grateful. Mama would have most likely taken his initial offer and prevented Theodora from arguing a higher valuation. "Thank you for the compliment, Mr. Brown. My father spoke very well of you, too. We can conclude our business today."

"I believe we can." He went to his safe and counted out the funds for half the gems, and put them in a small leather coin purse. He slid that across the desk to her, and remained silent while she put the funds into her satchel. "We're all very sorry to hear of your father's death, and your terrible loss. Honest men like your father are rare in my experience."

"We are managing as best we can without him," she assured him, and it wasn't a lie. She was challenged every day, navigating in Lord Templeton's complex world. She did not understand why Quinn wasn't more excited by a future filled with endless possibilities.

"Your father would be pleased you landed on your feet, and now find yourself engaged to marry an earl who will be a duke one day," Brown confided.

Rumors of the engagement had spread quickly through the ton. But what Theodora hadn't expected was for a trader, wholly outside the upper circles Quinn moved in, to have already heard the news. Brown was usually the sole of discretion, and for him to have mentioned her situation was alarming. Someone had to have passed him information already knowing they had a prior acquaintance.

"The new Lord Templeton is a man of great character, compassion, and generosity." Theodora smiled. "May I ask who told you the particulars of our current situation?"

He scratched his head. "Mr. Litton and I were talking about the news just yesterday outside his shop. I told him I was well pleased to claim to know your family well, and that, should your lord ever be in need of a goldsmith, my shop would welcome his business."

She smiled, although unease gripped her. She had a slight acquaintance with Mr. Litton, but how *he'd* heard was beyond her understanding. He was a needle maker. One of her late father's old acquaintances.

Feeling exposed and a little paranoid about being the subject of speculation everywhere, Theodora clutched the heavier satchel against her thigh. She had not informed anyone of her destination today because she had been carrying Mama's gems and would be returning to Newberry House with a small fortune. "I must be going."

"Oh aye. Best not linger here when you've somewhere better to be." He smiled kindly. "Not when you've all that to carry about. Make sure you keep your mama's fortune under lock and key from now on."

"Most assuredly I will. I have a carriage of Lord Templeton's waiting to take me directly home."

Brown peered down the street to where Lord Templeton's carriage had pulled up to wait for her. "Well, it's a fine thing to have a smart carriage like that to ferry you about London. Do give my condolences to your mother when you see her. Your father adored the ground she walked upon."

"Indeed, he did. Mother has taken his death very hard. I don't think she'll ever be the same." She shook hands with him like a man concluding business would and turned for the door. Mr. Brown's sons, openly impressed by the gleaming carriage, unlocked the workshop door, and slipped outside ahead of her.

Lord Templeton's carriage was very quick to appear before the shop. A groom jumped down from the back of the carriage and rushed to the carriage door before Mr. Brown's sons could even get a look inside.

Theodora stepped out onto the street and quickly clambered inside the safe, dark interior. "Why on earth did you close the carriage blinds, Mama? It's so stuffy in here now," Theodora complained as she placed the satchel on the cushion beside her. So much money. They would never want for anything again. "Do you have a megrim?"

The door snapped shut and at the very moment the carriage lurched forward, Mama cried out suddenly.

Theodora snapped up her head at the sound to stare at her.

Dennis Small, hiding almost beneath her mother, cracked Mama on the head with the butt of a pistol, and she slid sideways without another sound, eyes glazed.

"Mama!" Theodora shrieked, reaching across the carriage.

Dennis Small, very much alive, pressed his pistol into her temple to hold her back. "Screaming for your silly mother won't do any good."

"Mr. Small? What are you doing?" She took in his ragged appearance quickly in the dim light, chest tight with shock. The burn on his face was healing but looked quite awful. "You're alive?"

"Not that you care."

"Of course I care! You're my friend. My father's most trusted companion."

"Come now." Small snorted. "I was his *slave*."

"That is not true. We mourned you!"

"I doubt you gave me another thought once you'd wormed your way into the new earl's life. Just like you did with that fool Daniel. You went after him for a reason. You fluttered your lashes at Daniel so your father could purchase his shipments at a substantial discount."

"What discount? What are you talking about?"

"Oh, didn't you know your father had a deal almost stitched up tight as a drum that would have guaranteed him exclusive rights to trade with that company Daniel was partners in?"

"No!"

"Well, it would have, if dear old Daniel hadn't croaked." Small laughed callously. "Your father was so disappointed when Daniel's partner took one look at the contract we'd so carefully drafted and ripped it into shreds. Your father could have fought, but he wouldn't have won. Why do you think we came back to England so suddenly? He'd already bled his friends dry in India."

Theodora shook her head, dismissing Small's words as false. Father had been a good man. Fair and honest. "What do you want with us?"

"I don't want either of *you*." Small smirked. "But I want everything your father hoodwinked from everyone else. I want the gems that you have in that satchel."

He knew too much about her life. Theodora licked her lips. "What right do you have to any of it?"

"He nearly worked me to death! Sunrise till sunset and longer. Seven days a week. I poured over his papers for a pittance, until I almost couldn't see the letters anymore. When he discovered my weakened eyes were beginning to be a problem, your father began interviewing new candidates for my position behind my back. The only choice I had was to sink to his level and demand he compensate me fairly at last, for all my years of devoted service."

She swallowed hard, knowing Father had expected a great deal from Mr. Small, and recently had found him lacking. But she had not known about his eyes, or that father meant to replace him. But there *had* been a few strangers calling on Father for private meetings when Small was out. "You killed him?"

He shrugged. "Stupid old fool. Stubborn till the end."

Theodora closed her eyes briefly, appalled that she'd been right all along. It couldn't be true, but he never denied it. She opened her eyes and searched his face for any sign of regret. "I remember the day Father found you starving on the docks of London. We fed and clothed you, well before you began to work for him. Father invited you to go to India with us, and all you asked for was the position of his secretary. We made you part of our family."

Small laughed. "One of you? There was nothing he cared more about than his money and his clever daughter's future. He'd be so proud of the way you've secured yet another betrothal so easily. Playing the helpless damsel in distress again. Let's hope this new one lives long enough for you to actually marry his fortune this time around."

"It's not like that. I'm not—"

Small swung his pistol at her head.

CHAPTER TWENTY-NINE

"IT SEEMS YOU WERE CORRECT. Mr. Dennis Small is very much alive, and given the description you furnished, following the Dalton's about London, I'm afraid," Mr. Banks told him after a perfunctory greeting in Quinn's drawing room.

Quinn clenched his fists at his sides. "What is to be done to stop him?"

"There is no law against a man merely following a woman about."

"There should be, if he thinks he can touch one hair on her head."

"We must be vigilant."

Quinn would be more than vigilant. He'd never let Theodora out of his sight again. And if he caught sight of Dennis Small anywhere near her, they'd have more than a few words said between them. "What else did you learn about him?"

"A few things. Small has taken lodgings at the White Goat tavern. It's a mean place, and he only talks to one other man staying there. Keeps to himself, but they do walk past this house each day, which is quite a distance from his lodgings."

Quinn ground his teeth. That was more often than he'd considered likely. "What's the other fellow look like?"

"Big, terrible smell about him, and one of my men concluded he's not quite up to snuff in the intelligence line."

Quinn remembered another man beside Small on the night of the fire. He'd thought them strangers at the time, but he suddenly remembered Small had prevented the other man from speaking for himself. "What would a former secretary be doing with someone like that?"

"Nothing good, given the way he treated the fellow last night. Small is the brains of the pair. The other hasn't the wits to stay out of the rain when it's falling."

"And Small is most likely the most dangerous of the pair," Quinn reasoned.

"You still wonder about the fire, don't you?"

"I do. Even more so now that I've learned Mr. Small faked his own death. He hasn't fled London. He followed us from Maitland House to Newberry House, and follows Theodora when she's in my carriage. I would say I have reason to wonder what more he might manage if she and her mother were making calls on their own."

"There's absolutely no evidence to point in his direction about the fire."

That was the worst of it. Small couldn't be convicted without presenting evidence of his crime. Their hands were tied unless Small made a move against the Dalton women. "I know."

"The gems would certainly have been motive, but he didn't get them, did he?"

It made no sense to light a fire to drive everyone out so he could steal, and then remain in the vicinity weeks after. "I wonder if Mr. Small didn't know where the gems were that night. There are not too many men who would wear their wives' jewels about their neck instead of keeping them under lock and key."

"I agree that he might not have known." Banks smiled quickly. "I doubt that was Dalton's intention when he donned them. Most likely he planned to reveal them to his wife later, in the privacy of the bedchamber. It is a good thing they are safe now. Do be careful with them."

But Quinn didn't have the gems anymore. Mrs. Dalton had requested them back last night after his engagement dinner, and he'd gladly deposited them in her hand before he'd retired to bed with Theodora.

Now, he was a little worried about the matter of their safekeeping. A greedy servant could be bribed to steal unsecured items of value. It was an unpleasant thought. But there was a safe upstairs in another room he could make available to Mrs. Dalton for their continued safety. He would offer the use of it to Mrs. Dalton immediately.

He stretched out his hand to Banks. "Thank you for coming to see me."

"Of course, my lord. Always a pleasure to be of service. Do keep an eye out, and when you can, please convey my apologies to Miss Dalton. I doubted her telling of events, but what she said might have merit."

"I will do so." Immediately. Theodora would like to know her instincts about the night of the fire were right.

He waited for Banks to leave the building then made a beeline for the study, ignoring the whine of Mrs. Dalton's dog above him.

Theodora wasn't at her desk, and he looked to the other secretaries. "Sever, where is Miss Dalton?"

"I'm not certain, my lord."

"Kemp?"

"She never does say where she goes, my lord, but I believe she and Mrs. Dalton went out some time ago."

Quinn stilled. "Do you know why, or where they went?"

"No milord." Kemp stood. "Miss Dalton prefers not to confide in us."

Quinn wasn't surprised by that. Kemp had proven himself particularly disapproving of females who work. He would deal with the man later, but for now he was more concerned about where Theodora and her mother had gone. "Mother will know," he muttered, and hurried upstairs to his mother's private sitting room.

He found Mother, Sally, and Hastings, and, surprisingly, Lord Deacon sipping tea and ale together. Mrs. Dalton's pup, leashed unhappily to the leg of mother's chair, whined piteously.

He got straight to the point. "Where is Theodora?"

Hastings smirked. "Chasing her already?"

"I haven't seen her since breakfast," Sally advised. "Shouldn't she be working?"

"No, she and her mother went out." He glanced at his mother, who was frowning in silence. "Mother, where are they?"

"Gone to sell Mrs. Dalton's gems, I'm afraid."

"Now?"

"Indeed. Very rash, I thought. I told her she needn't bother with another house. We have plenty of room here. I expected them back by now, too." She glanced sourly at the dog pawing at her for attention. "Miss Dalton claimed I'd need to amuse Soot only an hour."

Quinn grew cold. "When exactly did they leave?"

"A little after ten. Mrs. Dalton is determined to waste no time in buying a little house for herself."

He raked a hand through his hair. "Christ."

"Language, Quinn," Mother chided.

He stared at Hastings. Theodora was nothing but efficient. If she was considered late, then it was entirely out of character for her. He had an uncomfortable feeling about the reason for her late return.

Hastings stood. "What is it?"

"I was right. Mr. Small lives, and he has been watching the house."

Hastings swore, and then kissed his wife. "I have to go out, love."

"I'm coming, too," Deacon said, as he stood and joined them without being asked to come along.

"Why? Devil take it," Sally protested. "What is going on? Who is this Mr. Small you speak of, Quinn?"

"It is complicated, but it seems Mr. Dalton's secretary faked his death, most likely killed Theodora's father, and has taken to following my betrothed about."

"You never said you had found a bride, too," Deacon complained.

"I couldn't find you. I intended to mention it when I finally tracked you down," Quinn promised. "And ask you to stand up with me at the wedding."

Deacon beamed. "I couldn't be prouder to."

"Oh, dear heavens, Quinn," Mother gasped. "They're defenseless."

"They will be fine, Mama. I'm probably worrying for nothing. My men are with them."

"I couldn't bear to lose either of them," she claimed, bursting to her feet with the dog now wrapped tightly in her arms. "You must hurry."

"I will," Quinn promised. He strode for the door and rushed downstairs—only to be confronted by one his own men, his coachman, staggering through the front door, holding his head.

"My lord, I have grim news. We were attacked, and the carriage was stolen."

"And the ladies?"

"Taken with the carriage."

Quinn grabbed the man by his coat. "Why didn't you follow them?"

"I'm the least capable. They hit me hardest," the fellow warned.

Quinn quickly released him as he noticed dried blood at the man's temple. "I'm sorry."

"No apologies necessary. They took us by surprise. The others are in pursuit, along with the fellows from the merchant your betrothed patronized this morning. We could have news at any moment."

CHAPTER THIRTY

THEODORA CAME AWAKE SLOWLY, head pounding and her senses lurching from one memory to another. When she tried to move, she discovered her hands were bound behind her back. She glanced up at Mr. Small's smug face. "Release me," she hissed through gritted teeth as a wave of nausea rose.

"Ah, the helpless damsel awakens at last." Small bent down and poked his face uncomfortably close to hers. "What's wrong? Don't you care for your new surroundings?"

Theodora quickly took stock of her location. She'd been brought to squalid stables. Her mother sat at her side, bound too most likely, already conscious but quiet. "Mama?"

"I'm so glad to see you awake. It's been hours since he brought us here."

"Quiet," Small warned. "And no more tears."

Theodora licked her dry lips and made a further quick study of her surroundings. They had been placed to the side of the large animal enclosure, leaning against a hard post that rose to a punctured roof overhead. Beams of light pierced the walls and ceiling and cast a cruel illumination over their captors. Mr. Small and an accomplice were all she could see at present. Her satchel sat on top of a barrel. The contents clearly visible. Money and the gems were stacked in neat piles out in the open.

"What are you going to do with us?"

"I cannot very well let you go. You know too much about me as it is."

"What threat could we be to you?" she cried out.

The light piercing one wall dimmed, and an eye appeared and suddenly disappeared from a gap there.

Theodora shivered. Mr. Small's accomplices most likely surrounded them. There could be dozens outside like that ill-kept fellow picking at his teeth by the far wall. She deliberately lowered her voice to mask her panic at what might become of them. "You've taken everything we have of value. You have a ransom in gems. Please let us go."

"No," Small snapped. He played with the gems. He held one up to the light, admiring the color. "Your father was quite attached to these, wasn't he?"

"They were a gift to Mother."

Small grinned. "At least you pair gave me much less trouble than your father did."

"You knocked over the lamp."

"His refusal to give them to me without a fight deprived him of his future."

"So you did kill him."

"I left him to die, screaming in agony."

Theodora's stomach clenched and Mother sobbed. "You're a monster!" Theodora told him.

"I discovered that to get ahead in life, you have to be willing to get your hands dirty."

"How did you learn that?"

Small smiled and fell silent, while Theodora desperately fiddled with her bonds behind her back. The rope seemed thin and soft, and not as tight as it could be around her wrists, too. She could move a little, but was it enough to free herself and then her mother? She tossed her head suddenly, determined to buy them as much time as she could to think and come up with a plan for their escape. "What trouble had my father ever been to you? He treated you as part of the family."

Small shook his head. "If I was a family member, I'd never have had to scrape for a living, would I, Nelson?"

"No, sir. He never treated you right," Nelson answered. "Manners are important."

"Indeed, they are." Small squatted down next to her and reached out to touch her black gown. "If Dalton had shown me the proper respect, you wouldn't be wearing mourning now. I even asked for your hand, and he refused me."

"You wanted to marry me?" Theodora stared at him in shock.

He shrugged, and his fingers drifted down her legs. "I could have learned to put up with your bookish nonsense eventually, I suppose."

She shivered at sensing Small's sexual interest in her that he'd never revealed before. "I was never going to love anyone after Daniel."

"Liar, but whoever said love was a requirement of marriage when there is money involved?"

I do.

Theodora's heart began to clatter. She did believe in love and marriage. At that moment she realized she was already in love, and Quinn could never know she'd fallen for him. She'd given her word that she'd never want to marry him. What a fool she was to have promised that before really knowing him.

"My husband treated you well," Mama protested, finally

speaking up. "He gave you far more liberty than anyone else in our employ ever had."

"Still a servant to his fame, and a man none of you took seriously." He inched Theodora's gown up her legs to reveal her stockings. "He cared more for the beggars on the street than for the people who truly needed his funds. Not that it matters now."

"How much is for me?" Nelson asked loudly, interrupting Small's perusal of her garters.

"I'll explain one last time." Small sighed and quickly stood, leaving her legs exposed. He hurried to Nelson, who was pushing the piles of coins around with the tip of his stubby fingers. He knocked her empty satchel off the table carelessly, and an emerald rolled into the straw from within, unnoticed.

The payment she'd acquired from Mr. Brown kept their interest for some minutes. Theodora used the moment to twist her arms and fingers, hurriedly trying to free herself. She found the end of the rope and tugged just as Small glanced her way. "You'll only hurt yourself if you keep struggling," he warned.

The moment he turned away, she tugged. The ropes became loose around her wrists, but she did nothing about it for the moment. She held herself still, knowing she could be free if only she had a plan for escape that rescued her mother, too. She had to bide her time for the right opportunity. "Let us go."

That eye returned to the peephole and stared at her.

"Now since I can't have you running to the authorities, or your new betrothed, about this we're going to take a short trip together," he advised in an offhand manner, barely glancing her way as he assessed their stolen fortune. He bit into a coin and then added it to a far pile, the one nearest Nelson.

He knew about Quinn. How long had he been watching them? How much could he know?

She turned to her mother. *I'm free*, she mouthed, careful to make no sound.

Her mother's eyes widened in surprise, and then she shook her head violently, warning her without words not to do anything foolish like trying to escape.

Theodora shrugged. She had to act soon. There was no telling what Small would do next, or where he would take them, but she was desperately afraid he could give them to his men outside as some sort of payment.

"Are you hurt?" Theodora asked her mother, after a quick glance at the men to make sure Small and Nelson were still occupied with counting their money.

"No," her mother said very softly. "Nelson made sure of that."

Theodora darted a quick glance at the little-known man standing beside Dennis Small. That was an odd thing for an abductor to do. Given Nelson's consideration for her mother's comfort, did that mean they had a secret ally in this room who might help them? He'd already distracted Small once from molesting her. Had he done it on purpose? And if so, could Mr. Nelson be persuaded to help them escape if given the right encouragement? She would have to be very creative about how she made helping them appealing. Offering more money was unlikely to sway him, given the fortune already in hand.

She swallowed hard and realized she only had one thing she could trade. Herself. "He's not my betrothed," she announced loudly.

Small turned. "What was that?"

"I said, Lord Templeton is not my betrothed," she protested. "He's only my employer."

"He *is* her betrothed," Mama protested. "And he will come to save us both because he loves her."

Nelson appeared to consider the matter.

Theodora's pulse raced with dread but pressed her advantage. "No, that is not true, Mama, and you know it. Lord Templeton hired me as his secretary because we were thought to be poor. Just ask him."

Small laughed. "I would never trust the word of anyone in that family ever again."

Theodora stared at him in surprise. "Have you had dealings with them before?"

Small glanced away. "Once I did, years ago, and believe me, the idea of destroying their happiness is quite strong still." A lusty gleam filled Small's eyes, and Theodora's skin crawled as he drew closer. He leered at her legs. "This will undoubtedly hurt *him* as much as his father's actions hurt me."

Theodora cringed as Mr. Small grasped her leg firmly. He was stronger than she expected, but she might just have the element of surprise on her side. She slipped her hands free of her bonds, ready to strike at him with everything she had in her if he moved his hand higher. But what would happen to her mama if she escaped? Mama was still bound, and may not have the strength to run away. There had to be a way to save them both.

Small's hand was clammy on her skin and revolted her. She tried to press her knees together as she addressed Nelson, who'd drawn closer to watch events unfold, frowning. "He's cheated you out of coin there."

Nelson's eyes darted up to her face, and then he scratched his head. "How would you know?"

"I'm bookish," she promised. Could she convince the fellow he was being swindled by his own friend? "I can count very well, and my father taught me to drive a hard bargain and never hold back a shilling that belonged to someone else. Small has given you the same number of coins, but his are worth far more than yours. He knows that."

Stinging pain burned her cheek as Mr. Small backhanded her.

She covered her head as she toppled sideways, unfortunately revealing her hands were free.

"Bloody hell!" Small exploded and then he grabbed her roughly and hauled her upright. She was shaken like a sack of flour, her feet barely touching the ground. "How did you get loose?"

Theodora buttoned her lips together. Implicating Nelson would do her no good. She needed Nelson's help if he could be swayed to their side at all.

Mr. Small, however, wasn't stupid. He glared at Nelson harshly. "You had one job to do! Make sure they don't escape."

"They didn't," Nelson promised, gesturing toward them. "You said I didn't have to hurt them."

Small rolled his eyes and shoved Theodora toward Mr. Nelson. "Here, have her. She's all yours."

Nelson caught her in his beefy paws, but he was far gentler than she expected he'd be. She was restrained in a grip she couldn't twist free of, so she stopped trying to fight him. Theodora couldn't leave without her mother. She had to stay no matter what came next.

Small turned and checked Mama's bonds, nodding as he discovered them still firm around her wrists.

"I'm not lying," Theodora whispered to Nelson quickly. "He has cheated you out of your share. I can prove it if you help us. Don't let him hurt us. I'll give you anything you want."

"For God's sake, don't ever listen to a woman's promises. What did I tell you? They all lie from birth till their last breath. Haven't I warned you about how they'll use their charms to get what they want from us? Haven't I always looked after you?"

Mr. Small checked his pocket watch. "There's still time for a little more revenge before we go. Give her to me, and go bring up our horses. Pity we can't keep that carriage, but it will stick out like a sore thumb where we're going and be trouble in the end."

Nelson's grip tightened on Theodora's arms. "What are you going to do with them?"

"With the mother, nothing. I'll leave her here in this charming cesspit. This one, however…she'll get what she deserves from me personally."

Theodora quaked. She leaned into Nelson. "Don't let him take me. I'm yours, remember."

When Small grabbed for her, Nelson blocked his path, throwing Theodora behind him like a rag doll. "You said she was mine."

"And don't we always share the pretty ones?"

Nelson's big head moved up and down, and then he shook it. "But you said she was mine. You did. I never had a woman just for me."

Small patted his back solicitously. "Next time you will. Miss Dalton has to pay first, though. Despite her words, I think I'll leave a message behind for Lord Templeton, to ensure his family never stands in my way ever again."

Nelson shook his head. "I don't want to share. We got the money. She won't say nuffin about us or where we're going," Nelson said stubbornly. He glanced at Theodora. "Will you?"

"No," she promised. "Never."

Small scowled, and then put his arm around Nelson in a reassuring manner. However, he palmed a knife in his other hand, the one Mr. Nelson could not yet see.

"Be careful! He's going to hurt you!" Theodora cried out a warning to Mr. Nelson that the big ox completely misunderstood.

"Friends don't hurt each other, do they Gently," he said.

"What did I say about using that name?" Small's jaw clenched. "It's not your job to do the talking or the thinking. It's mine! I'll explain everything later when we are away from here."

"Wait!" She knew that name. Quinn had asked her to look for a reference to the same name, but hadn't told her why. He knew

Quinn's family too. Even before she asked her question, she knew the answer. "Are you *not* Dennis Small?"

Nelson cringed away from his friend. "Sorry, Gently."

"Mr. Roman Gently," she asked just to be sure.

"That weak fool is gone," Small, or rather Roman, snapped.

Theodora shook her head. "But he's not forgotten. Someone important is looking for you."

"They're too late." Roman Gently tightened his grip on the knife as he tensed, ready to strike out at poor Nelson. "Nelson, come closer."

Nelson didn't. He turned suddenly at the sound of a boot scuffing the straw at the doorway to the stables.

Quinn! Her heart burst with adoration at the sight of him coming to her rescue.

"Yes, do come closer. But I think you've said more than enough to ensure you both hang," Quinn announced as he stepped into the filthy stables. He planted his feet wide in the doorway as he held two pistols, one pointed negligently toward Mr. Nelson, but the other aimed squarely at Mr. Gently's head.

Quinn's face was frightening "Give me an excuse to fire. I beg you."

CHAPTER THIRTY-ONE

QUINN TOOK in Mr. Gently's shock at seeing them with great pleasure. If not for his groom's quick thinking, Theodora would have come to harm in the hands of this monster. The men Quinn employed for his carriage had all followed the stolen vehicle on borrowed horses, sending back urchins wearing pieces of their livery to Newberry House, to warn him of their heading.

He took in the poor state of the stables, Mrs. Dalton bound on the ground, Theodora's bruising cheek as she backed away, and his temper soared. He'd arrived too late to protect Theodora from harm. Whoever had struck her would pay dearly for that.

"Drop the knife," he demanded of the man his late sister had once loved.

"I ain't got no knife," Nelson complained, then glanced at his partner in crime. Clearly slow to comprehend that he'd been moments away from being stabbed, it took another painfully long moment for him to see the knife Gently held at the ready. He turned to face the other man when he did. "Why do you have a knife?"

"Shut up," Gently growled.

"You were going to hurt the ladies?" Nelson tilted his head to the side, blinking in surprise. "You can't do that. It ain't right to hurt innocents."

"Women are never as innocent as they seem."

Nelson tackled Gently suddenly, and wrestled the knife from his grip very easily. He waved it about. "Knives are dangerous. People misunderstand when you hold a knife for too long. You told me that."

Nelson threw it across the stables, embedding the point in a post far from reach. Quinn breathed a sigh of relief that he wouldn't have to shoot the dumb ox and moved closer to them, never taking his attention from Mr. Gently, who he now judged the only threat in the room.

"So I understand you're the man who murdered Mr. Dalton." Mary had loved this man, a fellow who had abducted *his* Theodora and her mother. "I believe you also knew my younger sister too."

Gently's face transformed for a moment then hardened. "Slut."

"How dare you say that?" Deacon bellowed.

"It's the truth."

The force of Deacon brushing past Quinn nearly knocked him from his feet. Deacon fell upon Roman Gently and slammed a fist into his face. "You used her and then abandoned her!"

"She used me too," Gently snarled, struggling against the much larger Deacon.

"Stop!" Theodora shrieked.

Quinn clenched his jaw briefly. "Why should I stop him doing what needs to be done?"

"Because he must be punished under the law for my father's murder."

Deacon threw Gently away across the room so hard the man staggered. "I'm glad Mary's not here to see the type of man you've become."

Quinn gaped. "You knew about Mary and him all along."

"I introduced them," Deacon mumbled, looking down at Gently in disgust. "Mary unwittingly helped your father undercut the business."

Quinn blinked. "Why didn't you tell me?"

"I promised Mary that I wouldn't ever speak of him again or tell you what she'd done," Deacon confessed. "She was ashamed. She knew you'd try to punish him for her mistake. But he was never supposed to return to England."

"*Her* mistake?" Quinn swallowed hard and quickly gestured to Hastings who was blocking the exit with his men. "Bind their hands."

"Don't hurt Nelson," Mrs. Dalton pleaded suddenly.

Quinn dropped down behind Mrs. Dalton to loosen her bonds before helping her stand. "Madam, he abducted you and forced you to come to this filthy place."

"He was only doing what he was told."

"Who are you?" Nelson asked, as he was restrained, though he did not fight them off.

"Lord Templeton," Quinn said.

The big man paled and struggled to retreat. "Lady Mary's father?"

The way that sounded, Nelson had some experience with his father, and it seemed not to be a pleasant sort of remembrance. "Our father died. I am Mary's elder brother, and the new Lord Templeton." He studied the blinking idiot. "I am nothing like my father, but I warn you not to cross me."

The big man relaxed, and allowed his hands to be bound by Hastings without further protest. He tested the bonds, and then glanced at Theodora. "You said Lord Templeton wouldn't come for you," he protested. The oaf's eyes widened. "You lied to me like Gently said you would."

Quinn stepped between Nelson and Theodora. "Miss Dalton

misunderstood the depths of my feelings about our engagement. Of course I would want to rescue her," Quinn promised. "A gentleman always protects the woman he adores."

He glanced at Theodora quickly and grinned at her shocked expression. He shrugged, looking around for Deacon without finding him. "Loves, actually. We'll discuss it later."

Nelson began nodding. "I took good care of them. Made sure they had nice warm straw to sit upon. I only had one coat for one of them. It's warm and cozy here, so I didn't think they'd suffer."

Quinn nodded too, baffled by the man's polite manner. Surely, he didn't think this location was suitable for any lady? Had the jug only been half full when Nelson was created? Gently was the real villain here, and the one to watch. "Take them out."

The men hurried to do Quinn's bidding, forcing a resisting Mr. Gently out to the waiting carriages. Nelson looked back once or twice, appearing confused by his situation. Quinn felt a moment of pity for the man. Clearly, he'd been used ill, but that was no excuse. He'd suffer for his actions today, probably without fully understanding why it must be so.

Once they were away, Mr. Banks poked his head back through the door. "I have heard and seen enough to press for hanging. What was that business about with your sister?"

"Nothing to concern yourself with," Quinn said quickly. "An old grievance."

And something Deacon knew more about than Quinn did, apparently.

Quinn turned toward Theodora once more, lifted her chin to look at her face and, seeing that she appeared fine but for that, kissed the top of her head. It was clear Theodora had survived the ordeal relatively unscathed, freed herself, and was even now gathering a fine temper, given the way she scowled at her abductors. "Are you well, love?"

"My cheek hurts," she confessed.

Quinn cradled Theodora's damaged cheek in his palm. "I wish I could take away this pain for you."

"Do not worry for me."

"But I always will," he promised.

"He never hurt us. Nelson, I mean. He doesn't deserve to hang for Mr. Gently's crimes."

"That will not be for me to decide," he warned her. "It is Banks who must be convinced to be lenient."

"Mr. Banks," Theodora called, pulling away from him. He smiled as she spoke eloquently on behalf of Nelson's situation and alluded to his misuse by the much smarter and more cunning Mr. Gently.

Quinn glanced down and plucked up a garment from the straw. Once nestled beneath Mrs. Dalton, laid over a pile of thick, clean hay, was a poor man's crumpled coat. He shook it out, noting the unusually large size, and then showed it to Mr. Banks. "Look at this. Mr. Nelson appears to be a gentleman abductor?"

"Interesting, but hardly relevant," Banks claimed. However, he did make a note in his pocketbook that Quinn hoped might help the man escape the noose.

"It is Roman Gently who is truly evil, Mr. Banks," Theodora insisted. "Mr. Nelson merely went along with everything he said like a child. He didn't know what Gently planned for our future, or for my father, I'm certain of that. He's not to blame. You must see that and help him."

"He assaulted the Duke of Rutherford's grooms, aided in the kidnapping of yourself and your mother, then held you against your will in filth. What sort of man would I be if I allowed him to suffer no consequences at all?"

"He should not hang," Theodora insisted. "But he could be helped by someone with the power and compassion to do so."

"Indeed, he should be, if such a man existed," Mama agreed before Lord Deacon escorted her outside.

"We will have to see what we can accomplish together then, shall we?" Quinn offered. He held out his arm to Theodora. "Hold on to me and let us leave this hellhole."

Theodora wrapped her arm through his and sighed. "How did you know to look for us here?"

"The grooms survived the attack on them and followed you."

"I wondered what had become of them. I am so glad they are all right."

Mr. Banks stood before Mrs. Dalton; his hands spread wide. "We never imagined he'd be as brazen as to try for an abduction. I should have acted as soon as Lord Templeton's suspicions were confirmed."

"We all should have," Quinn added, feeling guilt replace his anger.

"You knew he lived?" Theodora looked up at him with huge eyes.

"I saw him, but didn't believe my eyes at first. Only today did I know it was him for certain. When I went to warn you to remain at home, I was told you and your mother had gone out." He frowned at her. "Next time, please do me the courtesy of leaving a note behind."

"Very well," Theodora murmured, suddenly meek and mild and quite timid for a change.

It was most likely from the shock of today and surely couldn't last. He put his arm about her shoulders and squeezed. "You could always take me with you."

Mrs. Dalton grasped his arm suddenly. "I wish to go home."

Quinn considered Mrs. Dalton's request with the seriousness it deserved. "Your old home was leveled yesterday to make way for the rebuilding of the property."

Mrs. Dalton smiled quickly. "I meant Newberry House. I

discovered today that it has become home to me after all," Mrs. Dalton confessed, with an apologetic smile. "If it is no trouble, I would like nothing more than to remain a guest there. Your mother has already asked me to consider it a permanent arrangement."

Quinn was not surprised by anything his own mother did lately. Mother gathered good people about her like his father had collected grudges. Quinn nodded slowly, sensing an opportunity to be alone with Theodora and express his hopes for the future. "Shall I tell the driver to take you there now, madam?"

"Please," Mrs. Dalton replied. "I've had more than enough excitement for one day. Or a lifetime, for that matter."

"Mother, the matter of father's murder can be proved. We have much to do now that Mr. Gently has been arrested."

"Mr. Banks will tie up any loose ends, so you will not be bothered by the matter again," Quinn promised the older woman. "There's nothing for you to worry about anymore, Mrs. Dalton. Your husband's killer will be dealt with and punished. As for Nelson, we can speak up for leniency in his case, provided he's placed in honest employment far from you and Theodora."

"Thank you, my lord."

Hastings, who'd been a silent observer until now, joined them. "I'll escort Mrs. Dalton back to Newberry House and leave you both to sort this out. Lady Templeton will be quite anxious to know your bride and future mother-in-law are safe and sound."

"Thank you," Quinn said, happy with Hastings' decision to leave.

Hastings winked as he helped the older woman into a carriage, leaving Theodora standing at Quinn's side. Quinn smiled down at her. "Shall we finish this business together, love?"

For a moment, he thought she would protest, but she eventually nodded. "There is one thing we must do first."

Theodora approached Deacon, who was nursing his bruised knuckles outside the stables. "Are you all right, Lord Deacon, is it?"

"Right as I'll ever be, I suppose. A pleasure to make your acquaintance."

Theodora bit her bottom lip as she examined his hand. "About Lady Mary. I'm sure she would understand that Quinn needs to know a few things now, if he is ever to have peace about her death."

Deacon looked around and then sighed. "I suppose she would understand after today."

Quinn only needed one question answered. "Why?"

"She fell for Gently at first sight, but your father was only interested in what she could discover about his business dealings. She fell in love with Gently and thought your father would help him succeed so they could marry. But then she learned what your father was up to and told Gently. He became very angry and blamed her. Mary would have eloped I think, but Gently refused to marry her without a dowry. By that point he'd already lost his employment. She pined for Gently and always thought your father would come around, but instead he sought to marry her off. To me, actually. I went along with the talk at first, hoping Gently would come for her still. But Mary was never happy again. She met with Gently only once, with my help, and then she left London suddenly for Newberry Park, leaving a note to me, saying goodbye. She was carrying Gently's child the day she died."

Quinn closed his eyes, at the news. "You loved her."

"Like the sister I never had," Deacon swore. "After news reached me of her death, I went looking for Gently, and when I found him weeks later, he swore he'd never touched her. But Mary wasn't a liar. I took Gently to the docks. I told him never to show his face in England again."

Theodora sighed. "And my father found him and took him to

India, and when it was decided that we would sail for England, he insisted Gently return with us despite his protests."

Deacon nodded. "I thought I saw him the night of the fire, but lost him in the crowd."

Quinn remembered something of that. He grasped Deacon's shoulder. "Thank you for telling me about Mary, my friend."

Deacon nodded, turning away to join the Newberry carriage before it departed with Hastings and Mrs. Dalton inside.

Quinn glanced at Theodora. She'd lost her beloved father because of what his own had done to Gently, perhaps sending him on a path of revenge and greed. He'd known his father wasn't to be trusted but never how far the consequences could reach. He shook his head slowly. "My father."

Theodora grasped his hand tightly. "We couldn't have known of the connection. Gently never spoke of his past."

"Lord Templeton," Banks called out.

He glanced at Theodora. "I don't think I will ever become used to hearing that title."

"In time you will," Theodora promised him. "You give it meaning again."

He smiled quickly and led Theodora to Banks, where Gently was being questioned.

Theodora leaped into the thick of it immediately, helping Gently incriminate himself further by goading him to be indelicate. He was astonished by her effectiveness, and so proud of her zeal in righting a wrong. When Gently had said enough, Banks had him taken away.

Quinn caught the investigators eye. "Mr. Banks, you will keep us informed."

"Indeed, I will, and may I say, Lord Templeton has made a fine choice in his bride. My congratulations to you both on your impending marriage. I've just heard the happy news."

"Thank you."

Theodora blushed. "Thank you, sir."

Quinn led Theodora to his carriage and, once alone and on the way back to Newberry House, he turned to her. She did not need him. Not really. But he could have lost her today, and knew he'd never survive it again.

He took up her hand, playing with her fingers. "Marry me, Theodora Dalton."

"What?"

"Marry me," he repeated. "Become my bride in truth, and not because of that nonsense my mother told you in private the day you agreed to this charade."

Her eyes widened. "How do you know what we spoke about?"

"I listened," he confessed. "You were right not to entirely trust her that day, and you managed her nonsense exactly the right way— and you may manage *me* to your heart's content for the rest of my life, too, if you want to."

Theodora tugged her hand back. "I don't know what to say."

"Say nothing yet, but think of all we could accomplish together. Your ambitions and experience combined with the wealth of the Templeton estates behind you. It could be a vastly satisfying life for both of us, I'm sure. You can even dismiss Mr. Kemp if he continues to put forth less than his best efforts. You would be his employer."

She wet her lips. "You couldn't want me as your wife."

"Of course I do. I have fallen a little more in love with you each day from the first night I held you in my arms. We belong together, Theodora. After the shock of almost losing you today, I demand you never leave me again."

Theodora fell silent, and Quinn clenched his hands together in his lap, knowing there was a risk she might never respond favorably to his proposal. He would give her time to consider the matter with a rational mind. He could be very patient to win her love.

"You love me?"

"Isn't it obvious? I have no secrets from you. No desire to have any other woman in my life. How many men allow strange women to sweep into their home, reorganize their furniture, and take over their lives so completely as I have allowed you to do? You stood up to my mother, too, and I couldn't be prouder of you for that. You dismissed my mistress and yet won't take that place, and quite rightly, too, because you deserve better. I want to share your bed for the rest of my life, so...marriage seems the best way to accomplish that."

Theodora pressed her hand to her chest.

"I'm not saying our marriage will be easy. There will be many challenges ahead. But I want you to know that I appreciate every-thing you do for me. I respect you more than you know. I would worship the ground you walk upon most likely, if given a chance. You make me happier than I ever expected to be."

Theodora turned into him suddenly, wrapped her arms around his neck and hugged him. "Oh, stop."

He pulled her fully onto his lap to hold her closer. "Why must I, love?"

"Because I love you, too," she cried before bursting into tears that lasted the whole trip back to Newberry House, where they both belonged together, forever.

EPILOGUE

TOUCHING THEODORA AGAIN WAS HEAVEN. Making her come with his mouth a pure delight. He nuzzled between her legs, drinking in his wife's scent, the flood of moisture on his tongue, and kissed her clitoris hard. "Tighten," he demanded as soon as he lifted his mouth.

She clamped around his finger, and he thrust inside her with it, noting his bride was panting and her skin was damp with perspiration again. She had her heels dug into the mattress, hands fisted in his sheets, and bucked and shook to his every touch. He withdrew, came up on his knees, and brushed the head of his cock against her parted lips. "Suck."

Teasing Theodora had quickly become his life's work. She was bold, uninhibited, and eager for him and new experiences. There was nothing he'd asked for that she'd refused. Not even the slightest hint of hesitation for anything that guaranteed her an orgasm by the end.

As her lips closed around the head of his cock, he thrust forward a short distance. Theodora scrambled, finding a new position to better accommodate his girth in her mouth. So far, they'd used every corner, every post of their new shared apartment at Newberry House in the pursuit of passion this night.

He kept his thrusts short and controlled, biding his time. He'd made Theodora come three times so far since they'd spoken their vows, but he kept his own release at bay. He was having too much fun exciting Theodora.

He was beyond glad they were husband and wife at last. Now he didn't care if the door opened; if anyone wanted them, they could wait or come in and be shocked.

He drew her dark hair aside, watching his cock disappear into her willing mouth. Despite no longer needing to keep their love-making a secret, Theodora remained an unusually quiet bed partner. The way he knew how she felt about him was in the frequency of her orgasms, the dampness between her thighs and the manner she held on to him, pulling him back when he paused to catch his breath.

He was close to orgasm again, so he pulled back and wiped the head of his cock across her damp, pink lips. "You have a talent, my dear."

"Thank you, husband. You have a talented tongue, too."

"Shall I prove it again?"

"Not yet," Theodora collapsed against the headboard, panting, drawing her knees together.

Quinn shifted down the bed, caught her ankles, and tugged her down the mattress until she was flat on her back once more. He flipped her over and crawled until he hovered over her body. "Shall I have you like this next?"

A moan left her mouth, causing him to grin.

"Or shall I have you on your knees?"

She buried her face to muffle her voice as she groaned.

"On your knees it is."

Quinn caught her hips and brought her up until her bum stuck out. He rained kisses down her spine, feeling her trembling under his touch. "Like this, and fast?"

"Yes," Theodora whispered.

He grinned at her request. He was already battling his arousal. He'd make Theodora come just once more before he finally let go of his seed inside her.

He slid into her body with a happy groan, and then brought his fingers to her clit. Theodora widened her legs with a contented sigh. "Is there nothing you will not do to torment me?"

"Pleasurable torment, my dear wife. Feeling you come around me is so perfect, it's a sin."

She laughed. "I'm feeling very sinful tonight."

He thrust hard into her and withdrew. "As am I, my love. Let me show you how much."

He took her hips into his hands and took her hard, fast, and deep. His pleasure built too quickly, though, so he stopped moving to tease her clitoris again. "Have you ever done it in a carriage?"

"Never," she replied, hanging her head as her breaths turned to soft little groans.

"Would you like to go out with me one night? I'm sure we can find some excuse to take a moonlit carriage ride together after the paperwork is done for the day. The sensations caused by the carriage bouncing us against each other will be exquisitely unexpected."

Theodora jerked and whimpered suddenly, tightening around him as she came.

He grinned. Theodora may not say much in bed, but his whispered suggestions for further pleasures never failed to arouse her. He had shared quite a number of his fantasies tonight, and he was beginning to suspect that, given the right circumstances and privacy, he might just do all of them with her. The only question was finding the time.

When Theodora relaxed a little more, Quinn let himself have all the friction he wanted. He took her hips firmly, and made love to her, only pulling out at the very last moment. He did not want her burdened by a babe just yet, and his seed shot out along Theodora's slender back in great long streams.

He mumbled out his apologies and hastily cleaned the evidence away.

Theodora collapsed, sprawled out with a huge smile on her face. "After that marathon, don't ever apologize again."

Quinn folded to the mattress, keeping close to her side. "I was apologizing for the mess."

"I didn't mind." Her smile was so sincere, he relaxed. She found his hand and kissed it. "It was nice to discover you're not always in control of yourself."

"Hardly ever around you." He brought her hand to his mouth and kissed her knuckles reverently. He grinned. He enjoyed touching her and being touched, and now they never had to stop. He smoothed her sweat-damp hair from her face and pressed a kiss to her temple. "Ready to go again, love?"

Theodora's eyes fluttered closed, and she inched closer, seeking more kisses from him. "I'll need a minute to recover."

He smiled against her skin and whispered, "I'll give you forever. Starting now."

The End

ABOUT HEATHER

USA Today Bestselling Author Heather Boyd believes every character she creates deserves their own happily-ever-after—no matter how much trouble she puts them through. With that goal in mind, she writes steamy romances that skirt the boundaries of propriety to keep readers enthralled until the wee hours of the morning. Heather has published over fifty regency romance novels and shorter works full of daring seductions and distinguished rogues. She lives north of Sydney, Australia, with her trio of rogues and pair of four-legged overlords.

Find out more about Heather at:
Heather-Boyd.com

facebook.com/HeatherBoydRomanceAuthor

instagram.com/heatherboydbooks

bookbub.com/authors/heather-boyd

goodreads.com/Heather_Boyd